C. M. HANO

# The Tale of Flame and Shadow

*TarotVerse Volume One*

Copyright © 2024 by C. M. Hano

All rights reserved. No part of this publication may be reproduced, stored or transmitted in any form or by any means, electronic, mechanical, photocopying, recording, scanning, or otherwise without written permission from the publisher. It is illegal to copy this book, post it to a website, or distribute it by any other means without permission.

This novel is entirely a work of fiction. The names, characters and incidents portrayed in it are the work of the author's imagination. Any resemblance to actual persons, living or dead, events or localities is entirely coincidental.

C. M. Hano asserts the moral right to be identified as the author of this work.

C. M. Hano has no responsibility for the persistence or accuracy of URLs for external or third-party Internet Websites referred to in this publication and does not guarantee that any content on such Websites is, or will remain, accurate or appropriate.

Designations used by companies to distinguish their products are often claimed as trademarks. All brand names and product names used in this book and on its cover are trade names, service marks, trademarks and registered trademarks of their respective owners. The publishers and the book are not associated with any product or vendor mentioned in this book. None of the companies referenced within the book have endorsed the book.

"The tarot cards used in this work are THE TAROT OF MARSEILLES BY PITISCI. © Copyright 2019."

First edition

ISBN: 979-8-8691-6579-4

This book was professionally typeset on Reedsy.
Find out more at reedsy.com

*TO THOSE WHO BELIEVED IN ME THE MOST.*

# Contents

*Foreword*     iii
*Acknowledgement*     v

## I   XORA

| | | |
|---|---|---|
| 1 | SERENA | 3 |
| 2 | SERENA | 9 |
| 3 | SERENA | 19 |
| 4 | SERENA | 29 |
| 5 | SERENA | 44 |
| 6 | SERENA | 55 |
| 7 | SERENA | 66 |
| 8 | SERENA | 85 |

## II   WHITFROST

| | | |
|---|---|---|
| 9 | ALWIN | 93 |
| 10 | ALWIN | 102 |
| 11 | NIYA | 114 |
| 12 | SERENA | 128 |
| 13 | SERENA | 138 |
| 14 | SERENA | 150 |
| 15 | ROSE | 161 |
| 16 | DAVI | 168 |

17  NIYA                                179

III  VWRIYNN

18  SERENA                             187
19  ALWIN                              195
20  SERENA                             203
21  ALWIN                              212
22  SERENA                             220
23  ALWIN                              229
24  SERENA                             237
25  ALWIN                              247
26  EPILOGUE                           256

*About the Author*                     257

# Foreword

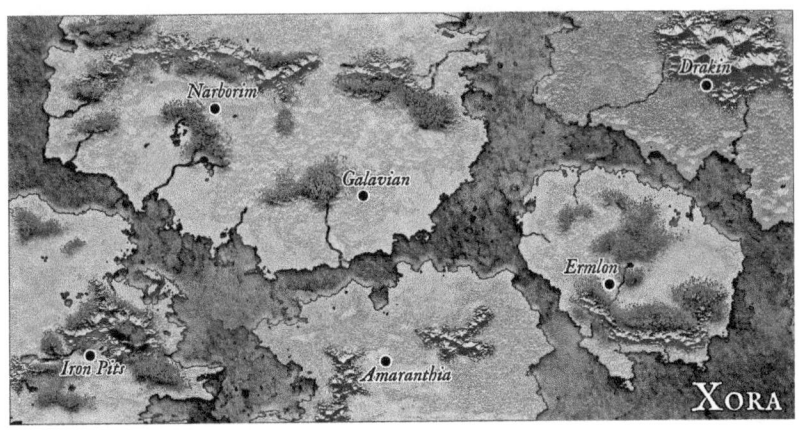

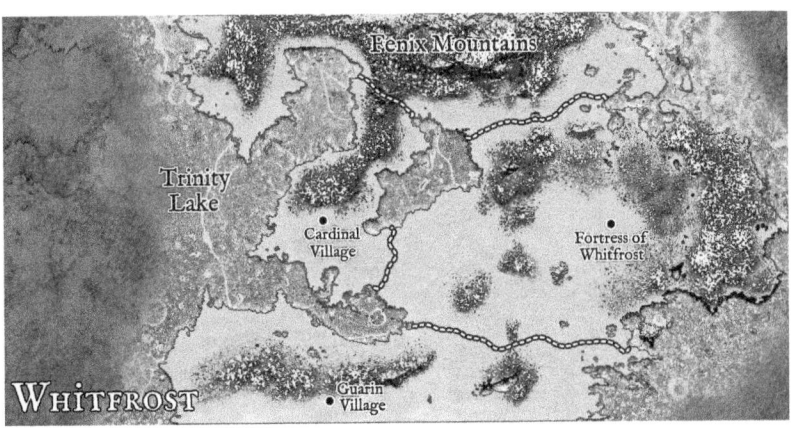

# Acknowledgement

**Michael Runk**
*Reiki Master/Teacher Intuitive Tarot Advisor*
    Michael completed his initial Reiki training in 2004 and his Master training in 2005. In early February 2020, he completed his advanced Holy Fire III Karuna Reiki Master training. As with his Reiki journey, his journey with the cards began in 2004, and they have been a part of

his life ever since. Michael has been reading professionally since early 2020, having read for clients worldwide. He now provides a full range of Reiki services and Tarot readings and teaches students who wish to learn either or both disciplines.

**Stay In Touch**

Michael can be reached at Reikibymike@gmail.com Follow him at:
Facebook: Reiki by Mike or Six of Cups Tarot Twitter: @reikibymike
TikTok: @six_of_cups_tarot
Instagram: Reiki by Mike/Six of Cups Tarot

**David Bailey**

*Rune Master*

I have been a paranormal investigator for nearly 13 years. I've read Tarot for almost a year and Runes for about six months. I am a Twitch streamer under the name DramaTroll.

**Stay In Touch**

TikTok: Divination David Website: www.paranormalhive.live

# I

# XORA

*PHOENIX AWAKENS*

# 1

# SERENA

The air was thick with anticipation as the question hung in the air.

"Are you ready?" Niya Riviera, my closest friend, posed the question, her cheerful expression accentuated by the smooth, straight black hair that flowed down her shoulders. Her hazel eyes were sympathetic, gazing upon the timid nature of her companion. Her beauty was undeniable, with a complexion of soft, fair skin that elegantly complemented her well-defined curves. Despite her modest frame, she stood tall among others. She was a *Justice* among elves, a towering figure that commanded respect and admiration.

"I suppose so," I responded.

Niya appeared glowing with radiance as she stood elegantly dressed in a furred jacket. With its short sleeves, the coat was made from the finest polar bear fur, a testament to her status and *Essence*. The sleeves of her jacket were long and extended down to her hands, adorned with a beautiful golden cluster of leaves, signifying her position as a *Confessor*. Her overall appearance was one of grace
and refinement, leaving no doubt in anyone's mind that she was a woman of great importance.

*Confessors* are the most respected beings in the realm. It could be more fear than respect, but that is because of their power. With the draw of one simple-looking parchment—their ability to bend you to their will with just one gesture, fear could be inevitable.

"Niya, where will you go? Will we ever see each other again?" As I cannot wield magic and come from a lineage of mixed blood, I am being transported to the illustrious training grounds of *Galavian*. This is where individuals like me, without the gift of magic, are trained to become skilled warriors or assassins once we reach the age of twenty-three. It is a rigorous and challenging process I am determined to undertake to prove my worth and become a formidable force.

"Of course, you will see me again. Once you complete your training, I will get you, and we will serve under the Queen's leadership together." Queen Lilac, the ruler of *Xora*, was known for her tyrannical ways, which she inherited from her father. Her father's reign allowed the *Dark Elves* to claim more than half of Xora, which led to a significant power shift in the region. Despite her subjects' grievances, Queen Lilac continued to rule with an iron fist, causing unrest and discontent among the people of Xora.

"Don't worry, Serena, you will do great." As she spoke, doubts arose, and my expressions must have given it away. Without saying anything, she hugged me, and as she did, I could feel the small leather belt buckle she wore, jabbing me in the stomach. It was a stark reminder of their traditional attire. Her silk satin white dress was adorned with intricate designs, and the belt added elegance to her appearance. Despite her kind and gentle demeanor, I couldn't shake off the feeling that something was amiss. "I can feel your doubt. Tell me, what is truly bothering you?"

Had she used her power on me? "I am an outsider everywhere I go," I could not stop myself. "My mother was a human that the

Gnaxtor took for having me. I have no clue who my father is. I don't have Essence, and for a person or abomination, as everyone else calls me, that isn't supposed to be normal." Her golden irises were staring directly through me.

"What if I escorted you to Galavian? Would that make it better?" I cannot believe she is using her powers on me.

"Niya!" Her eyes widened. "Stop using your Essence on me! We talked about this."

Ten years ago, the Old Father took me from my home and brought me to live in the local church. Despite its humble appearance, aged stained-glass windows, and wooden framework, the congregation gathered every Sunday to express gratitude to Ancient Marseilles for creating the Tarot Decks and the Essence that gave them their power. During these weekly gatherings, I often caught the eye of a young girl named Niya. She and her family would visit the church after lessons to spend time with me. The first time we met, she used her card on me, and even as an eleven-year-old, her Essence was formidable.

"You are right. I promise I will not use them again." Half of me believed her, but the other half, perhaps the human half, did not.

"Serena Ozark," the booming voice of an Iluminate came from behind us. "By order of Queen Lilac, you will be transported to Galavian to start your training immediately." It was one of the Queen's Guards at the door. I let out a sigh of defeat—or perhaps sorrow. And I looked toward my friend once more.

"Niya," I longingly looked at her, and before I said anything, she hugged me tightly and kissed me on the cheek. I blushed slightly.

"I give you a kiss of luck, my dearest friend. Be well. We will meet again."

# ALWIN

# THE TALE OF FLAME AND SHADOW

It's been a decade since the Gnaxtor made their appearance. They were tramping through Xora, taking half-elf children from their mother's breast. Narborim was their last stop hunting the *Phoenix* herself. On my orders, Odith has been watching her every day since the attack.

"How is she today?" The black coffee soothes my sore throat. It is the only invention humans have gotten correct in the last two centuries. "They are transporting her to Galavian." Looking through the pool of water, I can see her. Beautiful russet hair, bright sapphire-colored eyes, and flawless skin. "Do you want me to intervene?"

Odith understands the significance of Serena Ozark. Her untapped potential holds the key to liberating our community from the continuous persecution and slaughter inflicted upon us by humans. This prophecy has been passed down since childhood when the former Kings and Queens relentlessly pursued us due to my father's malicious actions.

"Alwin, there will come a day when the Phoenix is born. You must save her from the genocide that threatens our existence."

"How will I find her? Who is she?" Mother takes a shortened finger and reads along the written word within the Grimoire of old.

"The prophecy reads. Two centuries from today, the Phoenix will be born of a human woman. Hunted by all for the blood that runs through her veins, she will need protection."

As I observe her approach towards the palace, I can't help but be captivated by her striking beauty. While we must keep an eye on her, she must decide to join us of her own volition. Her presence is magnetic, and I can sense the power she holds. Standing beside me is

Odith, the pink-haired half-elf, who seems to share my admiration for the woman.

As I express my thoughts to Odith, she nods in agreement and admits that the woman is beautiful. Suddenly, her demeanor shifts, and she appears nervous. She turns to me and says, "Alwin, forgive me for saying this, but I have never seen you with a wife. However, she has the potential to be your Queen."

I follow her gaze toward the image of Serena, and I realize that I have never considered taking a partner for myself. I have never allowed a woman to enter my life, let alone my heart.

"I don't need a Queen. Serena has a far more important purpose. She needs training, discipline, and focus."

"But she will only get those if she comes here. To be with us and learn. If you let me use cards-"

"No, you will not use magic to persuade her. You know what will happen if you use the cards for nefarious means." Her head hangs low, with her chin almost touching her chest. Her shoulders slump forward as she appears lost in thought or sadness. "Odith, you are my most loyal soldier and friend. I accept your advice and guidance in all things. But finding me a Queen is not one of them."

"Maybe you won't be so uptight if you finally get laid." Her mouth twisted into a scowl, and she spat out her words with a sudden burst of anger, shocking me with her behavior's raw, uncivilized nature. "I just want to see you happy for once in your life."

"I will be happy once we are free of repression. Don't you want to be accepted for not just being a half-elf but wanting to be with another woman?"

"I want that more than anything." We both went quiet. "If you don't pursue a relationship with her, do I have your blessing?"

At that moment, a sudden burst of laughter escaped me, and to my surprise, she laughed along with me. I couldn't help but feel amazed at her resilience. Odith had been relentlessly tormented and chased out of town because she was a half-elf. She had even witnessed her beloved being captured right before her eyes, leaving her vulnerable and exposed. When I first met her, gaining her trust and making her feel safe took a lot of effort. But after a week of being by her side, she finally began to let her guard down and allowed me to enter her world.

"Serena Ozark's purpose is to embrace her true form and bring peace to the realm. I don't want her to be distracted by anyone. Plus, she has eyes for her Confessor friend Niya."

"Do I sense jealousy?" Odith teases.

"No," I answer. "Come, we need to prepare a room for her arrival."

"What makes you think she will say yes?" I gave her a smile that conveyed a sense of understanding. I'm unsure if she'll give me the answer I'm hoping for, but perhaps after speaking with Odith, she'll be more inclined to say yes.

While we haven't crossed Serena, she exudes allure and mystery, adding an enticing element to the prospect of getting to know her.

# 2

# SERENA

The trek to Galavian would be a three-day ride. The Iluminate were said to have the essence that controlled *The Moon Card*.

This gave them the ability to create portals. I wonder why they did not just open one up and march us throughout. It would be easier on me. It was a rough ride for someone not used to being on a horse.

"Why don't they just conjure up a portal?" I whispered to a scrawny brown-haired boy next to me. He did not answer me or even look at me. He must be afraid. The thing about being a half-elf is that everyone knows because you have an Elf's hair and body but a human's nose and ears.

"Because only certain Iluminate can conjure up one." A scratchy voice came from the other side of the boy. I saw an older woman with gray hair and wrinkled skin, reminding me of the old witches from the storybook Old Father read me. I did not dare speak another word. Someone who looked like that and ate her hog leg with sharp yellow teeth like it was her last meal gave me a slight panic in my chest. Or perhaps just a nauseous feeling in my stomach.

The rough leather saddle rubbed my inner thighs the wrong way.

By the time we reached our journey's end, I had friction burns that needed to be assessed by the Reiki Healers. I had never been on a horse before and never wanted to be again. But, for non-magic users, there was no other means of transportation. We could not conjure a portal using The Moon Card. Although, I would use that to go anywhere and everywhere if I had the chance. Maybe I could be like Niya. The memory of her soft velvet lips pressed upon my cheek sent a flutter through my stomach and made my heart long for her.

Of course, I have never told her how I felt, but with her power, I feel like she already knew. Being a Confessor and wielding that card means you may not mate with any other Essence. And there is the fact that we are both women. Both are forbidden, and if caught, it would cause immediate execution. If I could choose which Essence to be, it would not be to control The Moon. It would be to maintain the Justice. Then I could be with her. We could fly away on her Griffon. Find a place where the two of us can be together without any concerns for safety.

Confessors, like Niya, are given a Griffon. Due to their work, they must make it anywhere within an hour. Griffons are marvelous and majestic beasts. These charming but quite common creatures are a type of mammal. They are about the size of a horse and have four legs and a long tail with a small bushel of hair at the end. They have thick, smooth skin covered in short, coarse hairs, usually either bronze, light gold, or a combination of these colors.

They live with their assigned Confessor, but are raised in the high mountains. They are omnivores with relatively large beaks and narrow tongues ideal for eating various things. One flaw is that they are nocturnal and rely on their sight and extra senses to get around during the day. They have two symmetrical slits to smell their prey. And large, round midnight eyes sit well within their relatively gigantic heads.

These creatures are very peaceful and remain unconditionally loyal to their Confessor. I have yet to meet one in person, but when I see Niya again, I will meet her.

Upon dismounting my horse, I gazed upon the marvelous glistening city of Galavian. Seven cerulean thick, round towers penetrate the blue sky. Each is connected by massive, thin walls made of quartz stone. Quaint windows are scattered here and there across the walls in a symmetric pattern, along with asymmetric crenelations for archers.

A pronounced entry with thick metal doors, a drawbridge, and a large crenelation with guards to the only entrance to the fortress. It is the only easy way in, but easy is very relative here. Opulent fields of crops surround the castle walls and provide the inhabitants with food all year round. This citadel shows no signs of decay after being around for ages, but that is because of the Essence naturally flowing within the earth.

"So, you're the half-elf?" I turned my astonished gaze to the deep voice coming from behind me. "I was expecting more." Black, short hair, tight in a ponytail, reveals a round, warm face. Piercing brown eyes, set delicately within their sockets, look slowly over me.

Judging the abomination standing a few feet away from him. "Yeah, so?" I said, sounding frustrated. Everywhere I go, I am

judged because I was born differently.

"You are an abomination, and you shouldn't be given the honor of training in Galavian." The audacity of this man-child to sit here and call me that. Before I knew it, my fist was connecting with the small scar sitting atop his right cheekbone.

"Do you know who I am?" The look of anger in his wide, muddy eyes told me he was someone important. "I am Orlando Zain." He grabbed my wrists and restrained them behind my back. I tried to resist, but his strength over me was too much.

"Yeah, well, to me, you are a spineless coward who thinks it's right to insult someone based on their looks alone." I did not know who he was, but his grasp loosened as he apologized. I turned to look at him. Something is misleading about him. It is the sudden change of expression in my logical words.

It was paralyzing. He walked away with haste in each step, landing at his spot in the formation of one hundred other recruits. "Hurry, half-elf, the Queen waits for no one."

The Queen. The words bounced off my ears. "Why are we meeting?"

"Shut it and get in formation!" the soldier interrupted.

We marched in two by two. Shock and awe went through each row as murmured words of wow and so glorious were all I heard. The person walking next to me remained quiet. He was that skinny little man from the night before. He seemed like a ghost trapped in a body with barely enough meat on him. Pale white skin, cold to the touch. And lifeless eyes are afraid to look at anything but the path ahead.

"Hi, my name is Serena." I thought conversing would help ease his fears, but I remained mute. Maybe it is because of me. Some people shunned me my entire life, and others recoiled from seeing me. Old Father would say it is because I was the first half-elf to be born and survive. When news got out that a half-elf grew to the mature age of ten, that was when the Gnaxtor King sent his armies searching all over Xora.

Tears swelled in my eyes as the painful memory of my mother being dragged away by those dreadful beasts flooded my mind.

Soon, the images faded as we entered the corridor decorated with many unique fine art pieces. Narrow lanterns attached to the side of each silver column illuminate the entire throne hall and allow shadows to cavort where light cannot reach—the clear crystal of the windows in the dome ceiling dance in the flickering light.

"No wonder Narborim is so poor. All the money from the taxes gets put into this place." Instantly, I covered my mouth as the words spilled out. I pray nobody heard that. It appeared I said it in the lowest tone that only I could listen to. I glanced at my marching partner; even my treasonous words could not take him out of his trance—you poor boy. The Ancients will watch over us.

We stopped just short of the enormous steel doors that lead into the throne room. The General gave a loud knock with the bronzed Griffon-like handles. The large doors opened wide in seconds to reveal the most beautiful sight I have ever seen.

A cerulean rug runs down from the throne and splits to encircle the entire hall. Pointed banners with the crest of Xora at the center stand erect with pride. Between each pennant stands a large, bronzed chandelier; all have been lit and brighten the vast hall.

At the center, a radiant throne of granite graces the bosom of Her Royal Majesty Queen Lilac. She is wearing a regal red dress that leaves her olive-skinned shoulders uncovered. Her plunging neckline is embellished with cerulean ruffles. The front center of her breast is a brooch. She appeared to match the same colors on the Crest of Xora. A delicate red rose with a glistening circle of golden Griffins imprinted on the blue armor of each Iluminate Guard.

"Your Majesty, I present the recruits for your regal guard." Her matted red lips look down upon the General with a smirk of intrigue.

"Spread out." No one moved at the command. This made the General tense up.

"The Queen has commanded you to spread out. Move it!" He frantically waved his arms for us to split our formation of doubles into two separate rows. I was now looking at the skinny, frightened man that once walked beside me.

Black, straight hair hangs over a thin, nervous face. Frozen gray eyes watch timidly while the Queen makes her way down to each recruit, finding every flaw.

"What's your name, young man?" she gently asked.

"My... my name is... Trevor... Your Majesty." he answered with a stutter. I feel sorry for the lad. If the Queen does not like him, she could send him to the Iron Pits. That dark prison is full of the cruelest villains and monsters Xora had. Or that we have discovered. It was built over the lava mines just below the Black Rock.

"Trevor, you seem nervous. Tell me something, are you willing to die for your Queen?" he nodded, still trembling. "Why don't I believe you?" She snapped her fingers, and instantly, a hooded figure wearing all white appeared beside her.

Is that who I think it is? I watched in awe as the hooded figure raised a card and recited an incantation. In a blast of white, a transparent figure dressed in a crimson robe with gold embellishments and a golden crown upon his head. In his hand, he wields a majestic sword. The Sword of Justice. Niya. I could identify that level of Essence anywhere.

This is the first time I ever witnessed her, or any Confessor, use their Essence to conjure their Tarot. It was mesmerizing. My feelings of admiration for that woman grew tenfold.

"Do not be afraid." Her gentle hand was pressed against his pale face. "Answer the Queen with honesty."

"I am afraid, my Queen." Those words poured out his mouth like vomit.

"Very good, Niya. You may go." She retracted her Tarot, and The Justice disappeared. Niya gave a regal bow as she turned; our eyes met briefly. I sensed pain and worry in her. Something I have never seen before. Reading that boy must have hurt her somehow. I turned my gaze back to the Queen. Her hand was pressed upon Trevor's face. I watched as his trembling, scrawny figure transformed into a pile of ash. "The Queen has no use for scared boys and girls in her Guard."

The horrific sight that lay before me made my heart beat fast. What would she think of me if she did not like a scared human?

"Clean this up." Her eyes glanced around the room, looking for her next victim. My breath was only taken momentarily as her stone-cold eyes landed on me. "You," she said while pointing directly at me, "come here to me." I did as I was commanded and tried to swallow my fear. "You are a strange-looking Elf. Who are your parents?" she asked while scrutinizing me.

"My mother was a human, and my father was an Elve. They both died when I was merely a child." I said with the utmost respect. Her gloved hand, still smelling of burnt flesh, traced my body from head to toe, sending an uneasy feeling up and down my spine.

"What is your name, half-elf?"

"Serena, Your Majesty." She signaled the General to come to her and whispered something in his ear. I could not make it out.

"You may all be dismissed to Salma Hall to begin training with the Reiki Master. I expect you will do well to serve me proudly when the time comes." The crowded hall dispersed, and I followed the rest out, but not before my collar pulled me.

"You will stay for a moment. The Queen requests a private audience with you." I am going to become the next pile of ash. Niya, where are you? I searched the room for her, but she was nowhere to be seen. The Queen possessed Essence. I am not sure what kind gives you the ability to turn people into ash, but whatever it was, I did not want to be her next victim.

"Serena, I hope you don't mind me seeking a private audience with you?" Did she ask me that?

"It is an honor, Your Majesty." I attempted to curtsy, but I was no good at it and lost my balance. This gave the Queen a laugh.

"You poor child." She gestured towards her. "I need to get a better look at you. I am interested in you. I wonder how you came to be and why you have no Essence. A magnificent creature like yourself should have some Essence." I could sense the curiosity within her.

"I do not know how to answer." Before I could finish, a hooded figure appeared. I recognized the white-furred coat with the golden leaf cufflinks; it was a Confessor. Is it her? I hope so.

"Confessor, mildly use your energy to tell me everything about this girl." The Confessor kept her face covered, but the feel of her smooth hand was familiar to me. It was Niya. I hope you feel my love for you.

"Niya, it's me," I whispered as she approached. She said nothing except to answer the Queen.

"This half-elf is an orphan raised in Narborim, my Queen. There is no Essence within her." The somber tone sent chills through me. Why was Niya acting like this? Was it because of the Queen?

"Very well. Half-elf, you may join the others. But be warned, if you do not pass your training or you cause problems, I will have you sent to the Iron Pits." She sternly said, "I have eyes everywhere, girl. Please don't make me regret not killing you where you stand. Bad enough, I had to kill that boy." I tried to bow again, but I lost my balance again, "Someone should teach this thing how to curtsy properly!" Things? Now, the Queen insults me.

## ALWIN

Sweat drips from my brow as I block another punch from Pekka. Fighting helps me clear my mind and keeps me focused on the mission. To save our world and our people from the constant pursuit of her. Since my last conversation with Odith, I have thought about Serena.

The need to know her grows greater each day. This is new and dangerous. I shouldn't want her like I do. A thick fist connects with my jaw, making my mouth fill with my blood.

"Pay attention." Pekka spats. "Can I ask you something?"

"Did you forget how to block?" I shoot him a smile.

"When did you know Alina was your mate?" His face softened at my question.

"The moment I laid eyes on her, something clicked between us.

Like a broken bone snapping back into place. It was powerful, and I immediately felt her Essence illuminate her and combine with mine."

"Pekka, I didn't know you were a romantic."

"For Alina, I was." He doesn't speak much of his late wife. She was murdered for marrying a half-elf. I was too late to save them both, just like with Odith. That is why I continually watch Serena. I need to get to her before I fail again.

"Do you have a woman in mind?" he asks, snapping me out of my thoughts.

"There is one," I admit. Pekka seems shocked, but he smiles. "About damn time, boy. I thought you played for the other side,

which is completely fine if you do. You will seek no ill judgments from me. What is her name? Is it Odith because I thought-"

"No. It's someone none of us have met yet but will soon."

"What makes you think she is your mate?" When I look at her, I long to touch her, but I won't admit that aloud.

"I don't know, Pekka. I have only seen her through the reflection pool."

"Another charge to be rescued." he grunts, stretching before exiting the boxing ring. "You will know for sure once your eyes land on her."

After the training session with Pekka, I went to the war room. I am meeting with Braxor today. Upon entering, the tall, red, scaled dragon is already sitting on his haunches, waiting for me. His long black horns shift with his colossal head as those two black eyes look down on me. Braxor stands fifty feet tall, which is why the War Room is so grand. My friends need to be comfortable.

"How was your trip?" I ask while closing the door behind me. Drakin is a long journey for those of us who cannot fly.

"Brief as per usual." he answers in a deep tone. Braxor and I met in the first century of my life. He saved me the day my mother was killed by my father. Our bond hasn't faltered since.

"The plans for the war are progressing. We will have the last piece in play soon."

"You mean the Phoenix?" he questions.

"Yes." He lets out a fierce noise. "Where is the girl?" Braxor has known about Serena just as long as we have. Our future relies on her commitment to the war against the humans.

"In Galavian. I have sent Odith there to help persuade her to join us."

"I don't trust that girl," he snarls. Odith and Braxor have never gotten along, and he has never told me why.

"Odith has been a long-time loyal friend to me, just like you. I don't understand your disdain for her."

"She reeks of betrayal and manipulation. "

"You can smell all that? I wonder what I smell like." I mumble. "An uptight virgin who takes everything so seriously. But today,

you also smell of something new." He sniffs me, and I back away, feeling awkward. "Desire, lust, hmm, have the Dark Prince found a mate?" he smirked.

"Why does everyone keep assuming I found a mate? I am trying to prepare us for war, and all anyone can talk about is sex." Braxor bursts out in a thundering cluster of laughter that shakes the room.

"It isn't funny, Braxor, I didn't call you here to talk about me. I called you here to discuss your position in this fight." His laughter subsides, and he wipes the tears from his golden eyes.

"I apologize; yes, we are to take the aerial pursuit, I assume." "But you only use firepower if necessary. I don't want to cause

unnecessary bloodshed."

"It's war, Alwin. Death and blood come with it. It would be best to decide what future you want for the realm. Peace and unity, or just another usurper to take the throne."

# 3

# SERENA

I left behind my unpleasant 'private audience' in the palace,
I took the stone path to Salma Hall. It doesn't look very safe from the outside, but rightfully so. If I were to fail, I would be sent to work the Iron Pits. Plastered walls and marble details comprise most of the building's outer structure. It is tough to see through the windows, but the intense pressure from within can be felt outside.

When I entered through the hard metallic doors, a blast of cool air wiped the sweat from my brows. On the inside, the walls seem barren and plain, nothing glamorous like the Galavian Palace. The foyer leads straight into the vast library of thousands of original books.

"If you are looking for the rest of the recruits, they went that way." The annoyed tone from an older woman with a sharp nose stuck in a book pointed toward another set of metallic doors at the back of the library. Can this place get any more lavish?

I rushed down the narrow halls, passing by every door until I finally reached the back of the group.

"This is where the humans will stay, and this is where the Elves will be staying. Before you ask, yes, they are co-ed. That doesn't mean you can frolic and play with each other." His voice sounded annoyed. He must have given this speech a dozen times already. A new batch of recruits flows in and out of these halls yearly.

"Hey, what did I miss?" I tapped on the shoulder of the human girl in front of me, hoping she would fill me in.

"Back off, half-elf. You shouldn't even be here." Her snobby look sent a fire burning through me. Before I could retaliate, I heard another voice. "Um, where does the half-elf sleep? Because she is not human or Elve, she is an abomination. I suggest she sleeps with the hogs." The entire group laughed, pointed, and stared at me. I could not hold my anger any longer. In a sudden burst of anger, a girl straddled me, and my fiery fist connected with her Caucasian face. "Get off her. You are going to kill her." I was thrust back off the girl while she lay unconscious. Blood leaked from her broken nose and busted lip.

"She started it," I said, regretting the immaturity of my voice. Everyone was standing there in awe, looking at me with fear. I ran so far that I did not know where I was going. I settled down next to the lake, tears welling in my eyes.

"What is wrong with me?!" I hit my fist in the water. The blood seeps into it like little red ribbons. "Abomination, thing, insult after insult! I cannot take it anymore! Who am I? What is wrong with me?" I screamed towards the sky, angry at the Ancients for sparing my life.

"Nothing, my dear." I jumped and turned around to see a shadowed figure appear right before me.

"Who are you?" Wearing a black hood over themselves to hide their identity, no doubt.

"I am just like you. Nothing matters with who we are." "What? Where did you come from? Are you a teacher here?" I could not see her, but her sly voice and womanly features gave me an eerie feeling.

"I am what you call an Iluminate. The Moon Tarot is under my control." I gulped my rising fear down. "My dear girl, there is no need to be afraid," she uncovered herself. Her ears and nose exhibited a pointed shape, yet all other features retained a distinctly human appearance. "I am a half-elf, too. My human features are more pronounced than my Elf's. But we are the same. Just like our Essence." She smiled at me.

"No, I do not have Essence." Her mouth was full of teeth as white as the snow on the ground.

"Every half-elf is born with a certain type of Essence. Yours may be related to fighting, anger, and rage." Hearing her voice speak lit that same fire I felt before. Anger, rage, the burning sensation to punch her in the face. "I can feel yours now. You want to fight me. Kill me even."

"Get out of my head."

"You are too weak and untrained to keep anyone from being in your head. Now I can teach you. You can learn all the ways of the Warrior from me. All that built-up rage and anger can be let out hurting no one."

"How?" Her pink, short hair softly hangs over a beautiful face. She was barely hiding her darting purple eyes, with pink irises that glared at me with intrigue. Fair blue skin elegantly compliments her cheekbones and nose. There is something ambiguous about her; perhaps it is a feeling of seduction or simply her familiarity.

"You can feel it. I am just like you."

"How is that possible? I was told there are no others like me because humans and Elves may not bed with each other."

"Oh, Serena, there is so much I could teach you. So much more. He could answer all your questions without even thinking about it." He? Who was she talking about? How does she know my name?

"Who are you talking about? How do you know my name?" I anxiously awaited her answer. A slight smirk came across her face before speaking.

"Alwin, my savior, and he can be yours, too." Where have I heard that name before? "Think about what I said. I can take you away from here, and we can go to Alwin together." She smiled a fake smile.

"I will think about it." Her fake smile turned into a legitimate grin of sinful delight.

"My name is Odith. I will see you again, Serena." She faded into the misted air, and I kept thinking about everything she had told me. How did she know my name?

Back in the rear end of the hall, I sat in front of the Essence Master's desk. It was about the fight. She was going to send me to the Iron Pits or have me killed. Maybe I should have taken up Odith's offer. I have been a prisoner all my life. I was hiding within the musty walls of Narborim, waiting to be free. The clanking of heels coming from behind me tensed my muscles with anxiety.

"Miss Serena, it isn't customary for my recruits to behave violently on the first day." A slim figure dressed in a tight-fitting black dress sat across from me.

"If you would allow me to explain," she put a hand up, gesturing to me to stop my babbling.

"I understand perfectly, my dear." Her rose gold spectacles sat at the end of her pointed nose. Full-blooded Elve. "You are an outsider looking for a place to fit. I am here to tell you to stop looking. There are no other half-elves in this world. You are the only innate of your liking. Now, you must choose." Choose? What did she mean?

"You are neither Elf nor Human, but you can choose which side you want to convert to."

"I don't understand." How can they convert me to one half that makes me whole?

"Do you know what powers a Master like me can possess?" I shook my head no. She drew me in like the ocean as she spoke, "I can converge you. You can expel the unwanted half of you and become whole to one species."

"You mean I wouldn't be a half-elf anymore?" Interesting. "Precisely." Her wicked smile made me sick.

"What would happen to my other half?"

"Dead. The other half would cease to exist. You would be morphed into whichever species you see fit. This may not be very objective, but I would go for the Human half. Making rounded ears pointy can be pretty painful."

\* \* \*

As I sank into my cotton bed, I contemplated my conversation with the Master. Convergence. So far, I have two choices: go with Odith and learn from her Master, or stay here and become a complete human or Elve. Oh, Mother, what should I do? I prayed every night since the death or kidnapping of my mother. I was waiting for her to answer me in any way she could. I cannot imagine being anything other than myself. I must find out why Alwin's name sounds so familiar to me. Then and only then will I decide.

Morning came, and my night of sleep was restless, with the two intense conversations running through my mind all night. Break- fast included boiled eggs, sliced bacon, and freshly squeezed goat's milk. I had nothing so delicious.

In Narborim, all we ate was fish and fish eggs. It was pretty disgusting after a while. I sat alone because, of course, no one wanted to befriend the half-elf. Mostly, they all just stared and gossiped about the way I looked. It made me want to take the Master up on her offer—or even creepy Odith.

After breakfast, I scampered off to the library to research this name and the true meaning of convergence.

"Excuse me," I said to the back of a tall, gray-haired Elven Woman. Turning around, her rose gold spectacles did not hide the annoyance in her eyes. Does everyone wear rose gold specs here? Or is it an old elf thing?

"May I ask you a question?" She just stood there, giving me a blank stare. "Does the name Alwin ring any bells?" Her annoyed expression went instantly to panic.

"What did you just say?" She slowly removed her glasses and slammed her book closed, sending dust particles in the air.

"Alwin? Have you heard of him?"

"We do not speak of the Dark Elves within these walls. I could have you arrested just for asking me."

"I'm sorry. I didn't know." Dark Elve?

"Of course, you didn't. You are a stupid little half-elf." Her insults stabbed at me like a knife. That fire was burning to be re-released. I took some shallow breaths and held it in with all my strength. "Get out of my library before I report you."

I did as I was told and left the crude librarian to her books.

Only Niya could make me feel better. I thought of a way to contact her. But it was a loss. She had no time for letters or visitors because of her busy schedule and tending to the Queen. I miss the sweet smell of her cherry blossom perfume.

"Serena," a whispered voice echoed down the vacant halls, "psst, Serena come here." I looked behind me and saw her.

"Niya?" I said with the biggest smile on my face. "What are you doing here?" She pulled me into a small storage closet. "Why are we hiding?"

"I needed to see you and explain things." I touched her soft cheek. My feelings for her were trying to explode, but I suppressed them. "We cannot be seen speaking to one another."

"But why? You and I grew up together."

"Because I am a Confessor, and you are a half-elf." Hearing her say that word, half-elf, made my heart hurt. "Serena," she gazed into my eyes with a sense of longing, and my heart felt like it was going to burst.

"Niya, tell me. Something is going on. I can handle it, believe me." I reached out and grabbed her hands. Her energy flowed through me. It was warm, peaceful, and loving.

"You cannot go through with the convergence." She pulled away from me. Her words and actions stunned me. "I'm sorry, but this will be the last time you see me. You need to trust me when I tell you not to do it." I sensed the pleading in her voice.

"Niya," she pressed a finger to my lips, cupped my chin, and kissed me softly. The sensation of her soft lips on mine sent a tingling feeling through me. I pulled her closer, then my tongue reached the slit between her lips. She resisted me and pulled away with tears running down her cheeks.

"I love you, Serena. My love for you will lead you out of the darkest places."

I felt her drift from my grip and disappear between the shadows. She kissed me. She loves me. I knew it.

I could barely recall anything; the entirety of our conversation went out the window the moment we kissed. I felt her energy surging through me. I know she did not want to stop, and neither did I. Confessors are forbidden to love, especially loving a half-elf.

My mind was racing over the events of the last week. Leaving my home, meeting the Queen from hell, two strangers offering to "help me," and kissing the girl I loved ever since we were children. If I tried to wind down and think about everything, I figured answers would pop up. I was wrong. Niya's words echoed in my head. 'Don't do the convergence,' she sounded terrified. Afraid for my life. I wish I could see her again.

She doesn't want me to change who I am. Even if it means we cannot be together. I went back to the lake and called out to Odith.

I am leaving if I cannot converge and join the Queen's Guard as a half-elf.

"Odith," I called out in a hushed tone. She never told me how to contact her again. "Odith, I summon thee?" That sounds so stupid. I instinctively covered my face with my hand, trying to conceal the embarrassment that surged through me.

"Serena," I jumped at the sound of her behind me. "Jumpy, are we? The Master can help with that."

"Odith, I need to ask you a couple of questions before I agree to leave with you." A somber nod told me to go ahead. "Do you know about convergence?"

Her cheerful smile quickly faded. "It is a dark and painful practice. Why?"

"The Essence Master offered it to me so I could join the Queen's Guard and not be thrown in the Iron Pitts."

"I see. Well, convergence rips your soul in half. The side you choose stays, but it is weak and barely even a soul anymore."

"Why would she offer something like that to me?" We were walking and talking around the beautiful glass lake. The Moon glistened in on its reflection.

"Because the way she and your Queen see it, you threaten them. They want to destroy you. And if that means ripping you apart to do it, then so be it."

"And you think Master Alwin can help me? Save me?" She sighed before stopping to answer me.

"Serena, if you stay here, you will end up dead, half-dead, or in prison. I am offering you a way out. A way to be free amongst me and my people."

"There are others like us?"

"Not so much half-human half-elf, but there are other half- elves."

"Is your Master a Halfling?"

"Why don't you see for yourself?" She smiled, coaxing me into leaving with her. Niya's words echoed in my head once again. I grabbed the reached-out hand and was whisked away into a whirlwind of purple and pink. Energy flowed through me as we spun inside a portal. I have heard about them. Only the most potent Essence can conjure one up. They use The Moon card at night, when the Moon is at its highest peak, the perfect time to tune in on all that power.

## ALWIN

The thundering in my chest and sweating of my palms come as I watch Odith and Serena enter the portal. She came here,

why am I so nervous? What will she think of me and this place? Calm down, Alwin. I tell myself. She is coming to learn to help. I need to find out what Odith has told her before I ask her to join our fight.

Once they arrive, it will take about an hour for them to get here. Rose must ensure her quarters are perfect, and I need to call a meeting.

"Rose," I said as the half-pixie fluttered by. "Please call the council to the War Room and prepare Miss Ozark's room. She will arrive soon, and everything needs to be perfect."

"As you command." Rose started with a bow. I hated when she treated me like that. Bowing before me is what my father made all his subjects do. I may be a Prince, but I am nothing like my father. He was a tyrant and ruthless King of our people—the reason the peace within Xora was destroyed. I may have his power within me, but I also have my mother's.

She was good, loyal, and pure, and that is why he killed her. I sat as the doors opened and the council members flooded in.

"The Phoenix is on her way. We need to be wary of any conversations we have with her. Talk of her power and the war will come from me and only me. The girl has been scared her entire life. We all know how that feels. Please welcome her with open arms.

Council and train her, even if she doesn't know the reason." There was silence, which usually comes after a speech like that. They would all obey my orders, just like any other time.

"Is she going to bring peace to the realm? Kill the Gnaxtor King and usurper Queen?" Lena asked.

"I don't know if it will come to that. Both sides know about the legend of the Phoenix. If they get word that we have her on our side, perhaps we won't need to go to war."

"Here, here." Pekka cheered, and the rest followed suit. "Thank you, my friends. The meeting is adjourned."

Back in my room, I paced in anticipation. Gods, I am never like this. What is wrong with me is that she is just a girl. Someone I haven't even met yet. The sound of knocking came at my door, and then it opened.

"They are in the War Room," Rose stated.

"Thank you." I followed her out, and as she left, I ventured right.

Slipping in through the shadows, my eyes instantly land on her, and my pulse quickens. I feel it and hear it at the same time. The sound of a bone snapping into place. She is my mate, and I cannot believe it.

# 4

# SERENA

On the other side, colors intermingled, casting the world into an iridescent play of blue and gold. My eyes squinted as they adapted to the dazzling radiance of the sky. A brisk breeze danced around, causing marigold leaves to flutter and descend from the forest floor.

"Where are we?"

"Welcome to Ermelon Forest," Odith said with a smile. "Beautiful, isn't it?"

"Enchanting."

"Come on. I will take you to the castle." They have a castle. Who is this guy?

The walk was anything but boring. It was as if the forest was alive and wanted to show us golden mushrooms, glowing rose bushes, and whistling winds. The echoing of mockingbirds filled my ears with a sweet sound. The smell was natural, like a dozen flowers were blooming simultaneously.

"Have you lived here all your life?" I wanted to get to know her better. Part of it was curiosity, and the other was well…

"Unfortunately, no," she said as she guided me up a hill. "When I was sixteen years old, my parents were killed for having me. And my lover was killed for being with me. The Gnaxtor came for me, but Alwin got to me before they did."

"I'm sorry." Something we have in common other than our being half-elves and a lover being killed. I was never that brave to show my affection for Niya.

"I have had time to grieve. Alwin took me in and cared for me.
Showed me how to use my Essence to control my tarot cards." "Does everyone with Essence control these cards?" A small laugh

came from her, and I could not help but feel anxious.

"You poor child. No. Only certain powers can control the cards." I gave her a worried look. "Don't worry, if you have Essence, you will find out if you can control the cards."

We continued to walk for another hour. Odith informed me of her childhood with Alwin. He must be old, seeing as she is twenty- five. He taught her how to control her Essence and use it to Conjure.

"There are rules," she said. "If you manipulate or misuse the cards, they work against you."

"Has anyone ever tried that before?" She went quiet, and it worried me.

"There has never been nor will there ever be someone with that power. It takes a serious amount of control to conjure. You must be a god to manipulate the cards and make them do what you want."

"But, has anyone ever tried?" She just raised her hand and shook her head. My eyes followed her pink hand as she pointed to a vast fortress.

"Welcome to Ermelon Castle." It was a colossal stone tower connected by high walls lined with armed sentries. The black banners were decorated with silver phoenixes and danced with the wind. Steel lanterns were mounted to each pole to cast a luminescent glow over the fortress.

A grand archway was engraved with the phrase nonstate quod lux venit cum nubibus, "The light will come despite the clouds." It was a beautiful saying. Inspirational even.

The iron bars lifted as we approached, and the two guards straightened their posture as Odith and I walked by. The courtyard was busy with noise. Many creatures were here training, some eating and others socializing.

"Do they all live here?"

"Some live in the Castle, but the others have their own homes down in the town." There were Elves, Dwarves, Pixies, and even Humans. "Each one of those is a half-elf. Cast out and hunted by Purebreds."

"Purebreds?"

"All Humans or All Elves." Next time, I am going to call that girl a Purebred. It does not seem like an insult, though. We entered through a small door frame that led us down a narrow corridor. It was barren except for some torches to light the darkened halls. "Alwin is waiting for us in the War Room."

We entered through large wooden doors with two handles shaped like a phoenix. A round table with what appeared to be a drawing of the world was at the center. Narborim, Galavian, and so many other places. "Is this all of Xora?"

"All of what we know of." I strummed my fingers over the textured surface. I never knew our world was this big before.

"Where are you from?" Edith stopped in her tracks and quickly knelt. I was confused until I felt it. The slow breath coming from behind me. "Sneaking up on someone isn't the proper way to introduce yourself to them."

A hand brushed my shoulder, and my heart was beating out of rhythm when I turned around and saw him. Slick black hair pulled back into a bun. Blue irises danced within his gray-skinned face as he examined me from above. He was standing about two inches taller than me, and his face was plain. Handsome but plain.

"Welcome, Serena," his voice was cold and dark. Appropriate for a man of his age.

"Hi," that is all I could muster up. Out of my entire vernacular, the Old Father would be ashamed. Foolish child. That is what he called me when I was being ignorant. I cleared my throat, I wanted to step back from him, but I was paralyzed.

"Odith, darling, you may go." I did not move, but out of the corner of my eye, I could see a glimpse of pink hair pass me and hear the doors creaking as they opened and closed. "So," he started as he stepped away from me. I finally let out the breath which I was holding.

My eyes followed him as he circled the map. "Do you know who I am?" His broad shoulders and brooding face made me weak in my knees. I feel anxious, and I do not know why.

"Alwin," I answered, trying to hide the stutter of my voice. "Odith said…" Before I could finish, he was close to me again. This time, mere inches away from me. I could see the rise and fall of his chest with each inhale and exhale. Something was captivating about him.

"Odith said what?" He looked at me with those icy blue eyes. "You could help me." He leaned in, creating the expectation of a kiss, but instead, he stepped aside. "We shall see." Then he was gone. Like a ghost in the night. Here and gone again. I was left standing, alone, confused, and wondering what in the hell just happened.

"Come with me." A guard appeared behind me, and his voice made me jump.

"Who are you?" My question did not seem to faze him, for his automated stare stayed the same. "Where are we going?"

"He is escorting you to your chambers."

"Odith, glad to see a familiar face." She smiled as she approached me.

"So, your meeting with Alwin went well." How do you know? "Did it? He seems…"

"Intimidating?" "No." Yes.

"He means well. You will start your testing tomorrow." I shot her a worried glance. "Calm yourself; you will be fine."

"What if I fail? I have no place to go."

"Alwin will let you stay here, regardless. If you do not have Essence, you will still train to become a warrior."

"Why is he building an army?"

"He is trying to stop the ones that want us dead. To make Xora a safer place for everyone that is like us." Before I realized it, we had walked to the door that led into my bed chambers. "I promise you will know everything soon enough." She gave a respectful bow and then opened the door.

On the inside, a large canopy hung over a small bed frame. The sheets were lined with white cotton linen. The room was not grand but small enough for one person. A bath was drawn in the corner, and nightclothes were laid out for me to dress in.

I sank into that warm bath water. My feet were screaming at me for the journey that the day had on them. I sipped some jasmine tea leaves and let my body soak in all the heat. Niya, I miss you. I wish I could see you again. My thoughts went to her. The girl I grew to know and love. Her kiss still lingers.

Morning came with a loud knock upon my door. I blinked the sun out of my eyes as a blonde-haired pixie half-elf came in and opened my curtains.

"Good morning, I guess." Her face was stern.

"The Master wants you to dress and be in the War Room within the hour."

"Um, okay, thank you, I guess." She nodded her head at me and fluttered away. On my dresser, I saw a blue blouse embellished with golden lace. A small phoenix was embroidered on each shoulder. It was the most beautiful piece of fabric I had ever seen.

Accompanied with this blouse were black pants and boots. I fashioned my hair into two braids but let loose ends cover my ears. I have done it all my life to hide who I am from judgmental eyes.

I ate my breakfast, which was fruit and boiled eggs. The apples were unbelievably delicious. I could have eaten more if I were allowed. After filling my belly, a servant came and picked up the dirty dishes, and I made my way to the War Room.

I think it was this way. Of course, I would get lost on my first day.

"A little lost, are we?" My thoughts were interrupted by Odith once again.

"You sure know how to get around undetected, right?" She smiled at me. It made me blush, and I did not know why.

"It is one of my many powers. I can make myself invisible." I don't know if she is being sarcastic or not. She laughed, and before I knew it, we both were locking arms, laughing down the hall and into the War Room.

It was nice to make a new friend. I have not laughed like that since my last day with Niya. Then, my mood went from happy to sour in just one memory. "Did you sleep well?"

That brooding, smooth voice made me focus again. "Very well, thank you. Probably the best sleep I have ever had." He was standing right in front of me again. How does he move so fast?

"You seem nervous, Serena. There is no need to be. You are safe here." He reached out his hand, and I felt myself shrink down just a little. His skin brushed against mine, sending an electrical pulse through my body. "You do not need to hide your true self here."

He brushed my hair behind my ears and cupped my face so my eyes met his. My heart was beating again. I felt something I had never felt inside unless Niya kissed me. "What are you doing to me?"

No answer. I felt myself struggle to move from his grip, but my body was like stone. The electrical feeling soon turned into fear, and I heard myself screaming. And then, it happened. I felt the heat all around me and saw the embers reflecting in his eyes. A small smile formed on his lips, and he let me go. My body falls, but it does not contact the floor. Then, the room was black as I felt Alwin's powerful arms scoop me up. I last heard, "We will be in my chambers…"

When I came to, I saw a black canopy above me. And felt velvet blankets over me. I sat up, looking around to figure out where I was. The room was so dark that I panicked.

"Calm down." I looked toward the direction of his voice. "You will make yourself pass out again."

"What happened?"

"What do you remember?"

"I remember you holding me, heat, and then nothing." He approached me and sat at the edge of the bed. "You don't know what personal space is, do you?"

He smiled, and I felt my heart jump. Please stop it. You cannot fall for a guy you just met. Plus, he is like a billion years old. "We have discovered your Essence."

"Wait. No. I do not have magic. I am a useless half-elf…" Before I could continue, he placed a finger on my lips. Even the slightest touch sends a pulse through me.

"You are anything but useless. You have the Phoenix Fire." "What?"

"Did your Old Father not teach you about it?"

"It may have been mentioned, but it was just a myth."

"The Phoenix Fire is the most powerful of all Essence. Only certain people can wield this magic." I listened to him speak but still did not believe his words. "So, you coming here was probably the best decision. If our enemies got word of you, you would be manipulated into destroying all of us."

"What do you mean? Are you a half-elf, too?" He scooted closer, brushing my hair behind my ears again. There it was, the pulse surging through me. We were inches away from each other, one slight movement, and our lips would meet.

"I am half-elf and half-pixie. That is why I can move swiftly. I have the speed and stealth of a fairy." he whispered those words into my ear, placed a hand on my hip, and I was sure he would take me for his. I wanted it, but then I was not sure I liked it. His neck was so close to me that I fought the urge to kiss it.

"I think I need to leave." I got up before anything else happened, and the surge left with the distance between us. He nodded his head and then led me to the door.

"Serena," I looked at his half-disappointed face, "please do not think of me as too forward. I can come on strong in certain situations."

"You did nothing wrong. I am a big girl and can take care of myself. But I have just met you." I wanted to say, plus you are old, and I am in love with someone else. This was nothing but pure lust. That is the only logical explanation for me being so weak around him. I have never shared a bed with anyone, and Niya was my first kiss.

"We will start your training tomorrow." He smiled, and I quickly left his chambers and headed into my own. I slumped down into my bed. My body and mind are exhausted from the events of the day. You have Phoenix Fire. Those words echoed in my head.

How is it possible? I clenched my mother's amulet tightly and prayed to her. Uncertain of her fate—whether she's alive or gone—I find solace in holding this star. The following day, and mornings after, the same pixie girl came and went. She was leaving fresh clothes and fresh food. She took my dirty linens and laid my breakfast out before me.

"What is your name?" She did not stop at my question, so I grabbed her arm. "Please, if you are tending to my mess, I must know who you are."

"I am called Rose."

"That is a beautiful name. And are you half-pixie, half-human?" She blushed when I asked.

"Yes. Now, please let go of me so I can get back to work." I released my grip on her wrist. They were petite; my thumb and index finger touched at the center. She was as beautiful as her name. She had blonde hair, purple eyes, and pale skin, probably from her human half. Her wings were tucked in, but they shimmered like the stars in the sky when the light hit them. I cannot believe I am attracted to another one. What is wrong with me?

A lesson with Pekka will clear my mind. Pekka was a tall, Dwarf half-elf. The height was the only human thing about him. His red beard, scraggly hair, and brute strength were all dwarfs.

"Well, let's begin today with some hand-to-hand combat." His deep Northern accent was difficult to understand, but after a week here, I was making out his words. "Serena, I want you to show what you have learned this week."

I could not see my face, but the others snickered at the apparent fear I bore.

"Don't you think someone else should... okay." He pointed his big, burly finger at the mat, and I waited for him to choose my assailant. He scanned the class, but no one stepped up; I was unsure why. I was hardly strong enough nor skilled enough to beat anyone. "I am looking for a volunteer."

"Allow me," the entire courtyard got on one knee as Alwin approached the ring. "On your feet. You can't watch a fight from the ground." He removed his black shirt as he walked to reveal his defined muscles. My eyes followed each deepened line that outlined his chest, abs, and shoulders. The memory of those arms around me sent a hot flash through me.

"Are you ready?" I raised my hands and got into a fighting position. "Very good. Let us begin."

A big gray fist was heading straight toward my face in a flash, but

I must have kept something because I could dodge it and sweep his feet from underneath him. He made a loud grunt as he hit the ground. The crowd gasped at the sight of him on the stone floor.

"Stay down." I heard myself say it, but I did not believe it. He got to his feet, wiped the sweat from his brow, and bucked up to me. We engaged again; this time, he caught me and slammed me hard against the floor. He pinned my arms down by gripping my wrist and straddled himself on top of my waist. I struggled to get free, but he leaned down and whispered in my ear, "I usually like my girls on top."

A furious heat burned through me. I did not know if it was jealousy at those other girls or rage, but I was engulfed in flames again but did not feel the burn. I was unconscious mere seconds later. Just like last time, I woke up in Alwin's bed chambers.

"If you wanted in my bed, all you needed to do was ask."

"I don't want to be in your bed. I want to know why this keeps happening to me." He approached me; I did not let him get close to me this time. I jumped to the other side of the bed. "Stay away from me."

"Serena, I will not hurt you."

"I don't think you are going to hurt me, Alwin. You are the reason I keep passing out. Every time you touch me, it happens." He laughed at me. That gorgeous smile, I wouldn't say I liked the way it made my stomach flip. I was attracted to him, but I did not want to be.

"You pass out because you use your power every time you get angry, weakening you. Build your strength up. The more you use it, the stronger you will get." That makes sense.

"What about when you touch me?" He approached me slowly. Each step forward, I took a step back until I was up against the wall.

"What do you mean? What happens when I touch you?" He got close to me, leaned in close enough, but not touching.

"I need to leave." He leaned in, he brushed my hair behind my ears, and I felt it again. "Stop." He lifted his hand off me.

"I will bid you goodnight, Serena." He backed away. My heart was beating so fast I thought it would jump out of my chest. His back was to me; something told me not to leave yet. I grabbed him, pinned him against the wall, and kissed him.

I was not sure if he was going to kiss me back until I felt his arms around me, lifting me off the ground. It was intense. His hands were around my waist as he set me on the bed. Something inside me told me to stop. "I need to go."

In between breathless kisses, I pushed him back. "Did I do something wrong?"

"No, but this is too fast." I kissed his cheek softly, bid him goodnight, and left.

What was I thinking? Kissing him like that. What would Niya think? She said she would not see me again. I do not care and cannot wait for something that will not happen. I vowed to get Niya out of my mind and focus on me. Embrace my powers and everything about me. Alwin woke up something inside me; it felt good and powerful; I wanted more. I wanted him because he wanted me.

## ALWIN

She kissed me.

She pulled me into her and pressed those tantalizing lips against mine. It wasn't a soft kiss like a peck on the cheek from my mother. It was all-consuming, and the shield I formed around my heart melted. She doesn't realize it yet, but we are fated mates. The tension will grow between us if I don't do something quick.

I need her to focus on her training and not me. Leaving for a while should help take me out of the picture. A month should do just fine, and I can watch her progression through the reflection pool in Drakin.

"Don't tell anyone where I am going and why I have left," I told Odith as she summoned a portal. "Especially Serena."

"Why?"

"She needs to focus on training. I have a business to attend to in Drakin. I trust you to watch over and befriend her while I am gone."

"Of course." She shifted as the swirls of pinks and purples circled before us. "Why does she keep passing out when she uses her powers?"

If I tell her the truth and say it aloud, then it becomes real. "We are fated, mates, Odith. The longer she denies any feelings for me and doubts her power, the longer she will black out. I need her to focus on her Essence and not me. That is more important than any bond we will ever have." Before she could say anything, I jumped through the portal and landed on the other side with a grunt.

"Alwin, what a delightful surprise." Braxor's voice came from behind me.

I see that I have landed in the middle of the training yard. I have been to Drakin Fortress several times, but am always amazed at the

sound structure the dragons have morphed it into. A once-dormant volcano now houses the dragons of the realm. They do not have towers, no need for walls, and there is no threat to this kingdom.

Dragons have long since been extinct in the minds of the Gnaxtor and Galavian rulers, most likely because they have been focused on ridding the world of anything not pure.

Shooting into the sky behind him is a large black volcano with a vast hole carved into the bottom. Unlike the dragons, I am a speck of dust on a map. There isn't much else to this land besides the ash-covered ground and dry heat, which my shadows can protect me. The perfect place for dragons to live.

"Braxor, I need a favor." He looks inquisitively down at me. "You seek sanctuary?" he questions.

"Only for a month. I need to take time away from Ermelon. If it isn't too much to ask." The dragon ponders my request.

"Fine, but I need an explanation. You know we don't welcome others so easily without reason, and seeing as you are not bruised or bleeding, I'd say you didn't come here leaving a fight." That is the thing about Braxor: he is wise and observant.

"Should we go somewhere... private?" I ask as I notice other dragons make their appearance. Each of them has a variety of assorted colors, shapes, and sizes. Even the little ones could swallow me in one bite.

He didn't answer; he just waited for me to speak. Letting out a sigh and rubbing the back of my neck, I am nervous again.

"I have found my mate," I said with some relief. Braxor still said nothing, waiting for another more reasonable answer for my seeking sanctuary. "It is the Phoenix, and she is at Ermelon."

"I see. There is no real threat bringing you here besides your stupidity. Has she rejected you?"

"She doesn't know."

"Why are you telling me and not her?"

"Because I am a danger to her. She passes out when she uses her powers around me or touches me while using them. She can focus more on that if I am away."

"Alwin," he softly states. "You need to tell her and let her decide for herself what is more important. We need the Phoenix, but maybe being with her will help her become stronger. Did you think of that?"

I didn't.

"I have made my decision. If you let me stay here, I can help. With your permission, I also need to keep my training up and will watch over her through your reflection pool."

"Escort Master Alwin to some quarters suitable for a man. You realize we dragons do not sleep in rooms on soft beds. We prefer the soft ashes from the old volcano." The ground is covered in it.

As we make our way through a hollowed-out entrance at the bottom of the volcano, I take in my surroundings. It is all obsidian stone. The heat is not as unbearable as I imagined it would be.

Using my magic to cast my shadows helps shield me from it.

No bedrooms exist, but a room is prepared in a smaller, bizarre whole.

"Can you conjure your bed? Or would you like the King to do it?" a shorter, all-black, young dragon asked.

"I think I can manage, thank you." The youngling disappeared as I whisked up a bed using the incantation Mother taught me as a child. Not all Essence requires the use of Tarot Cards. I am not a master and have never wanted to become one. I am afraid of what I will become if I try.

My father didn't just use shadow magic to tear apart Xora. He used the Ancient Deck gifted by Master Vincent himself. He was manipulating the cards, twisting and turning the honorable practice, morphing it into something to be feared. I won't go down the same dark path as him.

With each passing day, I start a routine. I wake in the morning and run with shadows shielding me from the atmosphere. Eat a breakfast of charred meat, never ask which kind, and go on about the day.

Braxor created a makeshift punching bag formed from goose feathers and fabrics that the youngling fetched from the different territories. He was allowing me to keep up on my fighting skills. Usually, after a training session, he would join me at the reflection pool to watch over Serena.

A stone circle with the only water for miles sits at the center front of the mountain, glistening in the sun's rays. Because of the vast ocean connecting the realm, water is a resource we are all privy to.

"She is becoming stronger every day. You should be proud." Braxor murmured.

"She is, and I am." something caught my eye as I looked upon her and Odith sparring in the ring. A dark shadow cast itself around her.

"Do you see that?"

I asked as I pointed.

"An Omen," Braxor stated. "Serena is in danger; you must return to her. She hasn't embraced her true form and will be too weak to face whatever threatens her."

Rushing out of the room, Braxor's wing shoots out to stop me. "Beware of Odith, Alwin. Something isn't right with that girl."

Pushing past his wing, I move through the caverns until I am in the yard again. Calling out to Odith, a moment passes before a portal of purple and pink forms in front of me. Looking back, I see a line of dragons, and at the center is my friend, who bows his head in respect.

# 5

## SERENA

The following day, I am feeling happier than I have ever been. My thoughts are only on training to become a better soldier.

The kiss from last night helped.

"You seem rather chipper this morning?" I don't realize I am smiling when Odith sits beside me. "I thought after yesterday you would be in your usually sour mood. What changed?" Alwin and I

make out. That's what I want to say.

"I think I am ready to embrace all this. Tell me everything you know about the Phoenix Fire." She gives me a suspicious glance but doesn't push me any further.

"Well, it is said that the Phoenix Fire is only given to the most powerful beings. It is a blessing and a curse. If you can't control it, the power will consume you. Into the Dark Phoenix."

"How do I learn to control it?"

"First, you need to start small. Practice lighting torches or candles and gradually move up to campfires and eventually buildings." She sounds more excited than I am. "Listen, Alwin will not let you lose control.

When I was struggling, he was there for me through everything. I learned to control and use my power to conjure my first portal." What else happened between you two?

I swallow my rising jealousy. We aren't exclusive, so I cannot assume a man of his stature is a virgin. "Odith, have you and Alwin ever… you know?" I make a gesture, and she busts out laughing at me. "What?"

"Are you serious? Me and that lump of muscle? No," she steps behind me, brushes her lips, and whispers, "I prefer women." I jump when she slaps me on my butt.

"Oh," I say, blushing. "I didn't mean to…"

"Of course, I am single. The pixie half-elf left me about a month ago. She said she couldn't handle my essence."

"I'm sorry to hear that." We pause for a moment. "So, tell me more."

She tells me all about the legend of the Phoenix Fire. It was gifted by the Ancient Ones, who forged a fire out of the ashes of the first bird.

"It is said that when it is time for a phoenix to pass on, it will burst into flames and turn ash. They are reborn again in that ash."

"How is it I possess such power?"

"When the first Phoenix passed, the Ancient Ones took those ashes and blood from the reformed and consumed it." I shudder at the thought of them drinking ash and blood. "Many died, but the one that survived could control the fire."

"Why is it such a rare power to possess?"

"Because it hasn't been seen since the first Ancient." I look down at the ground, trying to remember everything she told me. "You are the first we have seen in centuries. And you are the first half-elf to possess such an Ancient power. You give us hope." The sad look in her purple eyes makes me nervous.

"It feels like a heavy burden. Why do you think it took so long for me to use it?"

"Well, I didn't know I had Essence until Alwin came for me. It isn't always dormant, and it can be for some others. Pekka didn't discover his powers until around your age, too."

"What about Alwin? How old is he?"

"I don't know. But he was raised by someone. He isn't much older than us, but somehow he is immortal."

"Do you think it is because he is half-pixie?" We look at each other and laugh at the thought.

"Pixies live an immortal life, that is true, but I don't know why he doesn't age." We continue to talk for hours. It is nice having a friend to talk to and laugh with. Niya was that for me growing up. But she isn't here now, and I won't ever see her again. The library is glorious. Shelves upon shelves of books chalked full of information. I am happy to study and train. Over a month, I trained hard and felt more robust and faster than ever before I got here. My control is flourishing. I can light a candle without passing out.

"Perfect, little one. Let's see if you can defend yourself without your powers." Pekka is constantly pushing me to be better. His lessons are complex, but I keep more than I give myself credit for. When he tries to sweep my feet, I am faster and punch him right in the gut.

"I am a fast learner." I smile. He doesn't return the smile, but nods and bows in respect. I look into the courtyard. My eyes are trying to find him. The one who kissed me with so much passion it burned and left a mark. I haven't seen or heard from him since that night. Whenever I ask someone where he is, I am told something different.

"Where is Alwin?"

"He is out on a mission. He should be back soon. Which is good because he will want to see your progress." Odith is proud of me. She practices and studies with me all the time. Each morning after breakfast, she comes for me, and we run the grounds, which I enjoy because I can admire the beauty of the forest.

Narborim is never this enchanting. After our run, we meet in the training yard with Pekka.

"Class, today we practice strikes and blocks." Pekka loudly exclaims. There is always a class of twenty students. "Simultaneously."

"Don't worry, Serena, you will be fine," Odith says as she pats my back. Odith is a skilled fighter who never wanted to spar with anyone other than me. I don't mind entirely because the others seemed too afraid to talk to me.

"On the mats in position. Begin." Holding my hands to block my face, Odith came at me with her right fist, which I stopped with my left forearm while thrusting my knee upward into her abdomen. It didn't seem to faze her as she shot me a smile when her left hook went straight toward my chin, knocking my head back and ringing my ears. Spitting out my blood, I charged forward. Our bodies interlocked as we wrestled each other to the ground. I have her pinned down and think I won, but I was a fool to let my guard down because she flipped us.

"Don't let your guard down, Serena. Not for one second." she muttered as I struggled to break free of her hold. A whistle sounded, and she helped me to my feet.

"Shower, meet Master Lena in the library for your magic lessons," Pekka ordered.

"So, you have been here a little over a month. Do you think you made the right choice?" Odith asked as we made our way to the library.

"I don't know yet." I was only saying that because of that grey-skinned man who lifted me and carried me to his bed. "When do you think he will be back?"

"Why do you keep asking about Alwin?" I didn't answer her immediately, but she got a shocked look and an accusatory smile. "You like him, don't you?"

"No," I lied.

"Oh, my, you are blushing like a little schoolgirl. Does he make your heart flutter when he looks at you?"

"No." I lied again. "I just wanted to know where your grandmaster is, that is all. I need to tell him how insufferable you have become." She punched me on my arm, which didn't hurt as much because of the new muscles that had formed. Odith and I spent every day together. She felt like a sister. We had so many things in common. We were half-elf orphans, with a human for a mother and elf for a father. The Gnaxtor King killed her parents too. She was a Conjurer who controlled different tarot cards. She is beautiful, but I did not feel what I had once felt for Niya and now for Alwin. Or think I feel.

Later that evening, as I delved into the pages of the book on Phoenix Fire, I once more experienced a chill. I grabbed my shawl and adjusted it over my shoulders.

"Serena." I thought I heard someone call my name, but only I was in my room. "Serena."

"Niya?" I must have been going crazy because I thought I heard her voice whispering my name.

"Serena, look at me!" Standing right behind me, clear as day, dressed in her white silk gown, her black hair flowing in the wind. I ran and tried to hug her, but my arms went right through her.

"How are you here?"

"I have little time," she looked sad, her face red from tears. "Why did you leave?"

"I wasn't given much choice when you told me not to go through with the convergence."

"I didn't want you to leave."

"Well, you should have said that then. Not giving me a warning that scared me. You could have explained everything to me." "Serena, you are not safe with them," I crossed my arms while

my anger was building. "Ermelon is not safe for you. The Dark Elf…"

"How do you know where I am?"

"Just listen to me. The Dark Elf is trying to use you to take over Xora."

"Stop calling him that! His name is Alwin." "Serena, what have you done?"

"Does it matter? I am finally happy and with people that accept me for who I am. I am stronger, and I have become my true self."

"You were happy with me. I have always accepted you."

"You kissed me. You kissed me and told me we would never see each other again. Now you come here trying to destroy my heart again. I love you, Niya. No, I was in love with you, but you broke me. Alwin and Odith have picked up the pieces, and I am better now." She was quiet. I couldn't bear to see her.

"You are in danger. The Queen knows about your Essence. She will come for you, and he won't be able to save you. She means to use you to take out the Gnaxtor King and everyone else who stands in her way. Leave this place before it's too late."

Then, she was gone. Just like that, I let the flood I was suppressing overcome me. Tears of sorrow and anger flooded my eyes and face. Why? Why did she have to come here and say that stuff to me? Before I knew it, my entire room was engulfed in flames. I was angry and hurt, and releasing my fire felt good.

"Serena!" Edith shouted as the room and I were drowned in water. "What happened?" I fell to the floor, my knees hitting hard, but I didn't care. Odith held me as I cried. Letting everything I was keeping in me all these years flow out: all the insults, stares, and Niya's voice. My tears washed it all away. When I was finally done, my eyes hurt from being so dry, my head ached from hours of crying. Edith stayed with me, holding me and rubbing my back like an older sibling. "Are you ready to tell me what happened here?"

"Niya." That was all I said. I heard the cold in my voice. "Who is that?"

"A girl I used to love." I sat up, and I saw the sympathy in her eyes. "She came to me saying blasphemous things. Alwin was the Dark Elf, and the Queen knew about Ermelon and me. She said that I was being used. A pawn in their game."

"No wonder you got angry. Alwin does not use us. As for your Queen, I have seen what she can do."

"I once saw her turn a boy to ash. Niya helped her do it, too." "I thought Confessors were honorable."

"I never told you she was a Confessor." She backed away from me, covering her mouth like she said something she was not supposed to. "How do you know about her power?"

"Serena, I watched you for months before I contacted you." "Why?"

"I needed to be sure you could be trusted. Bring you to my home and around my family."

"Why does everyone keep lying to me?" I felt my fire coming on again, but I simmered down. "Leave me alone. I need time to think."

"Let us take you to a unique room. One that hasn't been turned to ash."

I let Odith escort me to an unfamiliar room. I didn't sleep that night. I just sat by my fire, thinking about everything. I gripped my amulet and prayed to my mother again. I don't think she can hear me. Is she even dead? I must have dozed off because a knock on my door awakened me. I looked into the small mirror above the vanity; my eyes were glazed over with fatigue, and my neck was crooked from sleeping in a chair all night. The dark shadows below my sockets were the memory from the embers of last night.

"Serena, Alwin is back and wants to speak with you." Odith was dressed in a purple gown that made her eyes pop.

"Why are you in a dress?" Hearing the exhaustion in my voice was even more tiring.

"Because I am going on a date." No wonder she was chipper. She said she hadn't been physical with anyone in over a month. "Now get dressed. You are meeting him in the War Room."

Great. I thought to myself. I will jump for joy at the sight of my demise.

"Serena," my heart fluttered when he said my name, just like it did when he said it while my lips were on his neck.

"Alwin," I spoke. I was trying to hide the nervousness in my voice.

"I was told you have progressed amicably while I was away." We both started circling the map. We kept our distance, but I could feel the tension rising. "And last night. You burned down your room. Why is that?"

"I was angry." He smirked at me. I could not tell whether it was smug.

"Do you prefer my bedchambers?" I stopped. And then there he was. I felt his breath against my neck again. My heart was pounding, and I couldn't stop it. "I have missed you while I was away. I remembered your lips," he kissed my neck, "the feel of your hands on my body." He grabbed my waist.

"Stop it!" I stepped away from him. He turned, and his face was full of disappointment. "I am not some plaything. You cannot toy with me."

"Is that what you think I am doing here? Toying with you?" I saw hurt in his eyes.

"Well, you are older. I am sure you have had many women share your sheets with you." He let out a sigh.

"Serena, I have never even kissed anyone until you." My ears couldn't believe it. "If you don't trust me, I will ask the Confessor to use her power to prove it to you."

"I barely know you, Alwin. Are you the Dark Elf?" He stepped closer, and I stepped back.

"Alright. No. My father was given that title because of his terrible actions."

"How old are you?" "225 years old."

"Why don't you age?"

"Because once pixies reach the age of twenty-five, they stop aging."

"So your mother was a pixie?" "Now, who is playing games?"

"I am just trying to get to know you."

"Yes. My father bewitched her into his bed. She was killed when I was a child." His voice trembled while speaking. "My father tried to raise me to be a wicked man. But I ran away. I didn't want to be like him."

"Alwin," he stepped towards me. I didn't move this time.

"With your permission, I would like to kiss you." I nodded, and he kissed me. It was a soft kiss. "Serena, I would never hurt you. What your friend said…" "Ex-friend."

"It isn't true. Well, the part about me." I believed him. There was still a seed of doubt in me. He held me tight as if I was going to run away. I felt safe in his arms, and it scared me.

"Alwin!" Odith came bursting in the doors. Fear on her face. "What is it?" he asked, letting me go.

"We are under attack!"

## ALWIN

Odith disappeared into the chaotic crowd before I could ask her questions. Gripping Serena's arm, I pulled her with me.

"You need to get to safety," I yelled, but she didn't hear me as she tore from my grip, racing into the fight before us. Trying to charge after her, I am pushed into a wall by a Gnaxtor soldier with foul breath. My shadows release, wrapping themselves tightly around the creature and pulling him off me. It landed on the ground breathless as it dissipated. An illusion? No one here is that powerful or skilled except… Odith.

Running down the halls, I ignore the soldiers, and although they can still kill and wound, I am unafraid. The roaring beat in my chest quickens when I can't find Serena.

"Alwin," I hear Pekka in the distance. Turning, I see him toss a longbow and quiver full of arrows at me, knowing that archery was a skill I mastered long ago.

"It's an illusion, Pekka; none of this is real," I yelled back just as another soldier brought an ax down toward me. Rolling out of the way, the ax trimmed the end of my bun slightly. Knocking my arrow, I shoot it through the image, which dissolves.

"It may very well be fake, but the cuts and bruises are genuine." He spats, wiping blood from a cut on his brow. Sauntering over to him, we are encircled by an army of them.

"Where is Odith?" I ask.

"Last I saw, she ran out of the War Room."

"She did this. I don't know why I know." Pekka angrily yelled before we engaged with the army of beasts. Each of my arrows pierced through the images, leaving no damage. Unsheathing my sword from my side, I stopped wasting my ammunition and started swinging. Metal clashed with metal as sparks flickered into the cold air. They all vanish just before a sword is thrust through Pekka's back.

"What the hell happened?" he asked.

"It's over," I stated, both of us panting with sweat dripping down our brows. Looking around, I can see the damage that is left behind. Some bodies lay unconscious or dead in their pools of blood.

"Where is Serena?" I asked, looking for her anywhere. Pekka and I run helplessly around, searching for her. Panic rises, and I regret not telling her we are mates. That what she is feeling is accurate and meant for us to be together. The distant sound of Odith's voice catches my ears, and I run down a narrow hall, turning to see her. Serena is chained to a chair while a creature that sounds like Odith approaches her.

"You are mine," Odith states.

As I knock an arrow, it releases but misses.

"She isn't going anywhere with you," I exclaimed. "Braxor!"

# 6

# SERENA

Screams of panic and chaos echoed throughout the narrow halls.

Children are ushered through various portals; I felt a tight grip on my wrist, and looking up, I saw fear in Alwin's eyes. It was not fear for himself, no; it was fear for his people, for this sanctuary he built for people like us. They were burning down with the flames of dragon fire. Then I saw what was attacking us. The same people who took my mother from me. Their sizeable yellow tusk stuck out from the steel helmets.

"Gnaxtor," I murmured. A memory of their stench and the thick blood on my skin flashed into my head. I clutched my amulet tighter and freed my other hand from Alwin's hold. Running down the narrow hall, I see Rose pinned to a wall by a soldier. Willing my essence, I summoned a fireball, jolting it at the beast and smiling as his body turned to ash.

"Thank you," Rose said.

"You need to get out of here." The sound of stomping boots, clashing metal, and screaming snapped my attention behind us.

Four soldiers encircled Alwin. "I need to help him find an Illuminate to portal you out of here." Without another word, the fairy vanished. I felt my fire rising inside me, burning for me to let go. As I took down two of the four, my eyes landed on Alwin. A mist of shadows circled him. Two strands reached out to the remaining soldiers, gripping their necks. With a flick of his wrist, the sound of cracking bones filled the halls.

"What are you?" I asked as my flames burned out; those once blue eyes were nothing but pits of darkness.

"You know exactly what I am." he answered, the darkness fading. Before I could ask any more questions, a company of soldiers stormed the halls. We were outnumbered, outmanned, and outmatched. "Where is Odith?"

Alwin asked as his shadows rose again and my flames formed in my palms. "The last time I saw her was in the War Room."

We were on high alert, expecting an attack from any of the soldiers, but none of them moved. Standing like poised statues, I waited for Alwin to move, yet he did not. All of this felt strange and unwarranted. "Where is your leader?"

I asked since Alwin remained mute. None of them answered as I pressed my back into Alwin. The sound of clapping echoes from nearby; lowering my hands, I see her, and my heart breaks.

"Odith? What did you do?" I asked, not realizing that my flames had disappeared entirely and the firm back of Alwin had disappeared.

"I am taking what is mine." Her tone was harsh as she snapped her fingers, and the army of soldiers disappeared. It was an illusion. Then I saw the transparent figure of a horned beast with wings, the upper body of a man, and the lower body resembling a hawk. Its talons clutched a chain that connected two naked figures by their necks, walking behind him—the Devil card.

"You manipulated the Devil Card to create this delusion? Do you realize what you have done? The cards will punish you for this." I started all too calmly. She laughed, approaching me, her once friendly face now depicting pure evil. My arms tightened to my body, my head snapped down, and chains of iron wrapped themselves tightly around me, thrusting me back into a wooden chair. "Why are you doing this?"

She approached me, her image dissipating as another woman appeared before me. Midnight straight hair cut to just below her pointed ears, pale skin, rose-colored lips, and black eyes looked down at me. The dress Odith was wearing changed its form into nothing. The naked body of a creature I had never seen stood before me. A tail with an arrow-tipped end swayed behind her.

"What are you? Who are you?"

"I never lied about my name." Turning her back to me, I saw her body was covered in gray scales matching a dragon's. "Like what you see, dear? I know you enjoy the company of men and women." She turned her head to me and winked.

"What are you playing at, Odith? Where is everyone? Why all the deceit?" I asked, struggling with my bindings. With each move I made, they seemed to tighten.

"I wouldn't move. They are magical, set to tighten as you resist them." Another card appeared in her hand, The Moon card; she was going to portal us somewhere. Alwin, where are you?

"Let me go, Odith," I yelled as she summoned a pink and violet light portal.

"I can't do that, my friend. We are going home."

"She's not going anywhere with you." Our heads turned abruptly towards the man standing at the end of the hall, armed with a longbow and arrow. Without uttering another word, he let it fly, but Odith moved too swiftly to be caught. She blocked it with her powers, sending the arrow straight through the swirling vortex.

"She's mine, Alwin." Odith hissed and charged forward. They fought while I remained struggling, trying to summon my fire. The chains are pure iron, the one weakness all Essence has. Iron suppresses our abilities.

"She will never be yours, Odith." I heard the Elf laugh as they continued fighting one another.

"You think she is yours, Alwin? She belongs with her mother and father." Those words paralyzed me, and the fighting stopped. Both were panting with cuts and bruises.

"What are you talking about?" I asked. Odith gave us a wicked smile. "Tell me."

"Why do you think I found you? Mommy and Daddy want their little girl back home with them."

"She's lying to you, Serena." I did not want to believe her, even after everything.

"Who are you going to believe? The woman who saved you from Convergence, or the man named after the Dark Elf himself? Did he tell you about being fated mates?"

Before I could answer, the side of the wall splintered with fire. My ears were ringing from my head hitting the hard floor, blood trickling down my face—a large talon wrapped tightly around my still-bound body, lifting me into the air. Above me, I saw the underbelly of a red dragon. It is large, about fifty feet in height, and its wingspan just as large. My eyes fluttered close as my body fell unconscious.

When I awoke, I felt a thick bed underneath me; the chains were gone, but my head felt as if an anvil had pounded into it multiple times. Sitting up, I was in Alwin's chambers again. Was it all a dream? The doors opened, and the light from the hall flooded in. Rose walked in, holding a tray of food and water.

"What happened?" I asked, my voice hoarse.

"You better let Alwin tell you." she answered by handing me the plate of bread and cheese.

"How long was I out this time?" She ignored me. "Okay, where is he so I can get my questions answered?"

"I'm right here." That beautiful smile of his crept right inside of my body again. Rose excused herself and shut the door. He stalked toward me, sitting at the edge of the bed. Reaching up, he examined what I can only assume to be the source of my pain.

"What happened?" I asked before sipping the water.

"What do you remember?" he asked as he dabbed a cloth to the cut on my forehead. It smelled of herbs and eased my pain.

"Nothing. Just a glimpse of an attack. Some gray-scaled woman and the Gnaxtor soldiers." I took a bite of my bread.

"Are you sure?" he asked, placing the cloth on the tray. Then it hit me.

"Odith. She betrayed us. And I saw a dragon. But how? Why?" I wanted to ask about the last part about us being fated mates.

"I don't know. She disappeared the moment Braxor broke through the wall."

"Braxor? The dragon?" He smiled at me. "Yes. Braxor is a dragon and a friend."

"I didn't think there were dragons anywhere except the colonies." I placed my plate of food down, reached for his hand, and he smiled again.

"I reached out to him. Braxor and I share an understanding, a pact forged about a century ago: we stand as allies. When one seeks assistance from the other, the call is answered." We were silent for a few heartbeats, holding each other's hands. At some point, he moved behind me, my rear tucking between his thighs, as he draped his arms over my shoulders, and I leaned into him. At least this was not an illusion.

"What are you thinking about?" he asked in my ear. His lips brushed against it, sending heat through my body down to my sex. I did not answer; I craned my neck to give him better access. When his lips kissed my skin, I felt myself dampen as my arousal took hold. "What are we going to do about Odith?" He paused at my collarbone. "We could track her. But that is the furthest thing from my mind now." There was no need for me to ask. I felt how aroused he was behind me. I am not ready for that step. If we cross that line, what will that mean? Plus, a part of me still loves Niya. I cannot share my bed with him when I have not fully let her go yet.

"I'm not ready." I turned my head, our lips touching softly. "What did she mean by us being fated mates?"

"It means that we are fated to be with one another." He started so calmly while my heart was pounding in my ears. "But only if you choose to pursue that life with me."

"I…" I didn't know what to say. I knew my feelings for him were solid but robust for Niya. I am so confused. "I need more time."

"Okay." he said onto my lips. Pressing our kiss deeper, he broke away. He immediately changed the subject, which I didn't mind. "Odith has connections with the Gnaxtor King, and if what she said about your parents is true, I can only assume they are there, too."

"Where exactly? And we cannot trust that she was telling the truth. I never met my father, and the last time I saw my mother was when they were taking her." My hand instinctively went for my amulet. "Where is it?" Panic started rising as I shot up.

"Where is my amulet?" Scrambling to my feet, Alwin appeared confused. I chucked the sheets from the mattress, and the pillows followed.

"What amulet?"

"The one my mother gave to me. It is shaped like a star. I never take it off. How could you not notice it as many times as your lips have been near it?" He scoffed but helped me search.

"Serena." He approached me, trying to get my attention as tears started rolling down my face. "Serena, look at me."

Bracing both of my shoulders, he looked at me. I was brushing the tears on my cheek with his thumbs. "It was the only thing my mother ever gave to me. The last item left of her love for me."

"We will find it." He pulled me into his embrace. "I won't let her get away with any of this, Serena. I promise."

The following day, everything was back to normal. Those evacuated returned, the palace was rebuilt with magic, and my body healed. Alwin and the class leaders held a meeting to produce a plan. Find Odith and prepare for war. He even issued a search for my missing necklace.

"I say we bring the war to me." Pekka started lifting his ax. "Strike back and with a vengeance." Lena, the magic leader, said. "No." I heard myself say, and the room went silent as all eyes locked on me.

"The Gnaxtor King wants me. For whatever reason, there will be no more bloodshed because of me. My life isn't worth it." Alwin glared at me, but I ignored him.

Getting to my feet, I walked to the map, placing my palms on the table. "All my life, I have been insulted and judged for being born the way I am. The Gnaxtor King ordered his soldiers to march into my village, take my mother, and, I assume, kill my father before I ever had the chance to meet him. I don't know why he wants me, but it concerns my parents."

"I will summon Odith and go with her. That way, all of you can remain safe. Fortify your walls and prepare for war in case it comes to you. Once I get close enough to the King, I will strike. You all have taught me well, and I thank you for it, but now, I must protect you." The room was silent. Pekka spoke first, agreeing, and then the other leaders followed. My gaze landed on Alwin; he was seething mad, but I saw pride in his eyes. "Then we are all in agreement. I must kill the King."

"Leave us," Alwin ordered, and without protest, they complied. "You can't stop me." I crossed my arms.

"How dare you?" His voice was low and cold. "You think your life is worthless; you mean nothing to anyone?"

"I never have and never will." My voice raised. This was going to be a screaming match.

"You are a damned fool." He turned on me. He was charging at me, backing me into the wall. "You are a damned fool. Because if you think for one second, I don't," he paused.

"Don't what?" My words came out breathless.

"Nothing. You want to get yourself killed, fine, but just know this, Serena." He leaned into me.

"Say it." I gasped. He did not use words as his lips crashed into mine. His hands landed on my hips, hoisting me up as I straddled him. It was claiming, owning, and I could feel how much he cared for me. How much my words hurt him. He sat me on the tabletop, both of us panting. "Say it."

"You're mine." His blue eyes shone bright with desire. The desire to have me, to claim me, to love me. "And I'm yours, Serena.

Whenever you want to claim me, and tomorrow, when you leave to kill that murderous bastard, I want you to know that I cared. Please come home to me. But also, if you do not come home, this world will burn."

## ALWIN

I almost lost her.

Now, I have to let her go. I told her about our fated mates, and she accepted the idea. Tomorrow she leaves, and I should ask her to stay with me tonight. Getting to my feet, I walk out of my room and head straight to hers, stopping just outside with my fist raised.

"Serena, I know you are freaked about us being together, but I think that before you go on your suicide mission, we should be together," I mumbled under my breath before knocking.

"She isn't in there," Rose said from behind. "Where is she?" I asked.

"She left moments ago with Odith."

"What?" Pure rage coursed through me, and I ran to the reflection pool, willing to show her to me. I can't find her. Falling to my knees, gentle hands grip my shoulders.

"Trust her," Rose stated as she messaged my tense muscles. "I have watched her over the past month, and I know you have, too. She knows how to control her magic. She will not fail."

"Rose, I shouldn't have let her go alone." I sound defeated. "You love her?" she asked.

"After my mother died, I didn't know I could love again. Not until I see my eyes on her. Everything snapped into place. I have felt powerless being around her. It's all new."

"Did you tell her?" I shook my head. "When she comes home, show her how much you care about her. Women like action, not just words. If you want to be with her and want her to know you love her, then you need to show her."

"I have tried, Rose. She isn't ready for it. I never thought I would be. She said she needed time, and now we won't have any. Even if she defeats the King and Odith, we still have Queen Lilac to worry about. Gods, Rose, how fucked up am I to care more about Serena than the entire realm?"

"You are not fucked up, Alwin. You are in love." The sound of rushing boots came in, getting to my feet. I see Pekka and Lena charging towards me.

"Get off your knees, boy. Serena is doing her part; we must do ours." He is right. Sitting around feeling angry at myself will not help.

"Serena has twenty-four hours before we go looking for her. In that time, I want you all to prepare the troops. If she doesn't come home, I am burning this world to the ground."

The room erupts in cheers, not because of my speech but because they also know and care for her. Serena showed respect and maturity with her teachers. The humility she has is unmatched.

After they all leave, I decide to stay. I am using all of my magic to search for. I fell asleep at some point because a glowing red light flashed before my eyes within the pool. Stunned at the sight appearing before me, I watch as Serena is engulfed in flames with a dagger in her heart.

My mate is gone. I feel the pain in my soul like a thousand knives stabbing me all at once. She can't be. There is no way Serena is dead. Looking again, the water is back to normal, and I am left with a hole in my heart. Walking down the halls, I make my way to the open courtyard.

My world caves in as tears flood my eyes. Rain pours down, and I let it soak me. Wash away the pain, the memories, the flash of the dagger protruding from her beautiful breast. I was a fool to let her go.

"Braxor," I yell loud and into the roaring skies. "Braxor, come here."

"Alwin." He was here just like always.

"Get ready to burn this entire world down." I didn't sound like myself. A shudder ran through me at the memory of my father's voice running through my ears.

"What happened?" he demanded. Glaring at him, I answered, "Serena is dead, and the world will pay for its crimes against her." The dragon snarls at me.

"Get a hold of yourself, boy. The Phoenix is not dead."

"I watched as Odith's blade pierced her heart." A large paw came toward me, but I didn't move. Braxor wouldn't hurt me.

"Then why is your heart glowing red?" Looking down, I see it for myself. Dancing in golden embers under my skin is my heart. "You have consummated your bond, Alwin, but when your Mate truly dies, whether they reject you, you will know because it will feel as if your very own heart is ripped from your chest." My anger receded the longer I stared at my chest.

"I don't know what to do anymore. Ever since she came here, I feel lost. Every decision I make seems like the wrong one. I shouldn't have run to the colonies. That is the time I should've spent with her. Now she is gone, and I don't know if I will see her again."

"Having flaws isn't a terrible thing, my friend." "It is if you have a Father like mine."

"You are nothing like your father." He growled with the rain still pouring down on us. "Your father was a coward; you are not. Crossing paths with a dragon takes bravery, something your father never dared to do."

"Braxor, I was going to use you to rein your fire." He let out a muffled laugh.

"No magic, not even that of the Tarot Cards, could be used against us, dragons," I remembered his warnings about Odith. That is why her magic didn't affect him.

"I'm sorry I didn't listen to you about Odith. If I had, then Serena might be here." I paused, wiping the rain from my face as it slowed to a sprinkle. "Her magic didn't work on you, so you weren't deceived."

"Odith is powerful, but the deck will turn on her. Trust in the Ancients to seek their payment." He stretched out his wings, acting like he was about to leave. "If there isn't anything else, I must return so my army is prepared for war."

"Thank you, Braxor." He was gone with a flap of his wings, and I returned to the reflection pool, praying I would see her again.

# 7

# SERENA

"Odith, I summon thee." Last night, Alwin and I slept together. We did not have sex; we just held each other until I fell asleep. We talked all evening about my plan, my life in hiding. Alwin told me about his childhood and how his brother was killed for being a half-elf. We both have our scars, and that brings us closer together. Should I have crossed that line? No, will I regret it? I hope not. He asked me to wait another day, and I said I would, but I lied.

"Serena, you miss me already?" Whirling around, I find her appearing correctly. Knees, bowing my head, I raised my arms, clasping my hands together, showing my submission.

"A sudden change of heart? Do not take me to be a fool, Serena, Alwin, and you cannot defeat me. I'm stronger than you both."

"Take me to him," I repeated. Iron chains tighten around my wrist. A force pulled me to my feet, my eyes locked onto hers. "You were much cuter in your other form."

"I thought you liked your women naked?" She pursed her lips, winking at me flirtatiously. Pulling me closer to her, she said, "You know, Serena, I have mastered the entire deck of cards. Each one listens to my every word. It's something I could teach you to do." Her lips caressed my cheek.

"The Ancient Marseilles created them for a purpose, and it was not for manipulation. When the time comes, your dues will be paid. The cards don't take lightly to manipulation." I knew that much about them.

"Moon Card, I summon thee." Just as before, the transparent figure appeared, and a portal opened. "Move." I was pushed through the portal of luminescent lights. I was hitting the hard ground on the other side a moment later. The Moon was high in the sky; the air was dry and hot. There is no forest, no greens, nothing but sand for miles.

"Where are we?" I asked as Odith closed the portal. "Welcome to Amarathian."

"I see nothing but a wasteland." A smirk formed across her lips. She knew something I did not. Odith recited a new tarot incantation, and a gust of wind blew as another transparent figure appeared. A man with shoulder-length brown hair, dressed in a white robe, with a red cape around him, and an infinity symbol appeared waving a white rod. In a shimmer of light, a large Castle appeared before us. The Magician Card. She honestly uses every card she can to her advantage. If you hear my prayers, the Ancient one strikes her down before she continues to manipulate your power.

Ten thick, round emerald towers overshadow the skyline of this massive castle and are connected by strengthened, wide walls made of quartz. This King genuinely loves green. As we approached it, I could see the narrow windows scattered generously across the walls in an asymmetric pattern and enormous crenelations for archers.

"Did you use the cards to create this, too?" I asked sarcastically, earning me a scornful look. We stepped through a regular gate with great wooden doors and a moat that guards the inhabitants of this island castle. As we enter a corridor, a grand staircase shoots off to the left and right, meeting at a balcony in the middle. The walls are barren, and there are no other halls or doors.

Ushering me to the stairs, we take them two at a time; I avoid Odith's annoying tail, almost tempted to stomp on it if it did not mean I would fall to my death. At the top, we hastened through two vast metal doors into a large throne room. A large man sits center front on a stone of forged swords. To my astonishment, a human man, standing at about six feet tall with broad shoulders and brown hair, appeared. The silver strands peeking out from the sides of his golden crown hinted at his age. Clad entirely in black, a single sword strapped to his right side, his piercing blue eyes fixed upon me.

"Is this another illusion?" I whisper to Odith. She ushered us forward with a smile and a wink and then took a knee.

"My King, I present the phoenix fire to you, Serena of Narborim." Our eyes locked, but then his gaze trailed my body from head to toe.

"Come here, girl." He gestured with a gloved finger. I did not move, but it did not matter as the magic Odith was using pushed me. It's another card, I assume; I cannot figure out which one. "So, you are Hellena's daughter."

My mother's name. Getting off his throne, he approached me, cupping my head and turning it side to side. "What part of you is Elf? You look like a human."

"My hair is the color of chocolate, and my eyes the color of the sea. No pure-blood human has these features."

"Neither do pure-blood elves. Hmm. Yet somehow, you have the most powerful Essence ever known. How is that possible?" He went back to sit on his throne.

"Are my parents here?" I asked, my eyes darting across the room. The space held nothing more. No additional doors or windows graced the surroundings—just a solitary throne, the entrance we came through, and ourselves. How could this be possible?

"They are dead. Killed a long time ago." he said it so matter-of-factually that my blood was boiling. I need these iron chains to come off me, or else I can only kill him by sword or dagger. I will never get past Odith, not without my powers.

"What do you want with me then?" Odith rose to her feet at my question and smirked at me.

"I'm going to drain your blood and drink it. That Phoenix Fire belongs to me and no one else. You are not worthy of it." Just like the Ancients did.

"You will burn if you do this." They laughed at me, and then, disgusted, Odith kissed the King. It appears they are more than associates.

"On your knees, Odith, just like I like it." I heard him say. She undid his breeches, taking his rock-hard cock out, making the situation a thousand times more disgusting, and then sucked it deep in her throat. I tried turning away but could not; the magic held on me held me in place. "You will watch and learn from her. This is how you can earn your life, girl."

"I am no one's sex slave." His head fell back as he thrust his hips hard and held Odith's head down onto him. The noises she was making sounded painful, not pleasurable. With a loud grunt, his hips slowed, and Odith gently removed her mouth. She turned to look at me with a smug smile, then licked her lips clean. I did not hold my vomit in, heaving all the contents of my stomach onto the stone floors.

A gust of laughter came from both. A mix of a deep chuckle and a high-pitched cackle made my ears hurt. "Take the girl to my chambers, strip her bare, and then chain her to the wall."

"You won't touch me." I heard a growl leave from deep within my throat. It surprised me and earned a sneer of disapproval. The King charged at me, nearly slipping in my vomit, a thick hand wrapped tightly around my throat, lifting me into the air.

"You are mine; there is no use fighting it. If I want to fuck you, I will. If I want my pets, my guards, even Odith to fuck you, they will. You are a powerless abomination with no one left in this world to save you." I did not let my fear show the truth in his words.

"Fuck you." I spit in his face. Before I could catch my next breath, my body was hurled into the wall. My right shoulder cracked on impact, sending a burning pain through me. Before I could get to my feet, my back was pinned to the wall, and both of my arms spread out, injuring my already broken shoulder further.

"You will submit. I will have your blood," he approached me. My eyes darted to Odith, and I saw that this was all she was doing. All the Essence, conjuring, manipulation, it was because of her. And like a damned fool the King is, he cannot see the dagger that is about to be pierced through his back. The Fool Card. A blonde-haired, fair-skinned man with a shortened dress of sunflowers and yellow knee-high boots hovers above him.

"She is making a fool out of you." I spat. My blood was coating my mouth, the feeling of my limbs stretching and tearing; I was not sure how much longer I could take this.

"You should've never come here, Serena," gripping my throat again, his wide eyes, foul breath, and rigid body pressing into me. "She played you for a fool the entire time you were with each other. Odith is an immensely powerful Essence. She has mastered the deck, and those cards bent to her will just like you will." A memory of my time in study hall with the All-Father flashed in my brain.

Shortly after my arrival, he showed me the book the scribes created discussing Essence and Tarot Magic.

"If you master a full deck of cards, it can be a blessing and a curse." the older man said.

"Why?" I asked, looking at the incredibly detailed designs of each card.

"Because if another touches your cards, their allegiance will be compromised, and no one can escape that fate." The sound of my other shoulder cracking brought me out of my head. I did not cry; my body had become numb to this torture. I am unsure how it is because I am already dying.

"Show me your deck, Odith," I demanded. Ignoring the King was wrong, and the hard knuckles connecting with my face told me so. More blood filled my mouth as my left eye swelled. "Jealousy is so unbecoming of a King."

"I was going to make it more pleasurable instead of painful, but you love the pain. You are relishing in it, and that has me pissed and aroused at the same time." I felt the wetness of his tongue on my face, making me spit all that blood from my mouth.

"Why don't you have your pet release me from the invisible bindings so I can show how much pain I can inflict? I assure you; it will be more painful than pleasurable." I saw him ponder it before I felt my body thud to the floor. The chains were gone. Idiot. Looking up at them both, I could not help but smile. Getting to my feet, my arms are useless as they hang nimbly by my sides.

"You can't do anything with disconnected arms, Serena. Your threats are cute; I may even have some respect for you," Odith walked toward me, that dreadful tail swaying in tune with the direction of her hips. "Is this your last request before you die?" She was going to show me her cards. Any part of me that touches them could work.

"Yes." I started holding my chin up high. Odith snapped her fingers, conjuring a small round wooden table with a stack of tan cards with golden embellishments at the center. "Read me." I heard myself say.

"You want me to do Tarot Reading?"

"Yes. You both are so determined to kill me. I want to know what your cards think is going to happen." I saw her chest rise and fall faster. She is ruffled because I have cornered her. "Are you afraid the cards will betray you?"

"Sit." She snarled, and I sat in a wooden chair, her across from me, shuffling her deck. My eyes drifted to the king standing over her shoulder, watching. "I will pull three cards, and you see that death will be your fate."

She stopped shuffling, picked the first card from the top, and placed it face down on the tabletop. She repeated the same thing with the next two. The anticipation was killing me at what the cards, her cards, were deciding my fate. "Are you ready to know your fate?"

"What happens if the cards do not predict my death?" I asked. "It does not work like that. The cards are powerful, but they do

not decide your death. Just a workable course along your journey." She huffed out. "It doesn't matter, anyway. You will die soon after this, and the rest of Xora will fall to its knees before the King."

"You truly believe and want a pure-blooded human to rule all of Xora?" Dodging my question, she flipped the first card over. The Chariot: a masterful card of execution, confidence, and wisdom. A regal gladiator charging into battle. That is a good sign.

"The Chariot is your first card, which has many meanings, but the one I favor the most for you is the opposite. There will be no victory for you, no swiftness, nor achievement. You are going to lose."

"Do I sense fear in your voice, Odith?" She did not answer. I saw a slight tremor in her hand when she reached for the second card. A man is strung up by his left ankle, dangling between two cut staves.

"This is more like it. The Hanged Man, or woman, to be more specific. You are a sacrifice, which is what this tarot means if you weren't aware." She smirked, and I wanted to punch her in that scaly face.

"Flip the last one." Reaching for it, she hesitates. "Don't stop now, Odith, you are nearly there. Victory at your very fingertips."

"Death." we said simultaneously as my eyes landed on the image of a skeleton wielding his mighty scythe: transformation, rebirth, end of one cycle, and the beginning of another.

"Tell me, Odith, are the cards in my favor?" She looked up at me. She was afraid that her cards betrayed her. I did not have to touch them to turn them against her. She did that herself.

"No matter." Before she could snap her fingers, I slammed my head onto the table, sending the cards and splintered wood across the floor.

"What have you done?"

My head pounding, blowing my hair from my face, the warmness of a cut on my face dripping down to my mouth, I smiled. "Your cards are no longer in allegiance to you."

Those invisible chains wrap around my joints again, but not this time. I will not be a prisoner to be raped and killed.

"You're a worthless little abomination. Do you realize what you have done?" she yelled, backing into the arms of her king. His eyes are glazed over as if he is in a trance.

"Yes, insult me, call me whatever names you wish if it helps you feel better. My last card was Death, which terrifies you because it means transformation. My second card," I continued getting to my feet, feeling my bones morphing back into place, "the hanged man, which means sacrifice, but I have been sacrificing my entire life.

And you know what my last one will be?"

"What's that, little girl? Reuniting with mommy and daddy? Poor orphan Serena, I will gladly reunite you." Double swords appeared in her hands, and she shouted at me. My arms are still healing themselves, so all I could do was remember the defensive moves Pekka taught me.

"My first card," I started with a grunt as I dodged her cuts towards my neck from both sides. Reaching out my leg, I went to sweep her feet, but she jumped, dodging my moves.

"Pekka taught me, too." She sneered, and I kicked her in the back.

"Good, then this is an even fight." The feeling in my left hand returned, picking up a piece of the wood to shield her blows. I continued my distraction, stalling until I could fully embrace my fire. "My first card was The Chariot, which means I am going to achieve the mission I came here to do."

Stopping mid-fight, I let her blade pierce through my heart. The King was screaming, Odith's bewilderment, my world slowing. "In death, I am reborn."

Through the widened eyes of Odith, I see my glowing reflection looking back at me. As I watch my transformation, looking through the eyes of my enemies, my body morphs—beautiful iridescent wings of fire shoot from my back. My brown hair is adorned with streaks of crimson as fire morphs my bloodied, torn clothes into a shimmering red gown. The ice of my eyes melts into two golden suns. Transparent figures cavort all around me—figures matching that of every card in the deck.

"What have you done?" the King shouted. My eyes darted to him as he reached for the hilt of his sword. "Now, I can never drink her blood." Before he could pierce her through the back, I shot fire at him, but his blade blocked it. "Pure iron, not even Phoenix Fire can penetrate iron."

"You tried to kill me." Odith was hurt. I felt pity for her.

"You will pay for your sins against the cards and the people of Xora." Two blades of fire shot out from my hands as I charged at them both. They both have iron blades, blocking my magic.

Odith launched herself at me, going straight for my heart again. But I whirled away. As Odith struck the air, the King's blade came crashing toward me. Blocking it, I felt something pulling at my wings; it tasted of metal. I was pinned between one blade blocking the King and the other blocking Odith. Odith's magic fighting for control, the King's impossible strength pushing me to falter.

"Give up, Serena; you cannot win." the King yelled. But as I felt them moving closer, my magic lessening, the figure of a goddess and her lion appeared before me. She wore a crown of infinity upon her head—the Strength Card: Mind & Body. Through the silence, I felt her with me, willing strength into my soul. With dominant force, I pushed with all my Essence, knocking them against opposing walls.

Looking over, I see the King is unconscious, blood trickling from his mouth and nose. Odith is breathing heavily, confirming that the wind was knocked from her.

"Finish it, Serena." She heaved. I approached her with my blades, pointing one at her throat as she lifted her chin to me. Unafraid that I now held her life in my hands.

"No." I sheathed my fire, my wings tucking behind me, and then she laughed.

"All that power, and you can't even finish the job. You're worthless half-thing." Her words no longer affected me, but I turned toward her again.

"I am not a half thing anymore." She laughed at me, struggling to her feet, blades in hand.

"You're right." She charged toward me, our blades clashing, forming an X. "You are nothing but a whore's offspring. Worthless, piece of horse dung, undeserving of what was gifted to you."

"Your words are useless, Odith. I will not kill you, but I pity you because now you will live the rest of your days here with your King. Doing what you do best."

"Plotting your death." she inquired, pushing at me.

"Getting on your knees." With all the strength I had left, which was not much, I knocked her into the wall with a hard bone-cracking thud. Both enemies lay unconscious by my hands. The castle shook as the ceiling crumbled above me. I could conjure the Moon to portal me out of here, but I do not know how.

Trust is in the cards, Serena. They are with you. The familiar voice of my mother sang in my head. Without further hesitation, I formed a bubble of amber around me, feeling every hit of each rock, trying to break my shield. Pulling out the Moon card, I pressed my lips to it, asking for permission. A portal of golden light opened. I could not see through the other side, but I jumped through just as a large rock crashed through my shields.

I landed in a thick pile of snow; the sound of sizzling and the waft of steam circled me as the heat of my flames simmered out with the touch of the frost. Getting to my feet, I notice I am in a foreign tundra. Encircled in the mountains with snow caps, I stand center on a frozen lakebed. Unsure if I am even in Xora anymore, I feel for the cards, but they are nowhere to be found. I have lost them.

The sound of a screeching bird came from the skies above me. Shifting my gaze, I see the body of a magnificent griffin leading a flock to the tops of the mountains—Griffins, which could mean that a Confessor is nearby. Ancients watch over me. Spreading my wings, dusting the snow from them, I will myself to the skies.

Following closely in their shadow, but not too close to spook them into attacking me. Flying was a fresh feeling. The wind was a friend, aiding me with each movement.

I was expecting cold flying here, but my internal core acted like its own fire, warming me from the inside out. We flanked left, then right, and repeated the movement several times. I feel dizzy until I notice the tiny figure, dressed in all white, saddled on the back of the lead Griffin. Her hard eyes locked on me. The flock darted down, landing on the top of a small flattop of rock and snow.

Planting my feet firmly, the Confessor approached me, no weapon in hand. Common for them. Their Essence is the only weapon they need to bend someone to their will.

"Who are you?" The voice was familiar; the hood prevented me from seeing her face.

"Who are you?" I shot the question back at her. Her pure white-gloved hands dropped her hood, and to my surprise, I saw my old friend again. "Niya?"

Her expression cemented that my new appearance erased my old one. "It's me, Serena; I know I look different, and there is an excellent explanation for it, but-" She ran to me, throwing her arms around my head and crashing those soft lips onto mine. Wrapping my arms tightly around her tiny waist, my tongue piercing the slit of her lips. She gave in to me, tearing at my clothes. This was going to happen; it needed to happen.

With our clothes gone, her mouth explored my new body. I was pressing, sucking, nipping at the peaks of my nipples, making me moan. Cupping my sex, using her thumb to circle my clit, then dropping her mouth down there. "You're so wet, baby." She moaned and then licked my slit. My mind drifted to Alwin, and my body went rigid with regret.

"Niya." I gasped as she sucked on my clit, pumping two fingers inside of me. Reaching my hands to her head, I urged her to me. "I have wanted this for so long, but I need to tell you something."

"Whatever it is, I don't care about that, Serena." She kissed me again, and I tasted sweet on her lips.

"You need to know that I have feelings for another." She stopped mid-kiss. I could not decipher what she was feeling. But she has always been hard to read.

"If you want me, Serena, you can have me. You can have them. If you want us both, you can have us both."

"I love you." That was all I said, and then I got lost in passion's bliss. I was getting lost in the grinding of our wet lips. I lapped at her slit, thrilled by her moaning from her. This felt so good, but I still felt a slight betrayal of Alwin. I gave my maidenhood to Niya, and she gave it to me.

"Serena." She panted as I pumped two fingers into her sex, and my other found the puckered opening to her rear. Slipping it in and out in the same rhythm. I sucked on her clit, and she squirmed, coating me with her wetness. "Ancients, Serena, I'm going to." In a burst of white light, she climaxed all over me. My tongue lapped through it.

I crawled to her, kissing her softly as she came down from her high, the light slowly fading. "I love you, too, Serena."

We made love multiple times in the snow, using my wings to keep us warm. Over and over, the passion, the heat, giving into all the needs and desires for one another. We lay cuddling in each other's arms. My breast pressed into her soft back as our fingers interlaced.

"Tell me about this other lover of yours. Is it another woman? Or man?" Niya asked.

"His name is Alwin, and we haven't had sex yet." She chuckled, turning toward me.

"I can't lie and say I'm not jealous, but I also can't help but imagine what it would be like to have him between us." I dampened at the thought. She must have noticed because her hand went to my sex. "I think you would love that, wouldn't you?"

"We need to rest." I moaned breathlessly as she pumped into me. "Niya." As much as I did not want to stop, we needed to discuss everything.

"What's wrong?" she asked, removing her hand from me. "A lot has happened the past two months that we need to discuss."

"I know. You have wings." She smiled at me and then ran a finger on the inside of one. "How did that happen?"

"That is towards the end; let's start at the beginning." She listened intently as I informed her of everything after I left. How Odith tricked me into believing she was my friend. How I trained to defend myself, and how I fell for Alwin.

"I'm going to kill that traitorous bitch for hurting you," Niya remarked, and that was unlike her.

"I don't think she is alive. The ceiling was crumbling down as I jumped through the portal."

"We should go back just to be sure." It made sense. I did not exactly see them die. "Do you still have the moon card?"

"No. Somewhere along the way, the cards disappeared, but I don't think they belong to anyone now." She leaned in and kissed me again. "We need to rest, and tomorrow we will travel to Ermelon."

"How? I thought you went there by the portal."

"Alwin and I have a connection. It could be my new powers; I know which direction we need to travel."

"I love seeing you like this." she said with a smile. "Like what?" I asked.

"Confident, powerful, it's sexy as hell, and I think I am ready to ravish you again." Ancients help me.

We dressed the following day after having more sex. She said she wanted to have me all to herself before I shared my bed with Alwin. That way, she had an upper hand if I decided I only wanted one of them, which made me laugh.

The flight back was long, but we made it outside the castle by nightfall. "This is Ermelon?" she asked, unimpressed.

"Yes. Isn't it marvelous?" I asked as I interlaced my fingers with her.

"Sure." she spoke. I knew she would be unimpressed because this place is less lavish than Galavian. We were greeted by some guards, who escorted us to the War Room. I held Niya's hand tightly as we entered, and all eyes fell on us. Alwin's at once went to our joined hands.

"Serena, is that you?" He made his way toward me; I let go of Niya, ran up to him, and embraced him with a kiss. "I thought you were dead. We saw the rubble, but we couldn't find you."

"I know there is much to be discussed, but first," I gestured to Niya, and she approached, "this is Niya; she is here as an ally."

"Welcome, Niya; we were plotting how to take down the Gnaxtor armies."

"About that," she started, and I shot her a glance. "The Gnaxtor King isn't the only enemy you all need to be worried about. Queen Lilac has prepared her armies to march into war here."

"Niya, why didn't you tell me that last night? Or this morning?" "You two spent the night together?" I heard the jealousy in
Alwin's voice.

"We were preoccupied." she said as her eyes went to the floor. I openly admit that we did more than sleep last night.

"Well, come on, Confessor, tell us everything," Pekka ordered.
She approached the table.

"The Queen plans to invade from all angles." "How is that possible?" Lena asked.

"I'm not entirely sure, but somehow, she has a fleet of ships coming from the seas. An army fights from the skies and then plans to use the territory of Amarathian to combine both armies. There will be many Essence users and Tarot Masters on the front lines." When she finished speaking, the room erupted in angered shouting about the best approach. My mind scrambled to figure out what the best strategy was. The King wanted my blood, and the Queen wanted me in her Guard but only as a pure-blood.

I have always been a pure-blood. Just one of a kind. This means this war is not just about my power but about my allegiance.

"Everyone shut up," I yelled, and the room went silent.

"The Queen and King have something in common none of you are thinking about." I walked around them, stopping between Niya and Alwin. "They want me. The King wants my power; the Queen wants my allegiance. I am a Phoenix, the first since the Ancients walked the earth."

"You are not sacrificing yourself again," Alwin growled. "I'm not talking about sacrificing."

"Tell us, Serena, don't leave us in suspense." Alwin urged. "We bring them together. They want to take over our world,
purge it of non-humans, well I say to hell with them. We will not yield, we will not falter, and we will destroy them. Alwin, you will contact Braxor and get his aid, bringing the dragons to rein their fire down upon our enemies. Pekka, you will lead our army. Lena, you, and the others will remain here, fortifying the castle. We still want a home to come back to after this. Niya, you will gather as many loyal Confessors as possible to help bring justice."

"What about me?" Alwin asked.

"You and I are going to take them down." He smiled at me. "Alwin, you need to take lessons in leadership from her. She is
good." Pekka remarked.

"Well, you all have your assignments; tomorrow, we move." The room cleared all except us three, and an awkwardness filled the space.

"Niya," I said, turning to her, "I need to be alone with him. Talk about everything, especially with us going to war tomorrow."

"I understand." She cupped my cheek and then kissed me softly. "Find Rose; she can show you to some guest rooms." When Niya
left, I approached Alwin. I sit on the table in front. "Hi."

"Hi." he said and then nudged himself between my thighs.

"We need to talk." He brushed my hair behind my ears, just like always. "Niya and I, well we..." I trailed off.

"You had sex." he answered for me; my head dropped low with shame, and I was unsure why. "Serena," he tilted my head up to meet his gaze. I was expecting anger, but all I saw was lust. "I will not ask you to choose between me and her, but if you do, I will respect it."

"Tonight, I want you. All of you to be mine and me to be yours." I felt tears swelling in my eyes. He wiped them away. "I don't want to lose either of you because I love you both."

That was all I needed to say before we were whisked into his bed chambers. Kissing me deeply, passionately, sending sparks of heat through me. The Ancients felt good. Our clothes were on the floor, my back on his silken sheets as he hovered over me. "Repeat it." He moaned.

"You're mine." I gasped as he took my nipples between his teeth. His hardened cock rubbed at my entrance, and I wanted him inside of me. Flipping him over, I sank onto him. My wings were erected with the movement as he adjusted himself. His hands moved to my hips, and the stretching, the heat, all of it was overwhelming. I moved on him, my hips rolling as if I was riding a horse.

"Serena." He moaned, his hips meeting my rhythm. His thumb found my clit, moving in such teasing circles. I could not hold my release any longer, screaming his name as I let my climax drench him. He released, roaring my name, thrusting as he filled me with his seed.

Panting, our sweaty bodies entangled, coming down from our high, I kissed him again. "Holy shit." That was all he said.

"I know." It was unexpected, and I enjoyed it more than when I was with Niya, which made me feel awful. My time with her felt different, more out of the need to have her. With Alwin, I felt passion, fire, and love. If I choose, I know I will lose her. And that scares me because I just got her back.

## ALWIN

I feel happy as I lie awake with my girl wrapped in my arms, head on my chest. Her return to me was all I had yearned for in the twenty-four hours since she departed. Niya, her other lover, was with her, and I thought I would be furious at her for choosing to be with her first, but I was not. She told me the truth, and I knew from the moment I started watching over her the feelings she had for her.

I lost myself in her when she told me she wanted to be mine.

The feeling of our bond consummating was powerful. I won't make her choose between me and Niya. That is not who I want to be to her. A seed of dread formed in my head at the thought of her not choosing me. Would I be able to let her go? I already did once, and she came back. We go to war tomorrow, and I still feel like we need more time. It's time to get to know each other.

Niya was there for her for the past ten years. They had time to grow with each other, and now, I don't know how much time I will have before we are separated again. Gods, I sound jealous. I am jealous.

Getting out of bed, I walk over and pour myself a glass of water. "Alwin," I hear Serena mutter. "Come back to bed." Turning, I

see her sitting up, the sheet pooled at her waist, revealing her plump breast, making all my blood rush to my cock.

"As you wish." I kiss her softly, placing the glass down and creeping onto the bed. I feel her hand wrapped tightly around me, motioning it up and down.

"Ready for round two, love?" I ask. She giggled and replaced my hand with hers, sending my senses into overdrive.

Sinking lower, I feel the moist heat in her tight mouth as her tongue dances around my shaft. Lifting her head from me, I pull her face up and kiss her deeply, tasting myself on her.

"Serena," I say. "If tomorrow ends badly, I need you to know that you are the best thing to ever happen to me." She straddles me as I speak, sinking her wetness on me. "When you do, I can't concentrate."

"This?" She teases as her hips roll. I was slamming her onto the mattress. I pin her wrist down and thrust inside her, clamping my mouth onto her breast. Thrilling in the moan of her pleasure.

"I need you to know that I will love you no matter what the future brings. You will have my loyalty until I take my last breath." She was still looking at me with those beautiful, bright eyes.

"You will be my future, Alwin." She stated before motioning for me to continue. I take it slow, wanting this time to last longer. We both needed to be lost in the ecstasy and passion of the moment.

# 8

# SERENA

The following day, Alwin and I showered together, spending an extreme amount of time ravishing our bodies. I still have the
salted taste of his seed in my mouth after I went down on him. Something we both look forward to doing again. If we survive, I remember what he said last night, and I can't help but smile, knowing that Alwin will always choose me. No one has ever picked me.

"Good morning, Serena," Niya said in the war room. "Morning," I said, trying to avoid her eyes.

"How was your night?" she asked while taking a seat across from me. It was just us two; the others would arrive shortly.

"Good. And you?" This was too weird.

"Good, Rose kept me company." Her jealousy showed because she knew what had happened between me and Alwin.

"Niya," I started, but the doors opened, and the others walked in.

"As discussed," Alwin started as they all took their seats. "Braxor has his dragons ready. All the pieces are set except two. The King and Queen. How do we bring them to where we want them?"

"Odith, if she is still alive. Which I am sure that scaly bitch is." "How do you intend on getting her here?" Alwin asked.

"I summoned her, just like before. She can still summon portals, regardless of her abuse of the cards."

"And if she is dead?"

"Then I go to the Queen myself." There was silence, then nods of understanding.

"Let me do it," Niya said after a few moments. "Do what?" I asked.

"I am the Queen's personal Confessor; I can get close enough to bend her to my will and force her to reveal her true self to the kingdom." This is a new Niya. So full of rage and violence.

"That could work," Pekka said. The other agreed, but I remained silent, studying her. Something felt off and wrong; this was not the real Niya. It cannot be, but who is it? My answer came with a gust of wind that knocked us all from the table. The Fool's transparent figure stood before me, and I saw her. Odith was standing where Niya had been sitting.

"Where is she?" She smirked, but I saw what had happened when I left that crumbling castle. Her once flawless body was covered in scars, and her hair was matted, but around her neck, glinting off the light, was my amulet.

"This thing is powerful." she said as she followed my gaze. "Where is Niya?" I snarled, getting to my feet.

"Oh, she is right where you left here. With the Queen in Galavian." Gasping at what that meant. "Might I say you are a good lay? Even Rose shuttered at my touch."

"Fuck you."

"Oh honey, don't you remember, you already did. Over and over, tell me, was he as good as me?" She smirked, pointing at the fuming Alwin, who had his swords out.

"You can't compare." Hurling myself toward her with my blades, she knocked me into the wall.

"Like I said, this amulet is remarkable. You should've never lost it."

She toyed with it. "Your mother must have been a master to conjure up this magic."

"I don't need it to destroy you." She laughed.

"You're not understanding. You cannot touch me while I am wearing it. Adorned by blood magic, I can only assume. Nothing, and no one can hurt you. That is how you have been able to survive all these years. Shame, really, now I get to take your powers and destroy this pitiful place."

"Traitorous whore." Pekka yelled and came at her with his ax. Before it came down on her back, it turned on him, chopping his head clean off. Blood splattered the walls, and his body thudded to the floor—a puddle formed around him.

The others joined in, attacking from all angles, and she killed them with the flick of her wrist. All that was left was me and Alwin. Our eyes locked to one another, a silent conversation, as we charged at her. My body morphs into the golden figure of the Phoenix—Alwin's morphing into the darkened state of his shadows.

"You can't stop me," Odith yelled, holding her hands up, willing those invisible chains around us. "I am all-powerful."

My mind went calm, interlacing my fingers with his, a shield forming around us. I envisioned all the cards again, just like last time. Each one charged full force at the manipulator, breaking down her shield. Opening my eyes, I set forward, pushing Alwin out of the way. My hand clamped on my amulet, ripping it from Odith's throat. I felt the warmth of her blood on my hand with my blade in her heart. Then, nothingness as her life left her eyes.

Stumbling backward, I fell to the floor as my hands went to the blade sticking from my gut.

"Serena." Alwin raced to me, lifting me into his arms. Tears falling from his eyes.

"Hi," I spoke.

"Hi." He pressed his lips to me, and then his hands went to my wound.

"Alwin," I started, and he shook his head. "It's okay. When I die, I will be at peace."

"No, I can't lose you; I just got you. Please, Serena, do not give up; I love you." He was kissing me, holding me, his wet tears mixing with my blood.

"Alwin, when I die, bury me back in my hometown. I know it is not much, but it was my home. Promise me."

"No, because you are not dying." His hand gripped the hilt of the blade, pulling it from me, but I did not feel the pain. My body was numb, and I was dying.

"Look at me." I cupped his face, my blood staining it. "Thank you for saving me, Alwin, for loving me and giving me a home. You will be okay. Purge this world of the evil that is trying to destroy it. The Gnaxtor King, the Queen, our people will never be safe if they live."

"Stop, you can't die. You are supposed to be my wife." Sorrow filled me.

"You didn't ask yet." We both chuckled, and I was coughing, blood in my throat. There would be no coming back from this. "Tell Niya that I loved her; tell her what happened. Can you do that?"

"Okay." He knows, too.

"My life is complete, and knowing that I am dying, I will tell the Ancients that I died with love in my heart. You are my heart,

Alwin." My eyes fluttered close as he kissed me one last time. My mind shifted into darkness as my soul left my body.

## ALWIN

"If we burn her, she can be reborn out of the ashes," I said, putting Serena's lifeless body on the pyre in the middle of the courtyard.

"If this doesn't work, how will you fulfill your promise about being buried in her homeland?" Rose asked me.

"I will take her ashes, scatter them across the seas. Then, I am marching into Galavian and killing the Queen." Holding the torch, I lit the pyre, but a shout stopped me.

"Wait." Turning around, a small woman dressed in all white approached us. "It won't work."

"Niya?" I asked.

"Yes. You can't just use any fire to bring her back."

"What are you doing here? How did you know what happened?" she touched Serena's blood-stained face.

"I kept a connection with her. I never told her, but it was my way of protecting and monitoring her. When the connection broke, I knew it must have meant she died." She turned toward me.

Serena's attraction toward her was called for. She was breathtaking with her midnight-colored skin, green eyes, and black hair.

"That answers those questions, but what do you mean, the right fire?" I doused the torch in a bucket of water.

"She was reborn the first time Odith killed her. She was killing her half-human self. She was then reborn into her true form as the Phoenix. For her to be reborn again, we need fire from a phoenix."

"Impossible, they are all extinct."

"No, they aren't." She rummaged through a brown pouch she brought, opening a book to show me a page about them. "I have been researching this since I learned how to read. The Phoenixes are not extinct; they just migrated to a different realm."

"How do you suppose we get to it before her body turns to rot?" Rose asked.

"We use this," Niya pulled out a tarot with the picture of a regal woman dressed in an emerald gown holding a staff and shield. "The Empress can preserve her state and create it when the time comes to retrieve her soul from the spirit realm."

"How long will it last?" I asked.

"We have a week, maybe two tops, before the magic will dissipate," Niya answered. I pondered this, but it was the only way to save her.

"Do it," I said, and Rose tried to protest, but I let Niya do her work. The transparent figure appeared, placing a hand on Serena's forehead, and a glass coffin formed around her body. The Empress stayed poised in her spot.

# II

# WHITFROST

*RISE OUT OF THE ASHES*

# 9

# ALWIN

The morning, we had started misty and cold, with a moistness hinting at another snowfall's start. We set forth just before daybreak to see the Rune Master, three plus Natiri, the Confessor's Griffin. This was the first we had heard of this Master of Runes.

The portal had landed us here in a small village fully known for its furs and fish. A population of two hundred pure-blooded dwarves, they were not too kind when we showed up. An army of ten males wielding large axes encircled us.

That wasn't the worst part. When I tried to summon my shadows, they were suppressed somehow. Rose was unable to speed and use sleeping dust, and the Confessor could not use her persuasive touch. We only made it out of there because of her words of coercion.

We were just humble tourists on a journey from a far land. I stopped her before she could reveal too much. I don't know why Rose trusts her so much.

"Master," Rose's soft voice awakened me from my stupor.

"How often have I told you to call me by name?" I scorn her. I respect her loyalty and manners, but it is not needed here. And I no longer deserve that title.

My eyes trailed over the busy tavern, which smelled of brew and charred hog. The meat they serve has a spiced flavor that can easily be washed with a warm pint of maple-flavored alcohol.

The barmaids are serving pints to customers. The entire place seems unaware of the strangers that sit just a few paces from them. The Confessor's choice of clothing should be enough to note the strangeness of our appearance.

With her pure ivory colors and polar bear-furred cloak, she is anything but ordinary. Rose, however, has dressed herself in the colors of the earth—a long-sleeved green blouse, dirt-colored breeches, black boots, and a hooded cloak that matches mine.

Even in my all-ebony attire, we do not stick out like her. "Why must you continue to dress in those colors?" I ask.

"Because I am a Confessor. This is my true self. I am not ashamed of the attire I am honored to wear." She states back in a regal tone. The hate I feel for her is burning me up inside. Especially while she consistently shuffles those insolent cards.

"Will you stop that?" My harsh tone surprises her.

"I am sensing some negative energy coming from you, Alwin." Her eyes narrow at me. "Didn't Master Mikao tell you how dangerous that is?"

I narrow my eyes right back at her. She is mistaken if she thinks she can use any persuasion over me. We stare at one another, a silent battle of power, neither blinking—fighting for dominance.

"Seriously?" Rose slams a pint in between us, making us both flinch slightly. "Why don't you do a reading for Alwin? It may help him understand why he is so on edge." Rose narrows her eyes at me—a silent plea for cooperation. But I won't let either of these women control my decisions. Everything I do is for her. For my Phoenix. "I don't need a reading." Although I greatly respect the cards and their masters, I don't feel they will do me any good.

"You have never been read." the Confessor states with a pull at the corner of her mouth. "Don't fear the unknown, Alwin. A reading could do you some good."

Pondering the thought, I remember Serena telling me about Odith's reading right before her phoenix emerged. Perhaps this could guide me in the right direction as the cards coached Serena.

"Fine. Just one." I started, and Rose let out a noise of excitement.

"Apologies, but I have a great admiration for Tarot Masters." A slight blush rose in her pale cheeks as I caught her glance towards The Confessor.

"This will be a three-card spread. I will pull a card and interrupt it for you. What you must understand is that these cards are connected to the Universe. But their meanings are not concrete." Her demeanor was admirable, making me feel like she was passionate about her gifts.

"Proceed." I started as she stopped shuffling and placed the first card down.

"The Lover," Rose whispers in awe. Depicted upon this card were three figures. A man is standing at the center, with another man to his left and a woman to his right. An infant holding a bow with a knocked arrow floated above them. It looked to me like a wedding ritual was being held.

"What does this mean?" I ask. "Does this have to do with Serena?"

"The Lover card can be interpreted with many meanings, but I sense this is a testament to your commitment and devotion towards her." I thought I heard a pain in her tone. Serena loved her first. I know that, and The Confessor did, too.

The second card is labeled as Justice. A man sits upon a throne of gold with a sword and weighing contraption in either hand. "You seek redemption for failing to protect her."

The Confessor's words hit me hard and true. "I want to see the third one," I state, ignoring her previous statement.

"The World card," she states. "I sense you will find peace at this journey's end." She examines all three cards again, just as I do. "Alwin, this spread is telling me that although you are devoted to the mission of Serena, some internal turmoil may prevent you from achieving your goals. You will know peace at the end, but don't expect it to come without trials."

My heart is beating so fast it reminds me of a thundering herd of horses. Getting to my feet, I rush to

the bathing chamber and splash cool water upon my face. I cannot lose her. I will not fail her.

A hand lands on my shoulder, but before my assailant can harm me, I have them pinned to the back wall with my dagger at their throat.

"It isn't wise to sneak up on me," I growl. I stare into the dark chocolate eyes of a human man, about the age of thirty years, with mid-night colored skin and a scar along his right eye. He smells of oils.

"I am told you seek the Rune Master." His voice is hoarse and reminds me of the time I yelled so loudly my throat was sore for a few days. Only Rose's honey lemon tea could bring my voice back to normal.

"And who might you be?" I ask, jamming my elbow further into his collarbone.

"I am the one you seek." he states with a crooked smile. I lower him back to the ground, removing my blade from his throat. I easily tower over him as his head stops at my shoulders.

"How do I know you aren't lying to me?" I state. He moves to pull something from his right sleeve, which makes me point my dagger at him again.

"Easy, I am not foolish enough to attack a soldier like you." I don't drop my dagger too low as he rolls up the crimson-colored sleeve of his robe to reveal a strange imprint within his dark skin.

Three symbols of white: one has three lines connected at two points, the second has five lines connected by four points, and the last one is like the first one, but it is lined horizontally.

"This is the mark of the Rune Master. I am the only one alive who has one. It is passed down each generation." he states.

When we first arrived here, I recalled the Confessor mentioning these facts. Supposedly, she read them somewhere in the same book that told her about the location of the Phoenix Fire. The Rune Master is the only one who can take us to it.

"Take me to your Confessor. She will tell you if I am lying." he eagerly states. He must know our magic doesn't work here, but why would he ask to see her?

"If you are lying, my eyes will be the last thing you see as I cut your heart from your puny little body." I threaten, then push him towards the wooden door.

No eyes follow us as we return to the table where I sat before. Rose and the Confessor are engaged in some conversation, which they stop when we arrive.

"He claims to be the Rune Master," I state, then silently urge him to show her the tattoo. The Confessor's long fingers glaze over the white ink, and her eyes find mine.

"It's him," she states while letting his arm go. I push him into the seat beside mine before I plop down into the wooden chair.

"Where is the Phoenix Fire?" I ask. He pulls out a black bag tied with golden strings. I watch as he opens it and takes something out. Placing the bag down, he clasps the object, or objects, in his hands as he shakes them before throwing them onto the wooden top.

They are rounded marbled stones with symbols carved into them, much like his tattoo. There are four in total. One bares a mark that closely resembles that of the Latin letter 'R,' the next corresponds to that of the Latin letter 'X,' the following looks like two opened mouths might eat each other, and the last one is an intricate design that looks like the letter 'x,' but the sides are closed off.

"We must travel North. To the Fenix Mountains." he states while hovering his hands over the pieces of inked marble.

"Is that what all your pieces say? From what I saw over the horizon, that is a vast mountain range. It could be anywhere." The Confessor's tone and question surprises me.

"I will know more the closer we get. Much like your cards, the runes work in their way. I do not control them." he states.

"Rose," I start. "Take," I gesture towards the man, who looks curious, "your name? Unless you would like me to call you Puny.'" "Ah, you may call me Davi." The Rune Masters states.

"Take Puny here and get some horses ready. The Confessor and I will get some provisions." Rose gives me a questioning look before pulling Puny to his feet and moving towards the doors.

"Do you believe him?" I ask her, not looking at them until the doors swing shut.

"Even without access to my magic, I can tell he is not a liar." she answers while getting to her feet. "I will take Natiri and follow you from the skies."

"You will alert me of anything," I command rather than ask. She nods her head before leaving me alone at the table. I pick up the rune pieces and scoop them back into the bag. I am holding one in my hand. It's heavy for such a small piece. I drop it in with the rest and head out the door.

*Soon, Phoenix, soon.*

## SERENA

My skin is pimpled with the cold air swirling around me. I try to call on my phoenix for warmth, but I can feel the internal flames weakening the longer I am trapped here. There is no light to

see behind the shaky breath I release. My mind is dazed as I try to remember how I got here.

Images of a man with pointed ears and soft blue-gray eyes filled with sadness flash through my head. When I awoke, my skin sweated, and my wings dropped low. I forgot my past except for the knowledge that I am a Phoenix. Or part of one since I only have the wings of one.

Voices filled with sorrow spoke a name, my name, I presume. But I cannot locate where they come from or why they are sad.

"I love you, Serena." A male voice states, and my heart flutters with the declaration. My body seems to remember the voice, although my mind does not.

"I will not fail you." A softer, more familiar feminine voice echoes. Her voice sounds like home to me. It makes me feel as though I should know it, should know her.

I am fearful of what will happen if I move from my spot. A soft bed made from silk is where I have been—dazed and confused since I awoke. Cold and shivering. My mind races with unanswered questions while my body begs for warmth.

I am adorned in a white blouse, brown breeches, and knee-high leather boots. My long brown hair is braided in two, tucked delicately behind my pointed ears.

Someone took great care of my appearance. Finally mustering the courage and listening to my body's protest, I force myself to sit up. Looking around, I still see nothing but darkness. But movement might warm me. I am getting my blood flowing and all that.

Remember, Serena, you must warm your blood to fight the cold. A deep masculine voice rings in my ears, and the faint memory of a tall dwarf with red hair and a big ax flashes through my head. My heart squeezes and tears

prick the back of my eyes.

Something about that memory is full of pain. He must have been someone important to me.

They say talking to yourself isn't wise, but since there is no one else- "Hello," my voice echoes with the vacancy of this place, bouncing off shadowed walls. Hoping down, my feet hit something soft, and dust particles flew.

Bending down, I brave a touch. It feels soft, reminding me of an infant's skin, but smells of fire.

As I drop the earth, I move forward. I stepped slowly, placing one foot directly in front of the other: heel toe, heel toe. I stop dead in my tracks as something passes me. My skin pimples, and the hair on the back of my neck raises alarmingly as its fabrics graze my arm.

Placing my arms in front of me, I form a sort of fighting stance.

My body must remember how to do this, too. "It's been a millennium since I had a Phoenix in my realm." A hoarse voice states, sending a shiver through my body that isn't directly related to the freezing atmosphere. "Where am I?" I ask, not dropping my fighting stance and looking all around for this shadow.

"I am the Spirit Master," it replies. In the not so far off distance, two purple irises come to life in front of me. A warm smile of pearls followed me.

"How do you know who I am?" I asked.

"I know all things within my realm. All the dead, the living, the in-between." The last part doesn't settle in my stomach well.

"Am I dead? Is this the shadow realm?" I daringly ask the floating eyes and mouth. Curious how it can hear me with no ears. So that's what is interesting to you? Not the floating eyes and mouth? Serena, we are going crazy.

"You are only half-dead," it answers, and I swear my bowels turn to water at the truth of its words. "What exactly does that mean?" I ask it, my arms slowly dropping as my willpower lessens with this news. "It means that you are neither here nor there," he states.

"I despise riddles, creature." I snarl. It lets out a hoarse laugh, like nails scratching against a stone surface and sending pain through my ears.

"The fire doesn't laugh; the fire will soon face his wrath. Fly away, firebird, or soon you will be the next to face the sword." Then, the face disappears, and light beams through the space.

My eyes blink while adjusting to my new surroundings. A beautiful field of poppies lays before me, with a sizeable snow- capped mountain range cascading a shadow across it.

The sky's lit with shades of purple, pink, and orange. A warm breeze melts the frost from my skin while igniting the internal flame of the phoenix. A tranquility wave washes over me, making me release a deep breath.

"Serena? Is that you?" A woman's voice catches me off guard. Spinning, I raise my fists in defense as my eyes catch on her. The beautiful face I have seen staring back at me through the mirrors all these years. A face I know in my heart and soul that will never leave my memory.

I sprint towards her, enveloping her in my embrace as tears cascade down my face. She reciprocates the gesture with equal warmth. As her gentle hands cradle my face, I gaze into her deep blue eyes, my heart pulsating with joy in my chest. "Mother."

# 10

# ALWIN

Should I be ashamed for threatening the Confessor? Probably? But will I lose sleep at night knowing what I did? Not likely.

These women do not know who I truly am or what I am capable of. My father earned the title of the Dark One for a reason, and as I sit here looking at the snow-capped peaks of the Fenix Mountains, I feel myself inching closer to that name. I will do anything for her. For my Phoenix.

"Puny," I called behind me at the Rune Master, who was more of an idiot than I thought he would be. Part of me thinks it is just an act, and the other part wants to question why the Ancients gifted a man as daft as him with the power to control relics such as Runes.

He stumbles from atop his horse, his boots caught in the stirrups until the giant, unwanted Amazon warrior quickly lifts him. She towers over him by two feet easily. But Amazon Druids are known for their height and everything else. The warrior hasn't said one word during our entire day trip to the bottom of the mountains.

I did not realize it, but the ice vessel moved quickly, and we only needed to ride half a day to reach this point. The moon is now peeking up over the mountains, giving us a quaint amount of light to work with, but I do not want to stop. I don't sleep anymore anyway.

"Hurry, Puny," I yell as he rushes over to me after thanking the warrior.

"The name is Davi. You should learn to use it as you should learn to respect it, for without me, you will not get your fire." I am slightly amused at his courage to stand up to me, but I don't have time for kindness.

"How about you do as you're told? I won't kill you." I growl with a sincere smile. He wipes some snot from his nose before nodding and unraveling the map.

"The fire is just over these ridges; another day, and we should be able to get it." Puny states while pointing to the middle of the mountain range.

"We should make camp for the night. Natiri and I can fly ahead and find the fire." the Confessor states, sending fire through my veins. I despise that woman.

"How about you and your little pet go away before I eat it." The giant bird doesn't seem to like my suggestion as I feel a sudden nip at my ear, and it bucks up against me, flexing its wings.

"Natiri will kill you before you eat her." The Confessor chuckles and then soothes the bird. "Griffins are noble creatures; if you have no respect for their bonded master, they will have no respect for you."

"I don't need the approval from my next meal, nor do I care for it," I state, which is true. The bird is noble and loyal. I respect it for that, but that doesn't mean I have to like it.

"Alwin," a soft voice catches in my ears, and I turn to see Rose. "May we have a word in private?" I nod to her, and we move far enough away for only us to speak.

"What is it that is bothering you?" I ask her. She appears flustered, not just from the cold nipping at her nose and cheeks. She must not trust our company either. No matter, I can ease her worries. "Do not fret, my friend. I will keep us safe."

"You are being an idiot." She spits out, and I am slightly taken aback. "What do you mean?"

"You are treating everyone here like they don't matter, and you are just using us to find the fire to save Serena, who is probably dead." The urge to slap her for those words crosses my mind, but I don't move. Instead, I curl my hands into fists and let her speak her mind. "Look, back in Ermelon, you were the master of the castle, and everyone followed your orders, but we didn't follow you because of your position; we followed you because you respected us enough to do our work. You were never above cleaning stables or chamber pots. But now," she pauses, and shame overcomes me as my anger eases.

"Now, I don't know if I want to follow this new male you are becoming. It's like you don't care about anyone or anything unless it saves her. I understand she is your destined mate, but if you keep going down this path, I fear what will come out on the other side."

Before I could speak in protest, she moved away from me to help them set up a campsite. My chest is heaving with the weight of her words, and I know she is telling the truth. I am becoming someone I swore I would never become. I am acting like my father, and that is a dark and dangerous path, but what if it is necessary for me to become him to save her?

Swiping a hand down my face, I close my eyes and think of her.

Of my memories with her and pray to the Ancients that somehow, wherever she is, she will hear me.

What will I do if it is not for the one I love? It could be the wisp of the wind, but I could've sworn I heard a whisper in response.

"Alwin," the voice is clear as day now. I try to open my eyes, but they remain shut as the scene unfolds. My heart thunders in my chest, and I see her. My Serena is walking through a meadow with a woman who looks like her, but it flickers in the sun's rays. A mask hiding a beast. "Serena," I try to call out to her, but my words are silent. I am whisked through darkness and coldness. A single burning flame burns and gets bigger the closer I am pushed toward it.

It's her again, only she is not alone.

"A test of faith," those words catch in my ears as the rest are cut off, and I am pushed forward again, finding myself outside a white door.

"If you fail, all is lost, heals the wounds of the past. Beware of the agent who seeks to please; another master pulls their strings."

While I soak all this in, the door opens, and I hear one word spoken that makes my heart squeeze with pain. "Alwin."

My eyes open, and I suck in the cold air as I lean on a nearby boulder holding my hand over my calming heart. "Are you okay?" The Confessor's voice comes from behind me, and I wonder if I should tell her what I saw, but those words of warning echo in my head: Beware of the agent who seeks to please; another master pulls their strings.

"I am fine, Confessor." I am calmer than usual. If I am to figure out who the traitor is, I shall play nice. "Thank you."

"Wow. That looked painful to say." She taunts me, and I do my best not to growl.

"Do we have food?" I ask her. She raises a brow at my sudden change of attitude. I watch as she rubs her arms while glancing over her shoulder at the other three in our party. My eyes follow hers as she speaks,

"When you were taken, Amazon cleaned out your sacks. The only food provided to us is some dried seal jerky that our new friends so elegantly provided for us." I glance back at her.

"I asked a simple question, Confessor. Just say yes or no." Not wanting to say anything more or be alone with her further, I push past her and join the others.

"Come, sit," Puny says while waving to the log beside him.

When I don't move, he tries to persuade me further. "You will be warmer around the fire and body heat we all provide. Or are you too high up there to sit with useless peasants such as us?"

I look towards Rose, but she looks away from me as if trying to avoid my eyes. I am losing one of my most loyal friends. This needs to be corrected. I give them a smile before taking a seat on the log.

It's cold and challenging, but at least it is dry—puny hands over some jerky, which I take with gratitude. When I bite, I am surprised at the spiced flavor that overwhelms my pallet. The meat is tender and not too difficult to chew through.

I pulled out a water skin and washed down my first bite before taking another and looking around. The Amazon Druid with us makes my instincts go wild as she stands erect and unmoving in her spot.

"What's the issue, Witch?" I ask her. She turns her head ever so slightly to meet my eye. Her golden rings pinned me in place.

"All is well. All is safe." The only words she has spoken to us since we left the block of ice are called a ship. "You speak, but do you eat?" I ask her.

"We don't eat meat unless it's roasted penis." I instinctively place a hand over mine and watch Puny do the same. Bile rises in my throat, and I have suddenly lost my appetite.

"Get some rest; we will need to leave in a few hours," I say as I reach my feet. "Did your leader provide us tents, or shall we freeze to death?"

Saying nothing, the Druid moves her arms in a raising motion to the cleared area behind us. The ground shakes, and I watch as one large tent made from ice rises.

When the ground settles again, the Druid bows her head and gestures towards it. I look at her with a raised brow, feeling envious that she has access to her powers, and I still do not. I nod back at her in a thank you, walk over to the horses, and grab the furred bedrolls.

## ALWIN

As I approach the shelter, I look over to find The Confessor and her Griffin hunkered down in the snow. Now is the perfect time to play nice.

"Confessor," I called, and she lifted her head from behind the Griffin's wing. "You will both be warmer here."

She says something to the bird, but I cannot hear it, and they walk over. As they soon arrive next to me, the Griffin squeezes through the almost too-small opening and squeaks inside. I follow the Confessor and stop to admire the site before me.

Four beds, crafted from snow and ice, sit flush along the room's back wall. In the far-right corner is a space large enough for the Griffin, and to the far left are the horses. At the center is a large fire pit ready, with flames of blue already heating our shelter.

"Wow," Puny's voice carries as he enters, making me turn to see him, Rose, and the Druid walk through with the horses in tow. "This is amazing."

"This is Essence," Rose states proudly. She still doesn't meet my eye as she walks past us to place the horses in their spots. I will show her I am still worthy of her loyalty.

As we all settle in our furs, my mind drifts back to what I saw on the other side of that door. Her wings of flames, a gown of fire, hair of auburn, and eyes match the deepest shade of the blue skies. There was no mistaking who it was. It was my Phoenix.

Tonight, I will dream of you, my Phoenix. We are so close. Keep fighting. Survive for me. For us. For the realm needs its Fire heart. Without you, none will survive.

## DAVI
### A FEW MONTHS EARLIER

"Soon, my Queen. I will hand them all over to you." I say to her as I kneel on the stone floor of her throne room. The charred remains of her last victim are still sizzling beside me, making a nervous shiver run down my spine.

"See that you do, Rune Master. Or you and your pathetic pieces of marble will turn into ash." I meet her eyes before getting to my feet and turning to leave. "Davi," I pause mid-step.

"Yes, Your Majesty?"

"Remember what will happen if you cannot bring me the Dark One and Phoenix." Not that I needed reminding, but it comes with two guards and two prisoners. My heart pounds with anxiety. "Your wife and daughter will be added to my collection of slaves, or they will be rewarded with positions in my court."

I try not to look into my girls' eyes because I know it will only make me fall to my knees and beg. I can't do that again. I have the scar on my face to remind me of how much begging displeases the Queen.

"I will not fail," I said loud enough and mainly in the direction of my wife and daughter.

Turning on my heel, I hastily exited the throne hall and into the vacant corridor, heading towards my private chambers. It's at the opposite end of the front doors. And you have to go down two spiral staircases to get there.

My single red door is the only one down here. It used to be a part of the torture chambers until the late King passed, and Queen Lilac disposed of it. She didn't deem torture necessary. They either speak or die.

As I push through my door, I am instantly greeted with her scent—the woman in white who haunts my existence.

"You are running out of time, Davi." Niya lowers her furred hood to look at me. I move past her toward my desk, littered with old books. I was detailing all the Essences of past and present.

"And you are risking everything being down here." I hissed at her.

"The Queen does not suspect me. I am her loyal Confessor." she responds, and I wave her off. "What does the text say about her? About Serena? Could it be her?"

Sitting down, I look back over the book on Phoenix Fire. Only one can be re-born every ten thousand years. And the day that Serena was born was that day.

"Was your friend the only child born that day in the entire realm?" I ask the raven-haired beauty. "She doesn't know it, but yes. That is why many fear her. The only half-elf born on the prophecy written by the Ancients. Half-human and half-elf. A true descendant of the first Phoenix."

"Why have you never told her this?" I ask her while continuing to study the text. She paces slightly while speaking. Her small heels clicked against the stone floor.

"Serena has lived a hard life. What kind of friend would I be if I told her she was even more unique than she already is?"

"You'd be an honest one. It isn't like Confessors to hold the truth from the ones they care for." I said to her; she sighed before plopping down on the mattress.

"I do not want to tell her until I know how to help her. To discover what it means to be the Phoenix. She is already scared of being in these walls." She pauses and fiddles with her golden cuff links.

Getting to my feet, I make my way over to her. I was pulling out a chair to sit in front of her. Our knees brushed ever so slightly.

Niya is exquisite. I take her hands in mine, linking our fingers before brushing calming circles over the back of her hand with my thumb.

"Speak your mind. We have no secrets between us." I tell her in a reassuring tone.

"I kissed her." I don't stop my thumb but want to at the surprising confession. I am married, but men are permitted a mistress.

"Did she reject you?" I pray that she does because the past months I spent with Niya made me realize I want her to be mine.

"No, but I ran away after." She let go of me to palm her face. "I am such a fool."

"You are not a fool. Sometimes, we can only admit our feelings for someone through action, not words." I reach under her chin to lift her head so she can meet my eye. "What you did took courage; I envy you for it."

"Davi," I shush her by running my thumb across her lips, which she parts slightly. My eyes move from her lips to her eyes—a question she wants to ask but doesn't know how.

"Tomorrow, when you forget that I ever existed, and all this is over, I will remember how you felt in my arms. The way it felt to kiss you and make love to you the way you deserve to be." She pulls back, confused.

"What are you saying?" I smile because the only way she knows is to show her. Leaning forward, our lips inches away from one another, I ask her, "I would like to kiss you, Niya." I wait for rejection, but she doesn't move.

"Okay." I press my lips firmly to hers and savor the moment.

Pulling back, I look into her eyes, and she speaks. "Don't stop, Davi. Make me forget."

I deepen our kiss as she lays back on the back. My body is hovering over her as I pull the strings of her corset loose. My lips move to her neck as I slowly remove her dress while leaving a trail of kisses along her body.

When she is bare before me, I admire her curves and bountiful breasts. I undress quickly before moving over to her.

"Are you sure you want me to be your first?" I ask her. "Are you sure you want to risk becoming my slave if I lose control?" she asks with worry clouding her eyes. "Your magic will not work on me. It's the benefit of this." I show her the painted image on my forearm that marks me as the one and only Rune Master. "Tomorrow, we have to tell her. Promise me you will help me help her." she pleads, and I can't say no to her. "I promise." She nods and then wraps her thick thighs around my waist, urging me forward. I place my tip at her entrance and ease into her so she can adjust. "Are you okay?" I ask her, and it's taking everything in me not to pick up the pace.

"Yes." she states, sounding like a moan. I begin to pick up my rhythm. Moving faster as she arches her back, I clamp down on her right breast. She clenches as her orgasms soon approach.

"Davi," she moans. And I thrust harder, reaching between us to find her bundle of nerves to make her scream with release.

I soon followed her as it's been too long since my wife and I made love. Her tight sex just made it ten times better. When I roll off her, I grab a towel and clean ourselves up.

"Are you okay?" I ask her. Praying she didn't just regret that. She sits up quickly and then cries. "Shit. Did I hurt you?"

"No." She grabs the sheets and wraps them around her body.

"Tell me what's wrong, please." I am panicking now. Getting off the bed, I pull my trousers back on and rush over to my cupboard, eyeing the empty vial of the forget-me potion I concocted after reading one of the books. If I need her to forget about me, she needs to.

Rushing back to the bed, she stopped crying momentarily to look at me.

"I'm sorry, Davi. You did everything perfectly, but," she pauses. "I just felt nothing for you or any other man. I thought having sex with one would change it, but it didn't. I was thinking about Serena the entire time."

As if that makes me feel any better, but at least I know I didn't hurt her, or make her feel as though she had no choice. Without thinking, I place the vile in her hand.

"Drink this; it will calm your nerves," I tell her, and without question, she pops the cork and downs its hole. The potion will act quickly;

tomorrow, when she wakes in bed, she will forget all about me. "All our research will be on your desk when you wake tomorrow."

I brush strands of hair out of her sleeping face. "You may forget me, Niya, but I will never forget you."

*Present Day*

I never thought I'd see my charcoal beauty again. I look at her while she sleeps so soundly, wondering whether or not that potion is still affecting her. I'm sure if it wore off, she would remember me and our night together.

It would more than likely end in my death if she remembered me. Knowing what the Queen ordered me to do means that she would reveal me as a traitor to the Dark One. But since my daughter and wife are still locked away, it would be wise of me to keep my facade until we have the Phoenix and then take them both to the Queen.

However, Niya and the Amazon Druid conflict with my plans.

She will never surrender to Serena without a fight, and I am no fool for those Druids and their magic. But I have my runes to thank for my ability to block most types of Essence.

Sitting up, I quietly make my way out of the ice tent and squint as the rays of the rising sun peek. Making my way over to a boulder, I take my morning piss and then look around to ensure none of the others have awoken.

Reaching into my Rune Bag, I pull some pieces and sift through them until I find it. "I take your Essence with respect and honor.

Thank you for giving it to me."

Rolling up my sleeve to expose my tattoo, I position the rune over it and draw the magic from its intricate design. Something I started doing back when Niya first started helping me. In the book of the Ancients, I read that the first Rune Master did this to block other powers. He, of course, became addicted and died a painful death. I am not addicted. I do it enough to keep the wall around me strong sufficiently so no others can penetrate it.

When the Rune is a blank piece of marble, I kiss it and place it back in my bag. Looking at the last of the black wisps sink into my arm, I cover it back up and make my way back to the tent just as it falters.

"See, she was right." I hear Rose state to Alwin. They discussed dismantling the shelter because the Amazon was easing her arms down as the slabs sunk back into the ground.

"Where did you run off to, Puny?" What an ignorant bastard that elf is.

"To take a piss. Looks like you need to as well." I say, gesturing to the bulge in his pants that is sticking out of his furs.

"That is a human's problem. My cock is just that big." I hate him.

No matter. When I bring him before the Queen, we will see who the stronger one is.

"Davi," Niya's soft voice calls over to me. "Ignore him. He is trying to be more civil with us." I smile at her and take in her sweet scent. Flashes of my skin pressed to hers run through my mind, and I almost regret making her forget.

"Are you okay?" she asks while touching my arm. She blinks fast, looks at me confusedly, and then touches her head.

"Me? I should ask you." I try to steady her, but she regains her balance and smiles. "We best be off then. Your friend only has forty-eight more hours left."

"Don't remind me." she speaks. Her face was full of sorrow.

While the horses are set free, Niya and Natiri take to the skies to see if they can find the cave that holds Phoenix fire inside; as we trek up the mountainside, my mind races through the plan. Get to the cave, open the portal, save the Phoenix, destroy the Dark One. Sounds simple enough.

# 11

# NIYA

The air is freezing the further we fly into the clouds. My polar bear furs keep me warm upon Natiri's back. From this height,
 I can see the village below. The busy villagers look like tiny insects scurrying about their homes. I can see Alwin's black cloak dancing in the wind as he leads the other two north towards the Fenix Mountains.
 There is no other village for miles all around us. The ground glistens like beautiful pearls as the snow settles. You are reminding me that my home, Narborim, only looks stunning when the snow falls with the Winter Solstice.
 Home. Serena.
 When the news of her death reached me, I never knew what pain like that could feel like. When I placed that invisible link on her, it protected her from harm. Alwin believes he is the only one who failed her, but he
 is not.
 The day the Essence Master informed the Queen of Serena's circumstances, was when I realized I needed to protect her. I warned them that they would never accept her for who she was.
 When I pulled her into the broom closet, my intention wasn't to kiss

her. Or maybe it was, and I didn't know why like I do now. I always could sense her love for me went beyond friendship, but I was too much of a coward to return it.

Now, I fear I will never know what it is to love and be loved by her. She gave herself to Alwin. Would there be any place left for me?

A screech from Natiri breaks me out of my thoughts as I look to see what has alarmed her. Down below, I can see my traveling companions approaching an ambush.

"Down," I order Natiri with a nudge of my right heel, and as she begins to descend, I want to call out a warning, but as Alwin seems to turn his head slightly, he slows them to a halt.

"What did you see?" he calls me as we land. "Ambush straight ahead," I say, pointing from Natiri's back. He looked in that direction but could not see the moving bodies clothed in white and perfectly hidden by the blanket of snow.

"You cannot see them. They wear the color of the snow." I tell him to jump from Natiri's back. My boots hit the snow with a soft thud.

Walking up to them, I catch sight of Rose, who quickly turns away. "Is everything alright?" I ask her. She turns quickly, raising a brow as if I did not just catch her gawking at me. "Who? Me? Yes, of course." She waves her hand before placing it on her hip. I nod at her and then look at Davi.

"I told you this would not be easy." he states. "The runes never lie."

"Nothing can foresee hidden men," Alwin grumbles. "Only the Fates," Davi states, fumbling with his bag of stones. "They control the Universe, and the Universe controls all Essence."

I catch Alwin's eye roll as he scans the far area ahead. "What should we do?" Rose asks, walking up beside me. Our arms brush, causing what I can only describe as a spark to go off.

"Is there any other way towards those mountains?" Alwin asks Davi. Reaching into his robe, he pulls out a rolled parchment. Opening it, he reads the map of the world. "We are here," he points at the spot directly between a small frozen pond, Trinity Lake, and the path to the mountains. "The only way to avoid encountering these snow soldiers is by either going west towards the lake or back south towards Cardinal Village, but that could cause more delay."

"Give me a shorter answer, Puny," Alwin growls. "Right. The fastest way is to keep moving north." Davi answers.

"But that means we would walk right into their territory." Rose states. "I don't care," Alwin says, pulling out his sword. "We don't have time to waste. Serena doesn't have time, and I will cut down anyone in my path if it means I will save her."

I gently grab his arm, and as he turns to snarl at me, I state, "She wouldn't want you to die acting like a fool either."

"And what makes you think you know what she wants?" He snarls before shrugging me off. I shouldn't let him get to me, but he is right. I have no clue what Serena wants in life anymore.

"You are right. But I know that if Serena loves you, like you say she does…"

"We are fated by the Ancients themselves, Confessor." He snarls, getting into my face.

"Did she agree to the bond?" I ask him. He hesitates for a moment. The hurt in his eyes told me that she either said no or died before she had the chance to choose.

"It doesn't matter what she wants," Rose interrupts. "She will die if we don't get that fire."

I wait for Alwin to reprimand her. Tell her to shut up. "Rose is right. We have wasted too much time already." He cares for the fairy. "One day, I hope you will look at me like you do, Rose," I state for only him to hear. He gives me a slight smirk. Then he bares his teeth at me. "I will never look upon you with anything but hate. It's what you deserve after what you did rather didn't do for her."

He steps away from me and walks over to Davi. I don't hear their conversation as my heart breaks a little more. I could've saved her. I had Natiri, and instead of running away with her, I pushed her. Wiping the tears from my face, I gain my composure again. I do not have any Essence here, but at least I have my cards. Taking them out of my side pouch, I shuffle them a few times before pulling the top card.

"The Temperance?" I question them, and a slight vibration from the angled beauty reminds me not to ask them. This card has many meanings, but if I am to interpret my reading, I would say this is telling me not to let Alwin's words distract me from my mission but to use them as inspiration to push forward.

"Hey," Rose says, approaching me, and I stuff my cards back in my pouch.

"Hello," I say back. We stare at each other for a moment longer. "Is there something I could help you with?"

She looks down at her feet briefly before smiling at me. She appeared nervous, something I had noticed a lot about this woman. "Well, I came over here to check on you." she states, and her

kind gesture takes me aback. "Alwin isn't the only one who lost someone he cared for. Were you and Serena," she pauses, searching for a word, but I step in.

"We were childhood friends. We grew up together." I started and could have sworn I saw her shoulders relax a little. Why was she so concerned about my relationship with Serena?

"Right, so you two weren't, you know?" She made weird gestures with her hands, and I raised my brow in confusion. "Romantically involved?"

"Oh, well, we shared a kiss once but never went further." Not that I didn't want to. It was forbidden. You still could've found a way. Coward. I berate myself internally.

A blush rises in her cheeks, and I wonder why. I have known Rose for a short while. She is kind and loyal. I look deep into her purple eyes, searching for the missing puzzle piece I can't seem to find with her.

"Well, okay, I," she starts.

"Rose, Confessor, get ready to move forward. We may fight with our hands, but I'm not giving up the ground we have already worked so hard to gain." Alwin states that I give Rose a slight glance before turning and heading back to Natiri.

"Come on, girl, they will need your help," I say as I brush her head. She gives me a small purr before lowering herself for me to climb on top.

I will save you, Serena.

## ALWIN

I lead our small squad through the snow ahead. The sun is peeking over the top of the mountains I can see in the far distance. My sword is out and ready for the ambush, the Confessor stated was waiting for us. Nothing and no one will stand in the way of me and that fire.

Our horses' hooves thunder forward, turning the snow into powder around us. I won't stop, and we will not slow down until the horses need another break. The rush of the freezing wind sends ice through my skin, but as my mind drifts, I only picture my Phoenix.

Her sweet scent surrounds me; her smile makes my heart clench at the memory of her laugh. The night we shared haunts me because it was the last time I felt her close to me. I don't just miss her body; I miss her soul. Her presence. I don't feel whole without her.

The black beauty I am riding rears back suddenly, nearly knock- ing me off its back. With a loud neigh of protest, I look to see what has spooked her.

I cannot see anything, but the atmosphere is quiet once we stop.

The shadow of Natiri swoops over us, and I silently look at the

Confessor for any confirmation of an approaching attack. Before she could say anything, a battle cry rang out as forty soldiers, dressed in white from head to toe, jumped out of the snow and started charging at us.

"Rose, protect Puny," I shout, and I don't look at her. I know she will do what I ask. Not wanting to have my horse injured, I jumped down and prepared myself for a fight. I may not have my Essence, but I can still fight.

"I can protect myself," I hear him protest, but I ignore him and charge forward.

My blade connects with the first one; they only have slits for their eyes, while everything else is wrapped in thick white fabric. I sweep my foot out, trying to knock him down, when he does some flip over me.

I quickly turn before he can slam his blade through my back. We continued our dance as I heard more shouts in a language I could not comprehend. These soldiers are too tall to be dwarves, and I don't see human traits in them. However, I cannot tell with all the fabric they wear.

As I shift to the left, he mirrors by moving to the right, and this pattern continues. Every swing of my blade and his movements are anticipated effortlessly. It's as if we are in perfect synchronization. "Are we going to dance or kill?" I growl at him. Instead of continuing, he stands taut, sheathing his sword again. "I will not fight a defenseless man."

"Good thing I am not a man," it didn't register until I found myself bound at the hands, kneeling, with my sword at my feet. I look around, confused, as I see intricate ice cuffs enclosed around my wrists. I feel the faintest prick at my neck and see a shard of ice sticking from the ground.

"What are you?" I ask. And with the two golden eyes looking back at me, I can see it but cannot believe it. They were rumors and meant to be extinct.

"You know what we are." she states, her voice slightly muffled behind the cloth of the mask. "Bring the prisoners to the dungeons." Out of the corner of my eye, I see Rose and Puny being pushed onto the plank of a pure white ship.

How the fuck did we miss that? I ask myself. "Bring this one to my quarters." she states to two soldiers behind me. There is no point in fighting when I cannot access my gifts. Warriors such as these cannot be overpowered.

As I am escorted up a wooden plank, I step onto a frosted deck. The ship is made of pure ice, but it is thick enough you cannot see below deck or through any of the cabins. A beautiful blanket of snow gives it a shimmering ivory color.

I know little about ships, but one like this has been crafted using one of the most potent Essence I have ever read.

To my left, I can see a raised platform with two warriors holding a bow and quiver full of arrows. Adorned in the same all-white attire, I assume they are the watchstanders. To my right, there is another platform matching the other.

I am made to move to the center of the deck, where I feel the deck below me move. We are lowered beneath the deck, and I glimpse a griffin's wings as I look at the distancing sky.

The Confessor should follow us from the skies. In this place, we lack allies, and she would have no one to seek help from for our rescue. And these women, if I am accurate in my assumption, cannot be stopped by ordinary people or dwarves.

Below the deck, I am surprised by the colorful nature before me.

A cerulean satin rug encompasses the hull of the room, complementing the gilded colors of the furnishings. A double-panned window at the back is adorned with two cobalt-colored curtains with golden lace at the ends.

There is a single bed with ivory silk sheets and a polar bear-furred blanket covering the top. A settee is placed next to a glowing furnace that warms the room.

I am forced into a wing-back chair in front of the settee. I was left alone with my wrists and ankles bound to the chair by ice.

"This is not good. Not good at all." I murmur to myself. "Ancients, I don't have time for this. Serena needs me." I lean my head back to yell, but I am interrupted.

"Who is Serena, and why are the Dark Elves all flustered?" The same woman's voice fills my ears as I catch sight of her white clothes from the corner of my eye. I don't answer her because she doesn't care.

Her pure beauty instantly catches me off-guard when she enters my sight line. Flawless midnight-colored skin decorated with golden clusters along her arms. She is dressed in a pristine white dress, almost matching the Confessor's attire. But she is no Confessor.

"No answer?" she asks, and I don't look at her eyes. She has no hair atop her head, and her pointed ears are pierced at the tip and base with golden rings. "You've figured out what we are, and now you think you can go without speaking." She sighs, then turns to pick up something from the mantle atop the furnace. "I will get the answers out of you, Dark One," she states while turning back to me with a golden needle in her hand. "One way or another."

"If you're going to kill me, then just get it over with; otherwise, stop wasting both of our time." I snarl. She smiles at me before approaching me and then moves to straddle me. I turn my head away from her as she grinds on my crotch. She laughs before licking the side of my face.

"You taste like death, and I want to play with you. Let me play with you." She fakes a plea before piercing my neck with that needle—pure ice shoots throughout my body, numbing me in place.

"Callous bitch." I bare my teeth at her. The only muscles I can move are my tongue and eyes. She talks to me before placing a kiss on my lips. I need to move. I need to get out of here, but I must without my magic.

"Keep talking to me like that, and we won't have clothes on for much longer." she states before nipping my ear. I feel everything, but I cannot move.

"I didn't think Amazon Druids enjoyed the company of a male," I state, trying to persuade her to do anything further. My body is reserved for my mate. Not some murderous whore.

"We don't, but you aren't just any male, though, are you?" she states while pulling back to look at me. "Alwin."

"How the fuck do you know who I am?" I try to growl, but it doesn't come out in the tone I mean it to.

"You know about me and my kind. I know about you and yours. We are all alike; we all have one goal in mind. Rid the realm of the abominations that continue to disease the purity of the world."

"We are nothing alike." I spat back.

"Oh, that's right. Father and Son don't share the same beliefs. You want peace between the realms, not purity." She moves to get off me, thank the Ancients. "But that is a boy's dream, Alwin. There is no room for a species that isn't pure."

"Why did you take us? Where are my friends?" I ask, trying to avoid any further monologue.

"The pixie is being well taken care of, but the human, I have a special need for someone with his gifts." she states that she is filling a golden chalice with something red.

"You can have him, but let myself and Rose go."

"Tell me who Serena is, and I might." she argues before taking a sip of her drink.

"Nobody important." The lie tastes like acid as it rolls from my tongue. She is everything to me—the only woman to ever capture my heart.

"Don't think you can lie to me, Dark One. Is she a lover?" I don't answer her, and she steps forward. "No, a long-lost sibling?" She guessed, and again, I didn't move. "No, she is way more important than that."

She straddles me again. The smell of alcohol coats her breath as she presses her chest into me and moves over my crotch again. "Has the Dark One found his mate?"

I didn't mean to, but I allowed myself to blink slightly. A smile of triumph forms on the Druid's face. Her gilded eyes gleamed with the answer.

"Oh my, is that why I found you in the middle of my territory? Are you searching for her? Did she realize how pathetic love is and run away from you and it?" If I could choke her for speaking ill of my mate, I would. She leans in again, whispering against my lips.

"Simmer down; I am only teasing," she kisses me again, trying to push that vile tongue through, but I clamp my mouth down tightly. "Mostly."

"Whore." I let her see the fur in my eyes and hear it in my tone. I rarely insult women with a name like that, but this is no typical woman. Amazon Druids are masterful seductresses with the ability to bend any man or woman to their will. Much like a Confessor, they are evil instead of righteous.

"You know we could be great together; you and I. Create an heir with our combined powers, and our son or daughter would rule over the entire realm." The audacity of this woman to think I could ever betray Serena like that or even my people.

"Never," I growl.

"You'll need that anger where you are going." I cock an eyebrow at her. "You didn't think I captured you to keep you for myself?" She laughs. "Males are the inferior species."

She gets off me again, and the needle gets pulled out of my neck. The end is coated in my blood, and I grimace as she lifts it to her mouth and licks it clean. I try to be seductive, but her powers will never work on me.

"You may think you are immune to my Essence, Dark One, but all males succumb to it eventually. "

"You keep telling yourself that, whore, but I will never be disloyal to my mate," I say proudly.

"I admire you for that. I keep insulting me, and you won't make it to Fenix alive." Fenix, she says, as in the Mountains. What could be there aside from the phoenix fire?

"A mountain range. That is where your headquarters are?" I ask. I'm not trying to hint at anything else. "Oh, no. These are my headquarters," she states, gesturing to the giant ship of ice. "You see, I got word that a group of tourists were looking for the Rune Master. I thought to myself, why would someone want him?" I don't give away anything because she is trying to bait me.

"Do you know why someone would want him? Oh, you do because he is traveling with you." I swallow, praying that Puny hasn't already squealed on everything. "Don't worry, he hasn't told me anything yet. Except that you needed a tour of the Fenix Mountains. He said you didn't tell him why and that I should ask you."

"But you won't tell me since my charm doesn't work on you. I bet it would work on that perfect little pixie of yours, though, wouldn't it?"

"You stay away from her, or I'll—"

"You'll what? Kill me?" She laughs. "My dear boy, you are immobilized. You didn't think those dwarves produced the serum to stop others' Essence, did you?" If I could move to hit myself, I would. I should've known it was created by magic. Only magic can fight other magic, but it must be mighty.

"How?" I ask her. I know she may not tell me, but trying and coaxing it out of her is at least worth a shot. Maybe I can find a weakness in it so we can all get control of our Essence again.

"That's a secret I am not willing to share with someone who threatens and insults me," she feigns hurt. "But I will offer you a deal."

"What kind of deal?" If she wants me to fuck her, the answer is no.

"I need you to kill someone for me." That was a surprising statement.

"Why? You have access to your Essence and should be able to do it." She rolled her eyes before walking over to a shelf of books and rummaged through them until grabbing one. She flips a few pages before casually plopping the book onto my lap.

"That is the map of the Universe." she states, pointing at it with a long white nail. "Here is Whitfrost at the far North, Xora, where you come from, is to the west, *Vwirynn* is to the east, and *Ulorea* is to the south."

"What does this have to do with you not being able to kill someone?" I ask her.

"Shut up and listen," I do as I am told, which is strange, but I have never seen the universe laid out like this before. I knew there were more realms, but I didn't realize the extent of it. "At the center is the Spirit Realm, which you know is where all dead things go."

She flips the page over, and upon it is title Vwirynn: Shadow Realm. "This is where your ancestors are from and where the person I need you to kill lives."

"Why? Can't you just portal over there?" I ask here. "No, you fool, if I could've, I would have already." She bites back.

"How do you expect me to get there when I cannot access my Essence?"

"You will be able to once you are outside of Whitfrost. I will ensure you have everything you need." she states. "What did they do to you?" I ask her. When she doesn't answer, I know I struck a nerve with her.

"I mean, it must have been something terrible for you to go through all the trouble you did capturing me, trying to seduce me, and offering me a deal."

She turns her back to me, and I know I shouldn't, but I can't stop myself from tormenting her and making her feel pain for what she is doing to me. To Serena.

"Did they kill your lover? Or was it something worse than that?" She doesn't move, except I see the muscles in her back tense up. "I will not kill someone if I do not know their crime. I am not an executioner."

In an instant, she was in my face, no longer a playful emotion, but nothing but pure fur filled her eyes as ice coated her features— those golden pots of warm honey swirled into a rage of blue flames.

"You will not intimidate me." Her once soft tone is now a deepened growl laced with fury. "If you ever want to save your mate, you will kill my enemies for me."

She backs away, her anger seeming to simmer as she forms into her usual self.

"That's right, Dark One, I know you seek the flames of the phoenix, and I am inclined to aid you in your quest if you aid me in mine." she states while straightening her dress. "There is no use denying it; your Rune Master is not so immune to my powers. He spilled your secrets the moment I entered the room."

Stupid puny human. I say to myself.

"Do we have a deal?" she asks with an outstretched hand. "Oh, you can't move yet for another couple of hours. No matter, we can seal it with a kiss."

"No. You've already insulted me enough." I snarl. "The only way you will ever see your precious Serena again is with my help." I hate to admit it, but she is right. It doesn't mean I must trust her; I must work with her long enough to identify and exploit her weaknesses. I only have seven more days left until I have to get back to Xora.

"Fine." And with that, she presses her lips against mine, sealing our deal with a spark of magic between us.

## 12

## SERENA

"Mother? How are you here?" I ask, looking upon the face that reflects mine so perfectly.

"Come, my dear, there is much to be discussed." She gestures for me to follow her to a small cottage I didn't notice before. A few feet from the field, we are walking in a brown brick house with a straw roof, two small windows, and a brown painted door.

When we walked through, the smell of honey and lemon overwhelmed my senses, making my mouth water and my stomach growl in hunger.

"I didn't know spirits could get hungry." I joke, and she smiles at me before walking over to the open fire and using a long iron bar to remove the baked honey biscuits carefully.

"Do you remember when I used to make these for you each Winter Solstice?" she asks, putting two on a plate for me.

"How could I forget? It's the only happy memory from my childhood." The room goes silent, and I could slap myself for saying such a hurtful comment. "I'm sorry."

"No need to apologize, my dear. You, indeed, grew up in such a gray world. But now you are in a world where you can make your own."

"I'm dead," I state before taking a bite of my treat. Salivating over the honey-infused dough complemented with flakes of lemon.

"Besides that, I mean, look at you." she says, gesturing up and down my body. "You are a pure-blood now. I see you have grown into your wings, but where is your amulet?"

I reach for my neck, noticing it is gone, and a memory flashes again. Pain, betrayal, death. "It was destroyed by the woman who killed me," I admitted sorrowfully.

"No matter." I don't recall my mother's demeanor being this perky. My head feels dizzy, and my stomach cramps as I nearly fall over. "Oh, my, you shouldn't have eaten those biscuits."

"What?" I ask her, dazed and confused. When I find myself on the cold floor, my mother's image flickers until the entire place dissolves into something darker.

Bloodied carcasses hang from chain hooks attached to a stone ceiling. The smell of decay makes me want to vomit. A being replaces the image of my mother, its bony body, barely with black eyes and teeth—no hair litters its emaciated body, barely clothed with shredded robes.

"What did you do to me?" I mutter, my voice weak and barely above a whisper.

"I immobilized you so you won't fight me when I eat your soul." What? A soul eater. Shit, I am in terrible shit right now. Think Serena, think. Closing my eyes, I think about my wings. They are made of fire, meaning they should be able to burn through almost anything.

As I am lifted into the air so my face is lined up with his mouth, I clear my mind of all my distractions and call upon that fire—the heat courses through my veins without protest, burning through the magic the soul eater used. Opening my eyes, I see my reflection and another memory flashes.

The first time, I died and became a Phoenix. My eyes are alight with flames as my wings are erect, and I burn the soul eater until he is charcoal on the floor. I look around me at his many victims and decide to give them an honorable burial by fire.

Walking through the flames that do not hurt me, I open the door and find a different scene. There is no field of flowers but a replica of my home. Narborim has come to the spirit realm.

In the distance, I see two young girls, one with raven-colored hair and the other looking just like me. "This way, Niya." Niya's name sounds familiar; I must know it because I feel something for her. The familiarity hits me as I watch the two little girls run around a chapel.

"We can't go too far away, Serena. My parents will reprimand me, and I will never see you again." Little Serena's eyes flash with pain, but Niya grabs her hand and she smiles again.

I follow them as they wander down a stream connected to the ocean. I am amazed that as they walk, they seem to age. By the time they reach the bank, they will be adults.

"Want to go for a swim?" Niya asks Serena. I can see my cheeks become heated at the suggestion. And before the younger me could answer, Niya was in her silk undergarments, diving into the pool of water.

When she surfaces again, I remember my feeling at seeing her. The heat that rushed through my body and the thought of being able to be close to her like this.

The scene changes again, and I find myself in a room. I look around and see myself lying on a bed with black silk sheets, and at the back wall stands a male elf. His arms are crossed as he observes me.

When I look at him, my heart skips a beat, and the familiarity rushes through me as something snaps inside me—sounding like a bone cracking with a zap of magic connecting us.

I watch as he moves over to the edge of the bed, sitting close to me and gently running a hand over my sleeping face.

"You're my mate, Serena. I should tell you, but I don't know how. That's a coward's answer, but you are so strong and beautiful; I don't deserve someone like you." I try to say something to him, but my voice is silent, and I know I must watch this play out. "When you kissed me, I thought I was the luckiest person in the world. And when you gave yourself to me to share my bed, knowing you still had feelings for someone else, nothing else mattered to me. I needed to show you how badly I wanted you. I chose you, but you are the only one who has ever chosen me."

I feel the tears flowing down my cheeks at the memories of all my times with him. He never told me I was his mate. And now it's too late for us.

Falling to my knees, the pain of knowing this and knowing I will never see him again, feeling him touch me, is too much.

"Giving up already, Phoenix?" The Spirit Master's voice hits my ears, and I lift my head to see I am in complete darkness again. The only light is from my glowing wings.

"Why did you show me those memories?" I ask him. "I do not control the images that show."

"I am tired of your nonsense; just speak like an average person., I yell.

"Normal? Who wants to be normal? Normal is boring, bland; normal doesn't get you to your lover's land." The last two words simmer down my rage.

"Lover's land? Do you mean there is a way to get back to him? To Alwin?"

"A heart divided leads to a crossroad, a choice to make, another to break." Ancients, this isn't very pleasant. "Please tell me what you mean."

"The sands of time are sinking fast; a test of faith will come to pass.

But be warned, if two shall fail, a lovers' quarrels will end the realm."

"What does that mean?" My voice echoes far into the distance without an answer. "You could've given me a parchment and ink feather so I could write all that down."

Again, my voice echoes, and I think of his words. Test of faith. Lover's quarrel. Does he mean Alwin and me or Niya and me? Who am I kidding? Niya and I were never lovers. She kissed me once and left.

I gasp as another memory comes back into my head. Sands of time must mean that my time here in limbo will run out soon. I need to get out of here just as quickly as I came.

Looking around, I see no exit, but I don't give up as I close my eyes and picture a door that could lead to the realm of the living. When I opened my eyes again, I found a single door of pure white appearing a few feet from me.

Test of faith, here I come. Walking up to it, I place my hand on the fabulous golden handle and turn. When it pushes open, I am greeted with frigid air and the smell of iron.

## NIYA

Soaring above the slow-moving ice vessel, my heart races with the worry that Alwin, Rose, and Davi are being harmed. There isn't much I can do without my powers and the ability to convince these female witches to give them up without a fight. Not that I would use my Essence for anything morally cruel such as that.

Especially after having no say in the matter of my power.

An hour has passed, and Natiri is growing tired, and if we stop, I cannot keep up with them on foot. "Easy, you are doing great," I tell her while patting her head. She coos in response, and I know she will keep going until her muscles tense up. When I first met Natiri, she was nothing but a tiny infant. Merely the size of a kitten. Her fur was pure white, and her eyes were glossed over like a newborn should be. It was an honor when I discovered my Essence as a child, and my family was very proud. Being the first Confessor in the line of non-magic users was a blessing from the Ancients. Father took me to the breeding grounds to pick out my Griffin. Natiri caught my eye the moment I stepped into the stables.

I named her after the Ancient Warrior goddess because of her ability to fight for her right to survive. I remember the warning the Griffin Master said on that day I saw her. "A Griffin is a partner for life. They will give up their life to protect their Confessor; if you die, they die. But if they die, you will live on." the Griffin Master said. The thought scared me as a child, but we were both ready when our bonding day arrived.

"Step forward and place your palm on the forehead of your chosen Griffin." the Griffin Master stated. There were twenty of us, all the age of twenty-one. The nest of Griffins was fully matured, as we were. Natiri's pure white feathers stayed throughout her childhood, and her eyes stayed a frosted blue. When I placed my palm on her forehead and felt the magic of our bond zip through us, a piece of my heart filled up a little more.

A cooing sound from her snapped me out of my memory, and I looked below us to see the vessel coming to a stop. There is commotion atop the ship, and with a large grinding sound, a space opens in the deck, and bodies are being moved out.

"Fly lower," I ordered her. As she slowly dives down, I strain my ears to listen.

"This is as far as we go, Dark One," a bald woman dressed in pure white furs said to Alwin. I can see all three of them are bound by chains of ice and kneel in front of her. "Remember our deal, and we should have no problems."

"To cowardice to come with us?" Alwin taunts her. "My place is here with my tribe. But—" she pauses, and another bald woman, with skin the color of ebony, dressed in ivory-plated armor, wielding a white arrow-tipped spear, steps forward. "This is Lavinia; she is a great warrior and will help you find your fire."

I can see Alwin eye her suspiciously but nod his head in agreement.

"Alright, girl, let's enter." I signal for Natiri to land, and as we move lower to the iced surface of the ship, a wave of calmness overcomes me. A sense of familiarity and knowing comes to mind when my eyes lock on the leader. For a moment, I know this woman or have met her once in my lifetime. But that is impossible.

"Stand down." Their leader orders, and I didn't notice that a swarm of guards pointed their sharpened weapons at us. I get down from Natiri and slowly go to where my companions kneel. "Who are you?"

The woman's honey-colored eyes widen with curiosity, almost as if she senses the same thing I do.

"My name is Niya, and I bargain for my friend's freedom," I say politely. She gives me a wayward smile before speaking.

"Niya is the name of a Warrior, but a warrior is not who I see." She states as if to insult me, but I pay no mind. I am proud of my Order and where I come from.

"That is because I am a Confessor. My Essence is used to bring justice to the realm and does not cause pain or death." However, it has happened too many times. I try not to think about my past as I stand firm. The woman approaches me, standing nearly a head taller and just as firmly.

"And what would a powerless Confessor have that I could want? You are useless in this realm." That did sting a bit, but I did not lower my chin no matter what,

"I would give you my services as a Tarot Master. I could offer a reading." A noble offer. She would be foolish not to take it. Readings do not come easy, and many masters seek payment. I, for one, do not.

She moves to circle me. She is scrutinizing me from head to foot. As she passes me, my eyes shift to Rose's. Where I expected to see fear, I saw nothing but endearment. It only confuses me when I realize she must care for me, but why? We barely know each other.

My gaze moves over to Davi. Where I expected to see fright, I only saw annoyance, as if he was bored. He seems to be daft for someone as wise as the legends state. I see fire alight in those dark eyes when I look upon Alwin. They are two burning coals that could melt through anything and anyone—a resemblance of his pain for losing her.

"I will offer you a deal, Confessor." the leader states as she steps back into my line of sight. "Once you have completed your mission with the Dark One, return to me and be my bride. Then I will let your friends go back to their normal lives." I try not to let the shock show with her offer, but it does ever so slightly.

"A Confessor can never marry; it is not our way," I respond with logic.

"Oh yes, something about you can never bed your mate, or else they will be overcome by your power and enslaved to you." She waves it off as if it is no big deal, but it truly is. "If you haven't realized it by now, Confessor, my powers work here, and yours do not. I will not be affected when I have you in my bed."

The thought of marrying has only ever crossed my mind once, and it was only for a split second. If I were to marry her, would I be betraying Serena? It would betray my Order and all Confessors stand for, but isn't loving Serena doing that anyways? By the Ancients, what should I do?

"I will give you until you return to give me my answer. Otherwise, the Dark One knows what will happen." I look past her towards him and only see anger in his eyes.

"Agreed. I shall have an answer for you once we return from our completed mission." When I think we can leave, she grips my right wrist, and I suddenly feel ice closing around it.

"Just to remind you of what you just agreed to. I can't have you running away after you save the dead girl. Or whatever." She leans in to whisper in my ear. "I wonder if the Dark One is the only one taken by this Serena?" She purrs. "So you know, I would never choose anyone other than you. That's why I need a bride." She places a gentle kiss on my cheek before letting me go.

I shudder before moving forward to help Rose to her feet as the chains binding them melt away.

"I will give you three days to get back to me after that," the leader purrs and winks at me. "You are all mine."

The air is silent as we move forward on borrowed horses. The atmosphere is tense with the most recent of events. Alwin filled me in on what the Amazon Leader offered him. Assassinate a man in another realm after saving Serena—a coward and brute's way of doing business. I understand Alwin's hesitations about killing someone he does not know is innocent or not, but for Serena and his love for her, nothing will stop him from saving her.

"You will become her bride," Alwin growls, breaking the silence. "What?" I asked him to ensure I heard him correctly. A persistent chilled wind blows, making it challenging to hear muttered words.

"You will marry the Amazon Leader if it means saving Serena's life." he repeats, adding an instance glare to get his point across.

"Forgive me, Alwin, but you do not get to decide who I wed and who I do not. That is my choice and mine alone." He jerks the reins of his horse, and I stop next to him.

"You are useless, Confessor. Your powers do not work, you cannot fight, and even your cards cannot defend you. I will not lose my mate because of your selfish deeds." He emphasizes the words my mate added to the fact that Serena is his destined mate. I was deemed so by the Ancients through a sightless magic bond. Only Serena has yet to recognize or consummate this bond. He is correct about one thing: I am not a fighter. I never have been, and I pray I never will need to be.

"You are hurting, so I forgive you for your harsh words," he interrupts me by spitting at the ground beneath my feet—a significant insult to me and my Order.

"Take your forgiveness and shove it up your,"

"Enough," Rose states. "Alwin, what is wrong with you? You know better than to treat a woman, especially a Confessor, with such disregard."

"That's alright, Rose darling. Alwin's words do not affect me. A man gets like this when his pride has been wounded by a woman who is better than him." Rose's lips tip up in a smile as pride overcame me. Before my eyes focus back on Alwin, I sense the air in my throat being cut off, a thick hand wrapped around my neck, and I am forcefully thrown forward. I feel my feet dangling in front of me as I desperately scratch at Alwin's arms, pleading for release. "I will not hesitate to kill you, Confessor. When it comes to Serena, nothing and no one else matters. Do you understand me?" He snarls, and all I can do is nod as water slips from my eyes, and he releases me. I hit the snow-covered ground with a thud. Coughing and gasping for air. "You better get in line, Confessor, or else you will be left behind."

As I wipe the tears from my eyes and refill my lungs with the frigid air that only makes them burn worse, something inside me snaps. A possessiveness takes over the need to protect—a cranial
  instinct to kill any others who threaten me and what is rightfully mine. We will see who Serena truly belongs to, Dark One. When it is me, I will gladly squeeze your heart until nothing is left.

# 13

# SERENA

"Alwin," I walk to the other side and see nothing but frost and snow for miles. I could've sworn he was just right here. I was standing in front of me.

A gust of cold wind sweeps through, the sensation akin to a thousand needles simultaneously pricking at me. Instinctively, I encase myself with my wings, resisting the frigid assault. Even as the biting chill subsides, I choose to keep my wings tightly wrapped around me. I continue to use them to keep me warm. Turning around, I see the door is gone, and I'm curious to know whether or not I made it out.

"Hello," I yell. The only response is my voice echoing in the far-off distance. "Is anybody out there?" Nothing but the calm wind answers my call. When I move forward, the breeze blows hard against my back, pushing me faster until I am no longer in control as I am trapped in a vortex of wind and snow being hurled towards the mountainside.

Just when I think, this is how I will die—becoming a fire pancake on the side of the mountains. I come to a halt. In the far-off distance, I can hear voices. Looking below my feet, I see tiny figures moving up the mountainside.

As I low, they become more apparent.

"If you do it again without warning, I will filet your skin from your bone." Alwin's voice thundered with his threat. He was talking to a human male walking just ahead of him. Behind him, I see a fairy with bright pink hair, and I know her, but I don't remember.

"Alwin," I shouted, but he appeared not to have heard me.

Moving lower, I stand a few feet in front of him. Directly in his line of sight. He stops for a moment; he cocks his head to the side. His blue-gray eyes examined.

"It's me, Serena. I'm back." I smile, and when I move to grab his hand, he steps right through me, leaving me wide-eyed and confused. "Ancients, I'm no longer in the realm of spirits, but I'm still a blessed spirit."

I calm myself down just a little bit. But then I feel a chill move through my body as the human steps through me.

I look at his face, expecting to see a human, but I see something worse. A gilded helm with a domed top and two antlers sticking out the side sits atop the face of The Devil. Not the ones depicted in other stories but the one that matches that of the Tarot Card. A master of deceit and one that I have fallen for many times.

They do not know they have a traitor amongst them. I must warn him somehow.

After the human passes by, the next is the fairy. I prepare for whatever feelings she will bring about, expecting the worst, but I feel safe. A flood of memories comes to mind of my days at Ermelon Castle. She was the maid who brought me food, cleaned my room, and changed my chamber pots. Ancients, how could I forget her? I look past her and come face to chest with a tall woman. When I lift my head to meet her eyes, she narrows them at me as if she could see me. But then she walks through me like the rest did, and I feel stronger.

There is something about that woman that tells me she is no human. Her honor and loyalty to her mission keep her focused and prevent her from straying the right path. However, a stint of doubt lingers at something she was also ordered to do. I don't think my friends are in danger from her, but perhaps whatever master she has wants to strike them down.

I decide to follow them and wonder where Niya is. I don't know why I expected her to be with them, but I assumed she would be. A screeching noise catches my attention, and I see a pure white Griffin lowering itself to the rocky surface just before Alwin.

Jumping down is a black-haired childhood friend of mine. I move closer to look at her better and hear what she says.

"We found the cave. It's just over the ridge. Natiri can take two at a time. It'll be faster that way." That's a beautiful name for her, Griffin. I move to pet the beast and pull back, remembering that my hand will go straight through her, but I am surprised when she turns her beak towards me.

I look deep into her dark eyes, and she nudges me. I'm surprised when I can feel her beak's smooth, icy surface.

"Ancients, you can see me." I smile and move further up, running my fingers through her soft feathers.

"Can you tell them I'm here?" I ask her, and she just cocks her head to the side in confusion.

"Are you ready for two?" I hear Niya say as she steps right through me. The feelings I get with her are love, remorse, and confusion.

I stand there puzzled as Niya and the tall woman get on Natiri's back. They take off with two flaps of her wings and soar to where Niya said the cave was. I move to follow them but stop when I remember the human is here.

"Once we get inside, certain things will require us to get the fire." he says to Alwin and Rose. "Whatever it takes," Alwin says, and my heart flutters. "Good. Keep that in mind going into it." His human face is sincere, but the devil is smiling with triumph. "You will burn my hand if you hurt him," I yell at the human. Knowing he can't hear me.

Natiri doesn't take long; they are all on the mountain in three more trips. I followed along with Rose and Niya. I was seeing what I thought might be confusing, my dear friend.

Niya's hands are wrapped around Rose's waist, making the pixie blush. I remember the night she and Odith shared. I wasn't there, but Odith boasted about it while pretending to be Niya, so I can only assume Rose still carries a torch for her.

"Are you okay?" Niya asks her mid-flight, and Rose turns her head ever so slightly, catching the corner of Niya's lips before she has time to pull away.

"Sorry." Rose stammers, but Niya smiles and cups the side of her face, pulling her in for a kiss.

"It's fine. If a kiss from me will ease your nerves about flying, I'm all for it." I should say I am pissed she kissed her, but seeing her smile makes me happy for her. I pray that she will find her happiness regardless of what the rule of her Order deems.

Rose turned her head back to the front, her cheeks heated, and a pure white smile stayed plastered on her face even after they landed.

The cave looks eerie from the sticks of ice forming at the mouth of the dark interior.

"Someone light a torch." Alwin orders, and I move over to him, wishing I could give him some of my fire. I interlace my phantom fingers with his and feel something spark between us like flames flicker over coals. He lifts his hands, and to our surprise, a small fireball is formed in his left hand.

"Serena?" he whispers, and I long to answer. The fireball moves up and down, and I try something else. "Fly around his head." Just as I commanded, the flames circled Alwin, widening his eyes. When the ball stops before him, he reaches out to touch it.

"Don't burn him," I say, and as if he was touching my cheek, the faintest caress comes across as his fingers touch the ball.

"Show me, Phoenix." And as if it knew that I wanted it to listen to him, it followed.

## ALWIN

"Alwin," Rose calls to me, but nothing exists around me except her. I know she is here. My vision tunnels as I follow the light through the winding hollowed-out hole.

"Alwin, stop." A hand grabs me and tries to stop me, but I shrug it off. The crunching of snow blends with the pounding rhythm in my ears. The air grows colder with each step, and the scent of sulfur permeates my nose, yet I pay it no mind. I persist, forging ahead through the darkness. The light comes to a sudden stop, and so do I. I look around and see nothing outside the slight glow that lights up a few feet before me.

"There is nothing but rock and snow," I say. Heavy breaths come from behind me, and I look to find the others have caught up to me.

"Are you crazy?" Rose asks.

"Why'd you run off like that, and how do you know where you are going?" Niya asks.

"Serena showed me," I tell them, and they all exchange glances. "I'm not crazy; this ball of flames is her. Or a part of her guiding me forward."

Niya steps past me to examine the flame, which grows brighter with her touch. She gasps in shock at the feel of it.

"It's her," I repeat.

"It truly is. Serena, where is the Phoenix flame? Can you show us?" The ball doesn't move; it grows a little brighter—a test of faith. A voice echoes in my head. "We all need to touch the flame," I state.

"What?" they collectively ask. "We will burn." Rose stammers.

"How do you know?" the Druid asks.

"Have faith," I state, and my eyes land on the quiet Rune Master.

"What about you?"

"I say you are crazy, but," he pauses, then steps forward, "at least if it burns us, we will have someone to blame."

"Together?" I ask them, and they all form a circle around it. One by one, we place a hand on the growing flame. Neither of us gets burned, but something sends sharp pains down my arm, and as I try to jerk back, my hand doesn't move. We all cry out as we double over in pain, and then, one by one, I watch as they pass out.

As darkness clouds my vision, I am close to oblivion. I catch the faintest outline of her: those beautiful wings and jeweled eyes glowing with pride.

"Alwin," I hear my name and feel soft hands on my face. "Wake up."

My eyes snap open and catch on Rose. "What happened?"

"We all touched the ball of fire, passed out, and are now in some distinct part of the cave." She offers me a hand to help me to my feet. I look around and see nothing except a large stone ring at the back of the wall. Two lit torches illuminate the room, casting shadows all along the walls.

"What is this place?" I ask as I approach Davi, who has his nose stuck in some book.

"This is the door to the outer realms." he eagerly answers.

"We don't need to go to a different realm. We need to find that fire." I growl.

"This is how we do it." he states before returning the book. I turn away from him and find the three females waiting for what to do next.

"Is there a way out of here?" I ask.

"No. While you were still out of it, I walked a few feet opposite that ring and hit a dead end." Niya states. "Can you make things work?" I ask Davi. "Of course, I can. What do you take me for, a baboon?" I don't show any hint that I find him humorous. "Do you see the twenty-six symbols carved into the stone?" I nod, not sure why he asks. "Those are the Runes. And I am the Master, meaning I can read them and open the door."

"Stop with the lesson and get on with it," I state. "Everyone line up next to me, and whatever you do, do not move until I say so," Davi states, and we all do as we are told. "I call upon the runes of the first Master. Open your door to us, grant us passage. Fehu Uruz Raido Ken." Davi repeats those last four words several times, and when I think to speak, the ground tremors, and the ring moves, knocking ice and snow onto the ground as it turns. The wind whirls the louder Davis's voice gets, and the ring circles faster and faster until everything stops, and the noise dies out.

A shimmering blue light fills the circle where the wall used to be.

"It worked," I speak.

"Of course, it did. Hurry now, it won't stay open long." Davi ushers me forward.

"Aren't you coming?" I ask him.

"No. Only one can move through this door. The rest of us will stay until you have found the fire." Davi answers. "What? Why?" Rose asks.

"Because it's what the Runes permit. Only one can enter." "How will he get back?" Rose asks.

"The Runes will open it once he has completed his mission. Otherwise, we will all be trapped." Davi answers. "No pressure," Niya states, and I pull my furs tighter as I approach the portal. "Hurry back. The sands of time are almost up."

"Watch out for Rose, will you?" She nodded when I asked. "I'm coming, Phoenix." I step through the blue light, finding my footing immediately on the other side. I am slightly confused as it appears to mirror the one I just came through. When I turn around, the portal is gone. "Great."

I look around and see nothing with the dim glow from the torches. Moving forward, I bump into each wall. "What do you want from me?" I yell. The only answer is my words echoing off the vacant walls.

"Alwin," I turn to my mother's voice. Standing at the center, glowing as bright as the sun, is the spirit form of my mother. "My dear sweet boy, do not fret."

"Mother, how are you here?" I ask while approaching her.

Reaching out, I try to touch her, but my hands go straight through. "I wish this were a reunion, but my dear, you have work to do." she states.

"You were right." She smiles at me. "I found my mate."

"And now you must save her with this." In her hands is that same-looking ball of flames from before. Only this time, there are tiny flickers of blue, red, and orange. "It was you?" I ask.

"Your mate is strong and very smart. I was able to come this far with her help." she replies.

"She's here?" I feel tears escaping.

"Yes. But you cannot see her like me. Just know her time runs short." She reaches up to brush the tears from my cheeks but goes through me just as before. "Oh, my darling, I wish this could last longer, but you need to save her and be wary of the agent who seeks to please."

She echoes the words from before. "Do you know who it is?"

Her smile fades before shaking her head in answer. "What do I need to do?"

"You must give up the thing you love most." Her words baffle me because that would mean Serena. Wouldn't it? "Not as simple as you think it is, my child. Think of the thing you love all your life."

"No," I tell her as the recollection hits me.

"I am no longer in the realm of the living. It's time you let me go so you can move on with her."

"Mother," I stammer, but she quiets me.

"You have grieved me once before and survived. You can survive this, too. My ultimate death will not be in vain." she speaks. "I love you, Son, but you must take the ember before it dies."

Reaching out, I place my hands on either side of the flames and let her go. The piece of my heart that belonged to her. "Goodbye, Mother."

As she fades into the ember in my hands, I feel something growing inside me. Vines of flames begin to wind around my arms and torso. I am sending a searing pain throughout my body that makes me fall to my knees. I don't feel the impact as my body is on fire.

"Alwin," Serena's voice echoes in my mind. I fall onto my back, the ball of flames gone as my body is encased in a combustion of blue and red.

"Phoenix," I mutter, and I feel my consciousness slipping away from too much pain. But then it stops, and I feel myself get up.

Looking down, I roll up my sleeves to check my skin, and thereupon, both forearms are an etched phoenix of gold, blue, and red. Running my hand over each, the touch is warm.

I look around me to see if I can see either of the only two women who have ever captured my heart, but there is nothing except the glowing blue of the rune door. I guess that means I have completed my task. Here we go.

Without further thought, I run straight into the portal and nearly knock into a body on the other side. "Shit, you're back!" Davi exclaims.

"Did you think I would fail?" I ask him.

"It has been a mere five seconds." I didn't realize as I was falling into him, but everyone was still in the same position I left them in as if no time had passed.

"Did you get it?" Niya asks. I think about what Mother said, and I nod. I won't reveal to them I gained an imprint, as I am unsure how to transfer it.

"I did," I say, eyeing and gauging their reactions. Davi's mouth twitches slightly, but not enough to make me think it is him. The others appear to be neutral, except Niya, who is overjoyed. That doesn't mean it is her because I know what she feels for Serena.

"Great, can we get back to Xora now?" Rose asks. "Davi," they all seem shocked at me saying his name for the first time, but nothing else matters to me except saving her, "can your Runes take us back?"

"Yes, they should be able to." he answers, rummaging through his book.

"Don't forget Dark One," the Amazon starts as she approaches me. Those two golden eyes narrowed on me. "We go there, then come straight back with The Confessor."

"When all is said and done, I don't care what happens to her. Just know that if you prevent me or bring any harm to my mate, your heart will be removed from your chest because once we get back to Ermelon, I will have access to my powers again, and you won't want to mess with me."

I turn my back on her and head over to Rose. She finally meets my eye.

"I'm sorry for the way I have been acting of late. I did not wish to push you away." I admire her. "I'm glad you found the fire, but I need to ask you something," Rose states, then glances toward Niya. "You saved your mate; now help me save mine."

"The Confessor?" I ask her, and heat rises in her cheeks. "When did you know?"

"The moment she landed in Ermelon, it zapped through me. I haven't told her yet because I wasn't sure she could feel for me or would accept it because of her Order and because I know she is in love with Serena." I see the concern in her eyes. Watching your mate love another must cause unbearable amounts of pain. "That is until she kissed me."

I raise my brow at her while smirking slightly. "Don't look at me like that. It was just a kiss."

"I am happy you have found your mate," I smile. "Really? Because I got the feeling you hated her."

"Not so much now that I know you are her mate. Tell her before it's too late. I never got the chance to tell Serena."

"Will you help me save her from the Amazon Leader?" she asks me, and without question, I nod.

"You have aided me in this quest, so I will aid you in yours, my friend," I tell her while stretching out a hand to seal the deal. She takes it, and magic sparks between us. She pulls me for a hug and mutters a soft thank you.

"The portal is open. We need to move now. There are merely minutes left." Davi yells, and as I break our hug, I take her small hand in mine, turn towards the portal, and race through it.

My feet impact the hard stone surface I am familiar with, the courtyard where we left Serena and Masker Mikao. The air is excellent, and the scent of spices wafts through the air around me. Rose and the others appear beside me, and I look around to see the fading iridescent image of The Empress watching over my Serena.

"Welcome home." Master Mikao greets us with a bow and ushers us forward. "You must be quick; her energy is fading."

"Thank you, Master." I bow to him while peering over her. She is beautiful and looks at peace. When I answer, I think about transferring the fire from me to her. As if the flames themselves seek her out.

Removing the clothes from my torso, I hear gasps from all around and look to find not just my forearms covered in tattoos but swirls of blue intertwined around my torso.

"Everyone stay back. The energy must remain pure between them." the Rieke Master states. I look at Niya and nod to her. She calls back The Empress, releasing it from its duty just as I pick Serena up, cradling her close to my chest like a babe to its Mother.

"This is all for you, Serena. Come back to me, and I promise never to fail you again." I kiss her on her lips and give her all my strength and power. As it pours into her, heat engulfs us, and my body weakens.

"That's enough, Alwin. You've given too much." Master Mikao's voice rings, but I won't stop. Not until I know she is back. If I die, so be it. My Phoenix will survive.

She kisses me back as her arms wrap around my neck, breaking our kiss.

"Alwin," I opened my eyes to see her jeweled ones looking at me with wonder.

"My mate." The light around us fades, and I slump over. I run my finger along the side of her face, soaking in her feel.

"I'm back?" she asked me.

"Yes, my love. You're safe now." I move to stand but feel my knees buckle slightly.

"You both need to be healed." Master Mikao states, approaching us.

"I'm fine; look over Serena," I state, not taking my eyes off her. "It was not a suggestion." We both get to our feet, and I don't let go of Serena's hand, don't take my eyes off her, afraid that this is a card trick, but as she reaches out and touches my chest, placing a palm over my heart, her warmth spreads through me.

"Look at your chest, Alwin." I look down to see what she is talking about and see it. A golden phoenix with a tendril of black swirling around it.

"The image of your union." Master Mikao states with a smile. "Serena has accepted you as her mate." The broadest smile forms on my face. I lean down and kiss her deeply. She grips the hair at the back of my head and pulls me closer to her.

# 14

# SERENA

I can hardly believe I am back in my mate's arms. That's right, I have a mate. Something I never thought would happen to me, and although I do not remember my time while asleep, I look around at the other faces in this courtyard, some new, some old, and smile.

My eyes instantly catch the familiar black eyes of my friend. "Niya," I break my hold on Alwin and run to embrace her. "Serena, I've missed you." she says while hugging me tightly. "You came here for me?" I look at Rose and the other two figures I do not know. One is a human, and the other is a very tall woman dressed in pure white armor. She intimidates me just a little. "All of you?"

"You should know I will always come for you," Niya states. "Alwin needed a Tarot Master to summon the portal."

"What about you?" I ask, stepping up to the fairy.

"I couldn't have my Master going to a foreign land without proper backup." she states in a teasing tone.

"I'm not your Master anymore, Rose. You can continue to call me by my name." Alwin states, stepping up next to me.

"And who are your new friends?" I ask, eyeing them.

"This is Puny," I elbow him, so he calls the man by his actual name, and Alwin laughs. "Davi, he is the Rune Master. Without him, I would've never made it back in time to save you."

I reach out my hand to Davi. "Thank you for your help. I look forward to getting to know you."

Davi takes my hand and nods in response.

"And you?" I ask the very tall, terrifying-looking woman.

"I am called Lavinia. Amazon Druid of Whitfrost and a loyal soldier to my Queen."

"Also known as an Ice Witch," Alwin states.

"Your Mate is safe, Dark One. We must return with The Confessor, and you must keep up your end of the deal you struck with her." Lavinia states, and I look at Alwin with questions.

"Not until I have healed them." Master Mikao states. "With all due respect, time is of the essence, and I may not

allow any more of it to be wasted," Lavinia argues.

"You will make it; it will only take an hour or two. Then, you will all need to pack your provisions for your journey back to Whitfrost. This time should be better since you have firepower with you." Master states with a wink towards me.

"And my mate and I have some catching up to do," Alwin states, nipping my ear and sending a flutter of arousal through me.

"We will all meet back here when the sun rises again," I state, and they move about.

"Serena, may I have a moment of your time?" Niya asks.

"I'll be right there," I tell Alwin, and he reluctantly follows the Master inside.

"Come to Alwin's chambers when you are through." Master Mikao states, and I nod.

When it is just us, I look at her and no longer see the childhood friend who pecked me in a broom closet before my world turned sideways.

"You seem different," I told her.

"A lot has changed since we last spoke." she speaks.

"Indeed, it has," I speak. I'm not sure what else to respond with. "I would like first to say that I am happy you have found your mate. I knew you would always be happy whether you didn't know it." I should slap her for what she just said, but as her smile fades to confusion, my face says enough.

"That is why you wanted to speak to me? To tell me you're happy I am with someone else?" I ask her incredulously.

"Aren't you? You accepted the bond." she states.

"I was in love with you, Niya. Ancients, for so many years, I only saw you. I only wanted you, but I don't remember you reciprocating those feelings. Because of your Order or because if anyone found out that we were together, it would mean our heads. But do you know what?" I pause for only a moment. "I would've risked death just to be with you." When she doesn't speak, I continue to add to her pain. To make her understand.

"You know what that sad part is? I saved myself for you, and when I thought you had come to me, we shared a night of epic passion. I thought, this is perfect. This is what I have waited for. She loves me back. But a manipulative, lying creature used her cards to imitate you. And do you want to know who that person was?"

She doesn't move.

"The bitch that killed me. So, forgive me if I don't seem happy after being alive for five minutes." I finished.

"Serena, I'm sorry I didn't know."

"Don't lie to me. You knew, that's why you kissed me in a broom closet. You were just too afraid to act on it. But now that I have Alwin, I don't need you." Without another word, I turn on my heel, wipe the growing tears, and head inside.

Once the doors close behind me, I run straight towards Alwin's chambers, not caring who sees me. As I burst through the doors, he lies on his bed with Master Mikao's hands on his temple. A soft glow comes from where his fingers are connected. They do not break their concentration, and I calm myself as I gently close the doors.

"Come lay next to your mate." the Rieke Master orders as I make my way over to the silk-covered bed. It dips slightly as I settle next to Alwin, my wings spread out behind me but shrinking just enough not to touch the others. "Grab his hand as the Essence will pass from me to him and him to you. It would be best if you cleared your mind completely. There will be no negative energy permitted here."

I do not speak, do as I am asked, and interlace my fingers with his. Taking a deep breath, I release it, ease my mind of all that has bothered me, and focus on the feeling of my mate's hand in mine.

A wave of calmness washes over me, and I drift into the abyss of peace and serenity.

When I wake up, I find myself in brawny arms with a wall of muscle pressing into me.

"Are you well?" Alwin asks, somehow knowing I have awoken. I turn to look at him and run a finger along his jawline.

"Very." He leans in, kisses me softly, then moves to my neck, sending a surge of heat through me. I run my fingers down his back and urge him on top of me, gripping his loose hair and pulling his lips to mine.

"Are you sure?" he asks me, looking deep into my eyes. "Yes." He is soft as his fingers trail down my bodice, unlacing each string of my gown until it is loose enough for him to pull it off me. As it lowers, so does his mouth until his face is between my legs.

"You are not going to cum until I tell you to, understand me?" he asks in a profound, primal way. I nod, and he runs his tongue through my soaking folds, making my back ache with the moan that leaves my lips.

He licks again and places one hand over my navel to keep me in place as he sucks and nips most perfectly. His other hand moves to my leg, raising one above his shoulder and stretching me further.

"Alwin," I moan, and he pushes two fingers in while he relentlessly sucks on my clit. I feel the pressure building in my core, moving me closer and closer to my release.

"Not yet, Phoenix." he orders, and I can't hold on. Just when it pushes over, he stops.

"Please," I beg him, and he smirks at me. My juices are coating his lips, and as soon as he runs a tongue over them, I lose control. I was breathlessly moaning his name as I climaxed.

I watch as he removes his trousers, his hard cock making me gulp with anticipation. He hovers over me, kissing me deeply before coating his tip with my cum.

"Are you ready to consummate our union, my love?" he asks me, and I place my hand over our emblem, wondering if I will get one, too.

"Love me as I am, or not at all," I say, and he pushes into me. He is giving me time to adjust as it's slow and passionate. His rhythm increases as I kiss him deeper and feel my heart expand, filling with his love for me. My wings grow brighter, and his shadows explode from his body.

My fire and his shadows join in perfect unison as he continues to pump inside me.

"My mate," he says.

"My mate," I repeat back, and as my climax builds, he pumps faster as I clench down; a blast of Shadow Fire fills the room as he fills me with his seed.

Specks of flame and shadow dance around the room, reminding me of lightning bugs on a cool summer's eve.

"We are one," Alwin states while touching my heart. I looked down and saw that I now had the same mark as his.

I am awoken with Alwin's head between my legs, burying his face in my sex as he brings me to another blissful climax. I return with his cock deep down my throat; his hot seed is filling me.

While in the bathing chamber, we clean up and almost don't make it to the bed again before he has me up against the wall, fucking me so hard the walls shake.

"We should get dressed," I tell him as I clean myself up again. "I have you all to myself, and now I never want to let go." he says with his arms wrapped around my waist.

"As much as I would love to stay here forever, we have an evil tyrant to deal with. You know we're not the only ones she is persecuting." I told him.

"I suppose you are correct about that. Five more minutes." he asks.

"We have a lifetime to spend together." "That's still not enough time." He pouts.

"Tell me about this deal with the Amazon Queen? Who are they?" I ask, breaking out of his hold to grab my clothes.

My wings have developed a mind of their own for Alwin. They change their size to make room for him and grow bigger once they know he isn't near me.

I pull on black pants, a blue tunic, and black boots. My hair is pulled high atop my head in a long ponytail. Once I am dressed, I see Alwin nearly wrapped as well. His long black hair was tied in a bun at the back of his head.

"Amazon Druids are an all-female race who despise males. They have many abilities, and there are many tribes of them. We just so stumbled upon the ones who wield the Essence of Frost."

"Meaning?" I ask him.

"They control anything liquid or made from it, including ice and snow. They have manipulated it into whatever they want. Just as they can freeze and unfreeze any liquid to include the blood in our bodies."

"Any weaknesses?" I ask him.

"I would like to assume fire. It is good that you will be with us because I am powerless against them. We all are in that realm. You, however, might be the exception." he states while walking over to me.

"How so?" I ask him, placing my palms on his shoulders. "Because you are the first true Phoenix in two centuries. Your

power is unmatched." His endearment tells me he believes that. "We do not know my Essence is without issue until I have used

it properly."

"You are still a Phoenix. My Phoenix and the world will kneel at your feet when you order it to." he speaks.

"I don't want to rule anyone, Alwin. I want peace of all kinds. No laws should be against who you can be with no matter what species they are."

"I want that, too." He places his forehead on mine, stealing another moment before a knock sounds.

"Enter." In comes Master Mikao. "Good morning, Master." "I think you should both come see this." I look concerned to Alwin before we follow the Rieke Master out the doors.

## NIYA

I stand there stunned at how Serena's words process through me, I feel myself reach into my pocket, gripping my deck before pulling them out—their power hums to life at being back in Xora.

I shuffle them a few times before pulling the top card and staring at the depicted winged angel blowing her trumpet down at the three naked men. Judgment? Are my cards trying to tell me to recognize my truth?

"Pull another one," a soft voice states from before me. I look up and find Rose standing in front of me. She has changed out of her furs and is in a plain green dress that cuts off at the shoulders and knees.

"Do you know the cards?" I ask her.

"Not really, but from the look of doubt on your face, I'd say you should pull another one if you are not sure about that one." Her suggestion intrigues me. I smile as I look down and see the robed picture of a man with a staff, and my doubt fades.

"What does that one mean?" she asks.

"The Hermit can mean many things, just as all the cards can, but I think this one tells me to seek my true path," I tell her, and she steps closer. I remember the kiss I gave her when we were flying on Natiri. It differed from when I kissed Serena.

"What about the first one?" she asked, and this time, I took a step forward, smiling at her.

"The Judgment card means new awareness," I answered her, and we are now toe to toe. Her eyes looked directly into mine.

"What do they mean together?" she asks me, and I place my cards back into my coat pocket before answering her.

"They mean to tell me to realize my truth and stop running from it. Own up to what I feel and who I truly am."

"And who is that?" she asks, her eyes searching.

"I feel something towards you," I admit, and she sucks in sharply. "

"What about Serena?"

"She has found her true mate, and now I must find mine," I admit.

"And you think it is me?" Rose asks.

"I honestly do not know, but if you will have me, I would like to try and figure out what this spark between us means." I wonder if I have overstepped when she doesn't move or speak. "Unless I am mistaken and you-"

Her lips crash against mine in a claiming kiss as her arms wrap around my waist, crushing me against her. I grip the back of her hair, deepening our kiss as I pierce my tongue between her lips and savor the sweet flavor of her.

She breaks our kiss and pulls me towards the inside of the fortress, and we take off down the corridor. As soon as her chamber doors close, she has me pinned to the wall and kisses me hard like this is something she has been deprived of for her entire life.

I scratch my nails down her back, wanting to feel her skin pressed to mine. She pulls the furs from me and tears my gown from my body with incredible strength.

Her mouth lands on my breasts while one hand palms the other. I feel her free hand trailing down my side until she moves it to my throbbing sex.

"Are you sure?" she asks me, and I respond by running my hand up her bare thigh, finding her soaking folds.

"Yes." I plunge two fingers in as she does, sending me into overdrive. Don't lose control. Ancients don't lose control. I feel my power pushing at my skin; I jerk back.

"What's wrong?" She looks hurt and confused.

"I almost lost control," I confess. "If I lose control, your soul will be mine forever. Your free will gone."

She moves fast with her pixie speed and has me pinned beneath her on her bed.

"Then so be it." she snarls before kissing me again. She breaks our kiss to obliterate her dress, and I palm her peeked nipples.

She places her face between my legs and licks my soaking folds and my back arches.

"Are you ready?" she asks me, and I am confused. "Hold on."

I am about to say something when her tongue and fingers pick up speed, sending my nerves into overdrive. She's using her pixie speed. My powers surge through me as I climax with her tongue and fingers still moving at lightning speed, and I don't catch my breath as another one pulses through me, and her soul connects with mine.

"Rose," I moan, and she moves up to me, kissing me and allowing me to taste myself on her tongue.

I flip us over, slowly move down, and return the favor. When I kiss her and don't want to let go, I think for a moment that she could be my mate. How could she not after what we did?

"Rose, are you okay?" I ask her to see if she is still in control. "More than okay." she answers with a smile.

"Do you still feel your free will?" I ask her. "Yes, I don't think your Essence affected me." "But I felt your soul."

"And I felt yours." she says as she runs a soothing hand down my back.

"How is that possible?" She stops her fingers and props her head on her elbow; I do the same.

"It's what happens when you find your mate." she admits, and I am taken aback for a moment.

"What?" She flops down on her stomach and hides her face, seeming humiliated. "How long have you known?"

She answers, but it's muffled from her face in the pillow. "Speak up." She lifts her head.

"Since I first saw you here in Ermelon," she confesses. "But you don't have to accept it. It's your choice just as it is mine." I don't know what to say; I barely know her.

"Niya, we don't know each other that well, but I would like to. Don't say no and don't say yes, but allow me the chance to prove to you that I can be worthy of your love. Worthy enough to be your mate."

I still didn't know what to say, so I kissed her again.

"As long as you extend the courtesy to me," I whisper, pressing my forehead to hers.

"Deal."

When we awaken the following day, I take control and tie Rose's wrists to the bedpost while I bring her to climax three times before she burns through the silk fabric using her speed. Of course, she has me pinned to the wall of the shower, using that wicked tongue of hers to bring me to bliss.

As we dress, I find myself in need of a white gown. Rose reapers my torn one quickly after she dresses in a new green one. We exit her room hand in hand with smiles on our faces.

"Long night?" Davi appears out of nowhere dressed in a brown tunic and black breeches. Seeing him without a wool cloak to hide his rune tattoo is weird.

"Not really. We slept rather well." I tell him, and his eyes dart to our locked hands.

"Together?" he asked, almost upset.

"That's intrusive," Rose states, squeezing my hand. I look hard into Davi's eyes, and something inside me breaks. I let go of Rose and reached out to touch his arm. Flashes of him and me from inside Queen Lilac's palace flood my mind.

"I know you," I state, pushing my power into him, but it's blocked. More memories break through the wall I didn't know was there in my mind. Our bodies are joined at the sex. His mouth is on mine, and I am kissing him back.

With the force of a heavy windstorm, I am knocked back, taking out Rose with me.

"Ancients," I gasp as it all becomes more apparent. We get back to our feet, and Davi stands there. Emotionless and unmoved. "I remember everything."

"You know him?" Rose asks, pointing at Davi.

"Take the Confessor, kill the pixie," Davi states, and Lavinia appears out of nowhere.

"No," I put myself in front of Rose just as a shard of ice was thrown at her.

# 15

# ROSE

"No," I yell as Niya falls into my arms, her beautiful body cast in ice. "Niya, please no."

"I wish we had more time." she says as she reaches up to brush her knuckles across my cheek. "I'm sorry."

"Please, not my mate. You're my mate, I don't need more time. I say yes. It will always be yes." As her eyes close and the last of her body becomes encased in ice, a scream of fury rips through my throat, and I find my targets. "You took her from me."

"She was never yours; Niya will now and forever be my Queen's bride," Lavinia states while approaching us. "Give up now, pixie; you have lost."

"Never." I throw my pixie dust at her, but it has no effect as it hits an invisible shield. When I reach my feet, I stand before Niya, blocking the two traitors and preparing to fight.

"Don't be a fool, Rose. There is no need for you to die." Davi comments.

"You knew she would jump in front of me. But how?" I ask.

"Niya has a thing for the female species. I followed you after your little kissing session in the courtyard last night." I watch as he approaches her, kneeling to touch her. "She is quite beautiful."

"Don't you touch her," I growl and move to kick him, but I am frozen in place. My body is frozen in place.

"Tricky little witches these Amazons are. They can control any liquid, including what flows inside our bodies." He gets to his feet and signals for Lavinia to take Niya. "No matter. What's done is done."

Davi approaches me, slips something into my dress pocket, leans in, and whispers. "Read it after we have left."

Then, his fists connect with my jaw, making me fade into darkness.

"Rose, Rose, wake up." I hear Alwin's voice calling my name, and when I open my eyes, I look up at him and Serena.

"What happened?" Alwin asks as he helps me up. "They took her," I say, bringing my knees to my chest. "Who?" he asks.

"Niya. Davi and Lavinia took her." I wipe the tears as they flow. Then I remember what he said just before I passed out. Reaching into my pocket, I pull out the parchment.

"What's that?" Serena asks.

"A note from Davi; he says if we want Niya back, then the Dark One and Phoenix must turn themselves over to Queen Lilac." I looked up at them both, and then something Niya said before that ice pierced through her. "Niya new Davi. She didn't say how, but when she touched his arm, it was like forgotten memories returned to her."

"It is possible that Davi used a potion to do that." Master Mikao started from somewhere behind them. Alwin offers me a hand, and I get to my feet.

"We need to go after her," I tell Alwin. "We will." he promises.

"Davi seems to be more than just a Master of Runes." Master Mikao states. "Be wary of his need to please. His energy is clouded with the demons that haunt him. But with proper healing, he can be saved."

"With all due respect, Master, I will not save the man who took my mate from me. He deserves nothing less than death." I state, and Serena's head snaps to me. "You heard me correctly. Niya is my mate, and I will never stop fighting to save her."

"Then it is settled. We will journey to Whitfrost, save Niya, and kill anyone in our way." Alwin states. "But first, we need to take a trip to another realm. We might find some allies there we didn't have before."

"Why would we waste any more time on other people when my mate is being taken from me?" I ask him.

"Because nothing and no magic can impede a matting bond. If Niya accepts you as her mate, then no marriage will prevent that from being so." Alwin states, and I hear his words and agree.

"So be it. But I suggest we call in Braxor, so we have dragon fire to help burn that tundra down."

"You have me." Serena states. "I know we are not close, and whatever you may think of me, I still love and care for Niya. She is my best friend and will be for the rest of my life." I won't argue with that; I nod in understanding.

"I will call Braxor, and we will be on our way. Thank you, Master, for everything." Alwin states to the Rieke Master.

"I will always be here until the next Master is ready to take my place." Master Mikao responds while bowing his head.

## DAVI
### THE DAY THEY MEET THE AMAZON'S

"What is the Dark One doing here?" the Amazon Leader asks, pushing her Essence on me.

"They search for the Phoenix fire," I admit unwillingly. Damn, the one Essence I am not immune to.

"Interesting. And why is that?" she asks.

"To save some girl back in their realm," I told her. "But they won't without me."

"Do you know why I hate the male species?" she asks, and I refuse to answer. "Because you are weak. I barely push out my Essence; you squeal like newborn swine." She straddles me, running her tongue along my cheek, making bile rise in my throat.

"I should kill you, but I don't think I will. Not yet." "Why?" Stupid. Why question her? She laughs.

"Because I have a use for you. I will make a tiny deal with the Dark One, and I need you to see that he does not back out."

"How?" I asked. She pinches my lips close.

"After his mate is saved, I need him to handle a pest problem in an outer realm. You will do whatever you need to persuade him."

"What do I get out of this?" I ask after she lets my mouth go. "You have no choice in this, so why ask when you have nothing

to offer me except the flesh from your puny little bones."

"I can offer you a bride. The most beautiful woman you will ever lay your eyes on." Her brow raises with the inquiry. "She is flying upon a Griffin above us, no doubt. Her name is Niya, and she is of the Confessor Order. I will ensure she is married to you, and then you will let me live."

"You better not be trying to lie to me, Rune Master. But, if this Niya truly exists, how will I know?"

"Take us up on deck, stop the vessel, and she will reveal herself. It's who she is. She'll try to do the honorable thing and bargain with you." I can tell she is interested by the way she cocks her head sideways.

"Deal. You may live in this, and Niya becomes my bride. Shall we seal it with a kiss?" I don't get the chance to answer when her lips land on mine, and magic zaps between us.

## Present Day

I pull my furs tighter around me as the wind picks up. Lavinia still has Niya in her arms, and a part of me feels ashamed of what I have done. I shouldn't, though, because Niya made her choice long ago, and it would never be me.

Her once pale skin is now the color of blue, and I grimace at the site of that shard still sticking from her chest.

"Can we take it out now?" I ask her.

"Not unless you wish her to die," Lavinia responds, and we continue to wait. Watching for the large vessel of ice to peek above the horizon.

"I didn't think you would go through with it." Lavinia remarks. "I knew you and the Confessor had some history, and she remembers it by the looks of what she felt when she touched you. Tell me, did you do it because she rejected you, although you have your wife locked up in the palace back in Xora?"

"No. I did this to have my daughter and wife returned to me. Alwin and Serena will come for her, and I will take them prisoner once they do; their powers do not work in this realm, but mine do." She lets out a scoff.

"If you think my Queen will grant you sanctuary, you are mistaken. Males are only good and one thing only." She narrows her eyes at me. "For eating."

I gulped and then looked over just as the top post of the ice vessel appeared. With a stop, an ice plank is lowered, and we make our way up.

We are directed below deck to their Queen's chamber, which I prefer because it is warmer than doing business atop the deck. I am seated in a wing-back chair; they do not bind me to it like last time.

Lavinia carries Niya to a raised platform that was undoubtedly placed when she sent word of our arrival. Her black hair shines in the dim light from the glowing candles on a bed of polar bear furs.

"You have done well." the Queen states. "You may go." "Excuse me?" I say, getting to my feet.

"You have kept your end of our deal, and now I am keeping mine. You may leave with your life." she states and then pulls the ice shard out of Niya's chest without effort.

I watch in awe as the blue fades from her skin and the color returns. The wound healed completely.

"Leave now or die. Your choice." she warns. "Tell her I'm sorry."

"A little late for that." the Queen states. "Then tell me your name." She ponders it.

"I give you my name, and I give you power. I will say this once more: get out or die." Realizing I would not win this fight, I reluctantly left the deck and regretted betraying Niya.

## *IN A TAVERN IN GUARIN VILLAGE TWO WEEKS LATER*

"Hard day?" A husky voice asks from a stool a few feet from mine. I've been staring into my ale for nearly an hour. Thinking of all the foolish things I have done this year. "I bet I can make you feel better."

"Not interested," I state without looking at her.

"That's too bad; I've been told I'm a real treat in the sack." A hand grips my crotch, and I flinch at the feeling. Maybe just for tonight, I allow myself to get lost in the cunt of a whore.

Somehow, in the minutes between her offer, I have her pinned beneath me in her private quarters. Our clothes scattered on the floor, a sash tied around her wrists and ankles, and my cock buried deep inside her soaking pussy.

"You feel so good, Niya. Just as I remember."

"The name's Lidia," I clamp my mouth around the whore to shut her up.

"No, your name is Niya, and you're mine." I pump in and out, not caring if I am hurting her, but it's not enough. I pull out and loosen the bindings.

"On your knees," I tell her, and just like a whore, she does as she is told and takes me into her mouth. I don't look at her but fists her hair and force my cock in and out at a punishing speed.

When my balls draw up, I keep my tip at the back of her throat and spill my hot seed down it.

I pull out and get dressed, slamming the door and no doubt pissing her off. But I don't care. I got my distraction, but it wasn't enough. It wasn't her. And she is all I thought about, all I think about. Since the Dark One and Serena have yet to come for her, I realize that they never will.

It will be up to me to get her back. As I reach the bathing chambers below, my firm hand grips me by the back of the neck and slams me onto a tablet, opening abandoned glasses of ale to the floor.

"Hello, Puny."

# 16

# DAVI

I remember the first time I learned how to restore blank tiles. It's one of the first lessons each Rune Master must teach pupils. If there is the need to use specific combinations or to siphon off magic from them for a spell, I have not performed this spell since taking on this title and position in the universe.

There's something that these last few month's events have made me realize but never wanted to voice. Alwin and Serena will not need to know, but I feel Master Mikao knows what the future of these runs will be once I'm finished restoring them.

I've added each ingredient necessary: dragon's bone, blank tiles, blood from the master, and recited the incantation. There's not much left to do, but let the magic take its part.

"Davi," Serena's voice comes from behind me. I glance over my shoulder to acknowledge her and then return to prepping some more ingredients for other spells I've learned from the Grimoire. "How are you?"

Serena's friendly approach to me is like ice compared to Alwin's hot rage. I know I deserved their disdain because of what I did to Niya, but I hope my willingness to do so will earn me some forgiveness.

"Busy."

"How's the spell coming along?" she asks, her long fingers gripping an empty glass vile to examine it.

"Should be ready by tonight." My responses are short, but I don't wish to converse with her while slowly coming to terms with my revelation last night.

"What's wrong? Have I angered you?"

I sigh and pause my work before giving her my attention. "When you found out who you truly were, did it frighten you?" She raised a brow, not understanding. "When Alwin told you that you were the Phoenix and his one true mate, did you want to run away? Or did you accept what the fates had decided for you?"

She ponders it before answering, "At first, I couldn't believe it. I didn't want to, but I feared what it meant. You have to know that growing up in a small village as the only half-blood wasn't easy. I was ridiculed and judged just for being born. Plus, being that I had no essence and no skills at the time, I was seen as useless. Even when Niya's family took me in, there wasn't much I did except for chores. She was always the gifted one. Mastered her powers and cards at a young age."

I nodded.

"But after all that fear, I realized something when I was at Ermelon Castle."

"What's that?"

She smiled. "Fear can be used as motivation to do something great. That's what I did with mine. Took a hold of it and accepted my truth without allowing it to control me."

"I see." Of course, she was able to do that. "Is there anything that you can't do, Phoenix?"

"Master a deck of tarot cards or runes." We both chuckled. "Were you afraid when you discovered you would be the next Master of Runes?"

"Never really thought about it. I was focused on getting revenge when I returned to reality—after being in the Realm of Masters, time in Ulorea had passed significantly. My entire family was gone, and so was everyone I grew up with. Queen Lilac's father had taken possession of the land, and I was lonely."

"What did you use your new skills for? I mean, when you're not portal-ling from realm to realm, what does a Rune Master do?" she asks.

"Generally speaking, there is a lot I can and can't do. I have no power without the runes. Each is unique, and if I perform a reading, much like tarot cards, there is always one definitive answer. One of the things I can do is enhance another's essence. But that is not one many know about unless they are a scholar of the skill."

"You mean you can enhance my fire?" I nod. "Yes, but I wouldn't."

"Why?"

"Because you're already as powerful as you need to be. If we gave you even just the smallest boost, we wouldn't know the consequences." Serena looked around the room as if to find some comfort in my answer. "You have to understand something: every time the essence is siphoned from one of these tiles, they take something in return."

"What's that?"

"Depending on your use, it can take a piece of you. Your soul, blood, a part of your mind. That's why you have to be careful when dealing with them."

"But what about all the times you've portalled us? What has that cost you? And why?"

"Hasn't your mate already taught you? All magic comes with a price. The fates must get their payment in some form—the more power, the bigger the price. Portalling is usually just some blood, but that's after mastering and earning the trust of the tiles. Before becoming a master, it required flesh and bone."

She gasped in shock. "Yours?" Then her eyes went over me as if to search for missing body parts.

I couldn't stop the laughter from escaping me. "No, animals such as rabbits and mice are sufficient enough when first starting."

"I see. What does this spell of restoration require you to pay?" "Just some blood. Each tile is infused with the master's blood." I reach to my side and untie my pouch of runes, dumping them into my hands. "Every single one of these is connected to me. They will connect with the next chosen one when my time ends."

"When will that be?" she inquires, and I ponder telling her the truth. They've already sent me a vision of who it will be, but voicing it makes it seem too real. She must've read something on my face because her following statement had me putting my runes back up. "You already know, don't you? Davi, what will happen to you? When you finish training the next master?"

"That is something I can't share with you, Serena. I wish I could, but there are just some things you don't need to know."

"Davi, please, I only wish to help. To know you. I think we could be friends."

"No, Serena, we can't." I turn my back to her, my shoulders sagging because knowing what I must do when I return to Whit-frost will hinder any potential alliance I could've had with her. "Please leave me. I will meet you tonight in the throne hall when the tiles are ready. By tomorrow, I hope to have rescued Niya and Rose."

* * *

The throne hall was silent as I stepped into the center. My tiles were fresh in hand while Serena and Alwin were seated at the front on their new thrones. Alistair and Master Mikao were standing at either side of the new queen and king, everyone already bidding me well wishes on my solo journey.

"Davi," Serena walks over to me, something clasped in her hand. "When I was a girl, before the Gnaxtor armies took my mother, she made me wear a trinket around my neck. Growing up, I didn't know the significance of it until Odith revealed it to me right before I died." She reaches for my closed fist and puts something small inside of it. When she lets go, I look at it. "This is my token for you, Rune Master. A phoenix kissed to protect you when you come face to face with the Queen. Her powers and any others that may threaten you will be rendered useless."

The small silver phoenix is looped into a leather bracelet, which I slip on my right wrist and hide under my sleeve. "You'll need this. I don't know how long the illusion will last, considering this is the only time I could make the card work. But if you need us, don't hesitate. The phoenix kiss is directly linked to me. Just whisper into it, and I should be able to hear you. Master Mikao says the power of my phoenix can be felt across realms, no matter how far apart they are."

"Thank you, Serena."

"Bring them back to us, Davi, and no matter what happens, you come back with them." I nodded, which was why I didn't answer her this morning. When I go to Whitfrost, I won't be returning because if my apprentice accepts her destiny, training her will become my number one priority, and I can't do that in Vwriynn.

I hold the three tiles in my hand, take one last glance at the room, and recite them: Raido, Neid, and *Isa*.

*\*\*\**

The icy breeze hits me first as I approach the other side. I know this realm like the back of my hand, and the runes have placed me on the outskirts closest to the iced-over lake. In the far distance, I see the Amazon's ship anchored at the edge. With the decapitated head of Alistair secured to one side and the Grimoire in my other, I march on. They'll know that I've returned. She'll sense the essence of the book.

After fifteen minutes of fighting the winds, I'm greeted by three large Amazon Druids adorned in their winter clothing and spears. Leticia is the one I recognize from my time working with her on betraying Niya.

"I have what the Queen asked for. The book and the head of her enemy. Bring me the pixie and confessor; let's make a trade." I say it in the most commanding voice I can muster.

"Show me his head," Leticia demands.

*Please still be ahead.*

When I look inside the pouch, bile rises in my throat at how real the lifeless head looks. The skin is gray, the eyes dull, and the ring of dried blood around the severed part seems as natural as my neck. I tuck the Grimoire into my tunic, then reach into the sack with both hands. When it's out, I use one hand to grip his hair and hold it in the air.

"As requested, the head of Alistair." The druids don't move a muscle until I toss it into the snow at their feet. "Examine it yourself if you don't believe me."

Leticia steps forward, lifts the head, and looks it over.

"The Queen will decide if it's authentic enough to release the fairy. But I highly doubt the Confessor will be with her." she states.

"But what about the agreement?" I can't take Rose without Niya; that pixie wouldn't allow it.

"It wasn't my deal to squander. I'm merely a messenger and a soldier. Wait here while she makes her decision. My sisters will keep you company." Then she was gone.

The snow intensified at an alarming pace. Despite being clad in a wool cloak and winter attire, nothing could shield me from the relentless assault of icy needles piercing my skin. I pulled the scarf over my face and re-tucked my ears in the thick cloth I wore. It wasn't enough to stop my teeth chattering and shaking within my bones.

"Can I build a fire?" I asked, although there was no wood or flint for one.

Neither of them moved or responded.

The wind picked up a brutal force; I felt my toes digging into the soles of my boots as I held my hands up to protect my face. Nothing helped, and I started to get desperate. I gripped the phoenix kiss tightly in my gloved hand, wishing it would warm me.

Leticia returns mere seconds later with only one person in hand. "The Queen has been satisfied by the deliverance of Alistair's
death. However, if you wish to take the Confessor, there will need negotiations other than a magical book."

I look at Rose, who appears to be struggling to break her captor's hold. Her skin is paler than when I last saw her, and she has dark circles under her eyes, telling me her time as a prisoner has not been easy.

My bag hums at my side, the tiles sending vibrations through me, begging me to take her from them, and I know why. I swallow hard, looking at the sickly pix, and offer a hand.

"Whatever the Amazon Queen wants, I will give her in exchange for Niya's freedom." Rose's eyes locked onto mine; the fierce nature of them that ignited her hate for me was all but non- existent.

Leticia throws Rose into me; I must catch her before her small form touches the snow.

"The fairy knows what has to be done. Give us the Grimoire,
and you'll be free to leave with that one." Leticia demands. I lift Rose into my arms, feeling her strength manifest in the tight grip around

my neck. Our eyes meet, and she gazes back at me with a pleading expression.

Leaning down, I whisper in her ear as the vibration of magic from my runes grows stronger. At this point, I have no control over what will happen. They've made their choice, and now I must honor it. "Everything will be okay, Rose. We will save Niya, no matter what."

"Give me the Grimoire, Rune Master!" Leticia and the others form a defensive position, but I'm not afraid because we will be protected even if they decide to attack.

"Close your eyes, Rose." Before obeying, she gave me one last look, and I locked eyes with Leticia.

"Fuck you and your Queen, too." Then we were gone.

A portal unlike I've ever seen develops around us in a whirlwind of red and gold. My grip on Rose doesn't falter as I let the Runes take us where we need to go. My stomach tightens and loosens with each spin of the earth, and I finally relax when my boots land on soft grass.

I look at Rose, who has passed out, and readjust her in my arms.

She's practically skin and bones, and it angers me at the thought of them starving her.

It almost seems familiar when I glance at the surrounding realm before us. There are hills of green for miles around and a bright sun. A cool breeze keeps the temperature mild but not humid. I lay Rose down in the field of dandelions at our feet and walk out over the small hill before us to get a better look.

At the top, as far as I can see, there is a small village at the center of a valley, and I make it my next destination. After picking the pixie back up, I climb downhill and pray that this place is friendlier than the last. Much like the dwarf community of Whitfrost, I'd give anything for a kind race.

I'm drenched in sweat from my winter clothes when I finally reach the bottom. But making it to the gate was my first goal. After setting

Rose down, I knocked a few times until someone answered.

Their blue eyes looked at me with curiosity. "May I help you?" "My friend is sick, and we need a place for food and shelter. I only wish to seek sanctuary until she is healed."

The greeter looks at Rose, then the latches open to reveal who they are. A male fairy with golden wings flutters over to her. He's dressed in all green leaves covering his delicate parts but nothing more.

"What happened to her?" he asks.

"She was a prisoner of the Amazon Queen in Whitfrost. I've just saved her."

He lifts her into his arms and gestures for me to follow.

"If you don't mind me asking, what realm is this?" I follow him down a grass path; all the buildings are made of tree logs and leaves. There doesn't appear to be any advanced use of metal or other materials like in the other realms I've been to.

"This is Hollow Tree within the realm of Ulorea." I stop at the mention of my home.

"Ulorea? Are you sure? I thought the humans took it over?" I hasten my pace as he flutters toward a structure resembling an acorn for a roof, as if the acorn were intended for a giant. "That's on the other side of the realm. In this part, we're protected as no human can find us." he answers.

"But I'm human," I reply.

"Of course you are, but you must be her loyal and true friend; otherwise, you wouldn't have walked through the gate without being harmed." I swallowed hard and followed him inside the house. It appears covered in different values and salves lined on shelves and tables. He lays Rose down on a bed made from cotton and begins to work on something near the fire. "My name is Bryce Bell, and I'm the healer pixie."

"Davi, no surname, and I'm a Rune Master."

"Lovely to meet you. And your friend, I bet her name is Rose."

"How—"

He lifts her right arm, and just inside her armpit is a rose tattoo. "Some pixies get these, and others, like myself, don't."

I watch as he applies a green salve to her forehead. "Is she going to be okay?"

"She is weakened, but you coming here saved her life. Not sure how you found us, but be glad you did because only pixie magic can heal a fairy."

My hand went to the rune pouch at my side. They're quiet again, but this was what they were doing. They knew where we needed to go to save her. To save their next master.

"Will we be safe here?" I ask.

"Yes. I will speak with our Chief. All fairies are welcomed and loyal friends, too. For now, food can be brought, and you can stay here for the night. There is a guest-chamber up those stairs and a bathing chamber right through that door. The house will provide you with whatever you need." I listen and look at every spot he points out, unsure of what he meant by the house providing me with whatever I needed.

"Thank you." I stood and went to the bathing chamber, looking for a lock, but noticed they didn't have one. A steaming wooden tub awaited me, and the smell of fresh pine was enticing. I decided a bath would do me and my sore muscles some good. After stripping down, I sunk into the water and closed my eyes, keeping my head above the water.

I kept the phoenix kiss on in case the fairies tried anything, but something told me that the runes wouldn't have brought us here if it were dangerous.

"Rose is the next master, and I must train her. After she's healed, we'll go to the Realm of Masters to begin her training." I speak this aloud, knowing that no others will hear me and convincing myself that this is the right thing to do. The only problem is getting her to comply while our enemy still holds her potential mate.

# 17

# NIYA

*Cinnamon. Honey. Nutmeg.*

Smells of my childhood flood through my nose as my eyes flutter open, and I look at a frost-covered surface. I try to think of where I could be that would have a ceiling made of ice when I feel something soft and warm underneath me—polar bear fur blankets.

I slowly sit up and find myself in an unfamiliar place. A furnace sits behind a wooden desk while an enormous four-poster bed covered in more polar bear furs sits in the far-right corner.

"You're awake." A familiar voice exclaims, and I gasp in shock when a figure comes into view. "Don't be frightened, my dear. I will not harm you."

"How did I end up back aboard your ship?" I ask her.

"Davi brought you here after Lavinia sent an ice shard through you. I was the only one who could remove it without killing you." She states that the moments come back in flashes.

"He betrayed us."

"Indeed, he did. But it wasn't all his fault. I struck a deal with him just as I did with you." she exclaims, then offers to help me to my feet, which I take. Part of me trusts her. We walk over to the bed and sit down.

"What do you mean?" I asked her.

"I told Davi he could live if he brought you back to me," she says with a smile.

"I do not wish to be your bride," I tell her, remembering our deal and what happened between Rose and me. I would never betray her. It was not knowing what I knew.

"I'm sorry, but you no longer have a choice." I jerk away from her.

"What do you mean? Of course I do. I have found my true mate. Why would I marry another?"

"Sit down." I do it. "I'm delighted to know you have found your true mate, but I only ask you to pretend to be my bride."

I blinked.

"There have been rumors aboard my ship and amongst the people that I'm not a true Amazon Queen without a Queen Consort by my side and an heir in her belly," she said. She stood and grabbed a glass of wine. "I'm barren for reasons I do not wish to discuss with you. But if you could help me find my mate while pretending to be my bride-to-be, that would be." She stops and faces me. Swirling the drink before gulping it down. "I know what I'm asking is a lot, but if you could do this for me, I will aid your friends in the upcoming war against tyranny."

I swallow hard, unsure if I should do this or not. "I will help you find your true mate, but I will not bear false witness. I will not pretend to be something I am not. I did that for far too long."

She nods in agreement. "I won't force you, Niya, but you will be my prisoner if not my bride."

\*\*\*

## NIYA

I rattle the chains around my wrist and allow myself to fall into the bed in my private chambers. My mind thinks of my mate with her bright pink hair and glinting purple irises.

The addicting smile she has brightens my day. I should've known it was here the moment I saw her. But I was too consumed by my grief over Serena that I allowed myself to become blind to her.

Lying in bed, my eyes wide open, as the foreign body sleeps next to me, I fear I will never see my mate again.

## ROSE

"Tell us what you did with her," I yell as another fist connects with the already bleeding face of the traitor who took my mate from me.

"She is with the Amazons." he spits out. "It's too late. Niya has become their Queen's prisoner. She was locked in a cell made of ice. No one can get through it except for the Queen."

"Fuck!" I scream.

"Davi," Alwin states from behind us. We ended up in a private room to perform this interrogation after hunting down this bastard. The walls are barren, and the room only has one bed that smells like sex.

"Why does the Amazon Queen wish me to kill someone for her?"

"I do not know," Davi states.

"You knew her well enough to give up my mate," I yell, rearing my fists, but Alwin stops me.

"I only did it so she wouldn't kill me." He sobs.

"Coward. Niya is innocent, and she was anything but nice to you. Ancients, if Alwin weren't here to stop me, I would have you dead at my feet." I growl.

"What is her name?" Serena asks.

"She wouldn't say. When I asked, she said that a name is a powerful thing or something like that." he states.

"What did you have planned for me and Serena when we arrived?"

Alwin asks.

"Doesn't matter. I thought you wouldn't have your powers, but you do." Davi answers.

"Tell us." Serena states.

"Queen Lilac has my wife and daughter. She wanted me to take you prisoner for them." Davi confesses, shocking all of us.

"It didn't seem like you cared all that much about her with your cock down that whore's throat." I snarl at him, spitting at his feet.

"If you would have been honest with us from the start, we could've helped you." Serena states.

"You are a fool and a coward," Alwin growls. "So does this mean I can kill him?" I ask.

"No, please, I can still be useful. I can help you get Niya back and kill both Queens. I am still the Rune Master. If I die, you will never find the next one as easily as you found me." Davi pleads.

"What do you know about Vwirynn?" Alwin asks him. "Nothing. I have only been between Xora and Whitfrost." he
admits.

"Then how will I find you useful?" Alwin asks.

"Because I can use my runes to summon a portal anywhere. Not just through carved stone. Each realm has a set of runes dedicated to it. Like coordinates on a map. I recite the proper incantation, and the portal appears." Davi states.

"Do you trust him?" I ask Alwin and Serena.

"What else did the Amazon Queen say when she made her deal with you? By the way, I'm going to kill the bitch for touching what's mine?" Serena remarks, and I roll my eyes.

"She called it the Shadow Realm. Said it was where my ancestors are from." Alwin answers.

"Makes sense. You are the only person in all of Xora and Whitfrost I know who has shadow magic." Davi states.

"So, it's settled. We get reinforcements from the shadow realm and rescue my mate." I state.

"We have to grab one thing before we leave," Alwin states. "But it's going to be dangerous and difficult. We will have to be like phantoms in the night."

"What is it and where?" I ask.

"It's the Grimoire that the Amazon Queen had, and it was in her quarters last I saw it." he answers.

"No way. We would walk straight into a death trap and no doubt risking Niya's life." I protest.

"That's why Davi is going to get it," he states, and we all look at the puny human.

"The Queen will kill me," he starts.

"Not if you have something to offer her." Alwin smiles. "What could I have that she wants?" Davi asks.

"This," Serena pulls out an amulet I recognize as hers. I thought it was destroyed when Odith was. "This is an amulet of protection. Tell her it is infused with my blood, which means I can never harm her."

"You've had this planned since we let Xora," I state, and they smile at me. "You two are wicked."

"And if I die? Then what?" Davi asks.

"Then there is one less adulterous traitor human walking around us," Alwin states.

"Agreed?" I ask, and Davi reluctantly nods his head.

Hold on, Niya, hold on. While the rest of them continued to plan, I stared at the small emblem on my chest. A pure white stone dagger with pink pixie wings hovers over my heart. It appeared the moment I accepted her as my mate. Once she gets me, if she still can, she will have one to match.

*I will save you, Raven. The Queen will rue the day she takes what's mine.*

THE TALE OF FLAME AND SHADOW

# III

# VWRIYNN

*A COURT OF FLAME AND SHADOW*

# 18

# SERENA

The journey through the portal would've never prepared me for what greeted us on the other side. A gentle road that leads to a posted sign labeled 'Wethidarin Village' is somewhat discernible despite the many cracks and holes given to it by the elements.

Gardens are bustling with insect life who've made their home in the tall grasses and overgrown bushes.

Some doors look collapsed or were perhaps destroyed by looters or animals as time passed. Either way, they left a welcoming entrance for anyone needing shelter. There were signs of fires; in some cases, it was merely a trail of soot and smoke above a windowpane; in others, it was a pile of ash where once a building stood.

"Where are we?" I asked while continuing to look at this ghost town. There seems only to be wildlife and no sign of people.

"We are in Vwirynn," Davi answers, and I look at him. The book is still clutched firmly in his grip as his bag of runes sits tied to his hip.

"Did you get the coordinates wrong?" Alwin asks.

"No. The runes never lie. This realm is called Vwirynn, or, as the description in the Grimoire read, shadowlands. It looks pretty bleak and shadowy to me." Davi answers him. The temperature is cool but not freezing like Whitfrost. Our thick cloaks are unnecessary in this environment.

I move towards them and allow my wings to flex. "We should shed our thick clothing. I don't think we will need it here."

They both nod, and I glamour my wings while shedding my thick wool coat and tunic. "I was wearing a short black shirt, strapped in, and tan pants and boots." Odith's tarot deck is tucked inside my cargo pants pocket. I found it back in Xora, thinking she left it there before she killed me the second time. I'm not a master, but something inside me called to them as they called me.

"Is there a map in that book?" I ask Davi, pointing at it. He flips it open only in his black short-sleeved crimson tunic, pants, and boots. He thumbs a page before looking at me.

"Here. This realm is vast. I'm unsure where we will locate this king and shadow master." Davi admits. I took the book from him and looked at the map. The cartography is beautiful, capturing the different elements of each city and village of this world. To include routes directing us. I could fly, but I haven't had much practice. Then I would leave these two alone; I know Alwin might kill Davi if I do that. Despite my anger towards the Rune Master for what he did to Niya, we need him.

"We need to find civilization. But I do not see any place close to us that might have a semblance of a community." I let out a sigh. "Looks like we are in for a long walk. According to the map, we will need to travel south down this path until reaching a fork in the road and turn southeast along that small mountain range." But I will welcome this time needed for Alwin and me. It will give us more time to connect on an emotional level rather than an intimate one.

An hour or so passed, and we'd only made a few short remarks here and there about this world we're now in. It's awkward, and I know it shouldn't be. "Alwin, is something bothering you?"

He gives me a side eye before answering as the small rocks knock against our boots. "Just thinking of our mission. Of where everyone from home went during the fight with Odith. Master Mikao stayed there with a few to help rebuild it, but it still bothers me, knowing I won't be there to help. It will be new when this is all over with saving the Confessor and Rose and going to war with Queen Lilac. And perhaps–" He sighs.

"They won't need you anymore?" I finished for him. He nods. "I don't think that's true. Master Mikao, although I don't know him as well as you do, doesn't seem like the kind to keep you at arm's length. He'll need your help to replace the teachers that were killed."

"Perhaps you'll join me."

"I'm no teacher. I can barely control what power I have. How do you expect me to teach others how to control theirs? To master their weapons. Pekka was the master of combat." An invisible punch to both our guts at the memory of him.

Alwin stops briefly; we watch as Davi takes the lead further down the path. "When this is all over, we'll both be needed to guide the future generations in the new world. Half-elves will never go away, nor will humans who intend on our persecution." I drop my head, understanding what he means. His thumb and forefinger grip my chin, lifting it to meet his gaze. "Whatever we face, no matter what, we do it together. That's what these mean."

He places our hands over each other's hearts where our mate emblem is imprinted into our skin. A reminder of who we are to one another and the great lengths we will go through to be together, including death.

"Alwin and Serena, you both should come look at this." Davi's voice cuts through our bubble, and Alwin smirks at me before placing a chaste kiss on my lips.

"Let's go see what Puny wants. It's probably nothing but a dead snake."

We make our way to the Rune Master, and what I see is much larger than a tiny reptile. "As you were saying?" I looked over at my mate, who didn't seem amused.

"What happened to him?" Davi asked as I bent down to examine the corpse of a young boy who hadn't reached adolescence yet by the baby fat still lining his cheeks. His body is gray and laced with black veins popping out his arms, neck, and shins. Two black holes remain where his eyes used to be. I raise my hand to touch him, but Alwin snatches my wrist in warning.

"We don't know what killed him. It could be a contagious illness." he explains, and I nod.

"It was no ailment that took him." We spin on our heels, the three of us withdrawing weapons, ready for the stranger neither of us heard approaching. The voice belonged to an older woman, around her seventieth year of life, judging by the white hair and gray clouds mixing with what used to be bright blue eyes. A cane helps her walk towards us, the rags draped around her, leaving a drag mark in the soft dirt.

"Do you know this boy?" I asked, stepping between the men and her. My fire returns inside while I wait for the others to follow my lead. She doesn't appear to be a threat, but the caution has been there since my time in the in-between.

The older woman slowly kneels next to him, placing a hand on his forehead and the other over his heart. I watch her eyes close, and she hums a tune before swiping her hand over his lids to make it look like he is sleeping. "This shadow magic. The boy was a part of the punishment the villagers back in Wethidarin received for defying the King."

I help her to her feet, ensuring she's well-balanced before creating some space between us once more. "Who is the King?"

"He goes by many names, but most know him as Alistair." Alwin meets my eye at the name.

"Do you know where we can find him?" Davi asks before I get the chance to. The older woman laughs and then notices how serious we all are.

"No one finds the Shadow King. He rules from the blind spots of the naked eye. Using his magic to conquer and kill those that would defy him." She grunts and then begins walking further ahead, leaving us with the corpse. "If you want to find him, just go to where all the souls of Vwirynn end up."

I ran beside her, not wanting her to leave without further explanation. "Where is that, exactly?" She raises a brow at me but continues her forward progress. "We're not from here. I wish to speak with him. I have vitae information for him."

That catches her attention.

She turns to look at me, assessing me from head to foot before gesturing for me to bend to meet her eye.

"What are you?" Her hand presses against my forehead before I get a chance to answer, but she screams and jerks her hand away. The sound of sizzling skin and the smell of burnt flesh made my eyes water. When I look at her, those eyes are widened, and the humor from before is quickly replaced with terror.

I reach out to offer to heal her, but she flinches, and a firm hand grips my shoulder, pulling me back against a complex form. "We need to go, Serena. There's nothing you can do for her."

Alwin interlocks his fingers into mine, pulling me down the path until we sprint. We don't stop until we're a far enough distance away that Alwin doesn't fear for our safety. I raise my hands above my head, catching my breath as Alwin gets our water out. Taking a refreshing gulp, I look back behind us. I know she wouldn't be able to see us, but it frightens me knowing what I did to her.

"I burned her without calling my power." It escapes in a whisper, my words laced with confusion.

"You're a Phoenix, Serena; your fire is constant," Alwin explains. "I could've killed her. She still might die from an infection

because of burning her." I face away from him, close my eyes, and think of things that would cool me down being back in Whitfrost surrounded by snow and ice.

"You're not a monster, Serena." Alwin's in front of me. His scent washing over me had the calming effect I needed. His firm hands are on my cheeks, and he kisses me softly. "You don't burn me.

Clearly, your essence deemed her as a threat, and it defended you. My shadows have done the same for me. I've just had a much longer learning how to sense it."

"Will I ever learn to control it?"

"Open your eyes." he whispers, and I hesitate but listen. "You have more control than you think you do." I follow his gaze to the ground but then grip his arms as I notice they float in the air. My wings gently flapped behind us. "Whatever you feel comes to life. You wanted to escape, but not without me, so your wings answered the call. Use your emotions to communicate with your essence, Serena, and you'll be in command."

I think about landing, and slowly, we return to solid ground.

My wings dissipate once more, and I embrace my mate with gratitude. Davi clears his throat, reminding us of his presence, and we walk apart to approach him. He had the map out and began to tell us where we were.

"While you two were up there, I was deciphering what the old woman said. You see, we're here." He points to the backside of a mountain ridge. "Which, as you can see, is just beyond the horizon." We follow his pointer finger and see the pointed outline. "Now, there is something about her mentioning souls of this world and where they all end up. Just east of Nightingale City is the Sea of Souls. In the farthest southeast is an island with no name. I think that's where we're meant to go."

"Can you portal us there?" I ask.

He digs into his bag of runes and nods. "I can, but there's a small catch."

"What?" Alwin growls.

"I might not have enough power to bring us back to Whitfrost." We look at him, waiting for him to elaborate. "Runes are not just carved pieces of stone that automatically come with power. They're created. It takes certain ingredients and materials to make more. I siphon the magic from each piece I use, and once it's served its purpose, the stone turns blank and becomes useless."

"What do you need?" Alwin asks.

Davi shuffles in his bag, pulls out a parchment, and begins to read, "I'll need to borrow some essence from one of you. I prefer Serena since she's the more powerful one." Alwin snarls. "No offense, Dark One, but as you keep reminding her, she's the first true Phoenix in two centuries."

"You're not taking an ounce of my mate's power. Find another way."

"There is none. Unless you find another Rune Master running around the universe, then by all means."

I step between them, defusing the situation before it escalates further. "Davi can use my essence if we can get around quicker.

Remember, Niya and Rose don't have much time on their side. I'd hate to think what would happen to them because you're too possessive to let me lend a little magic." I narrow my eyes at Alwin, who scoffs but nods. "What else do you need for the spell?"

"Bones from a dragon. Wouldn't you happen to know any of those, would you?" Davi inquires, his gaze looking past me.

"Braxor wouldn't defile his death to help you."

"No, but he might if you asked him," I said, and Alwin went quiet. Running his fingers through his long white hair. "When the time is right, we must call him."

"There's no guarantee he'll answer from this realm," Alwin explains. "But I will attempt because it's what you want. And it's what we need to help Rose and the Confessor."

"Good, then let's get started," Davi states, pulling out his relics and reciting the magic needed to port us to another part of this realm. I grip Alwin's hand, neither knowing what danger awaits us on the other side nor knowing we're together.

"In this life and the next." he whispers. "Always."

# 19

# ALWIN

The smell is the first thing I notice, aside from the mud slick against our boots and coated against our skin.
"You couldn't have aimed us away from the mud pool?" I snarled.
"Portals are unpredictable, Dark One; you, of all people, should know that by now." Davi wipes his hands down his shirt and then looks ahead. I do the same searching for Serena. When I don't see her, my heart rate begins to rise as the last time I couldn't find her, she was drying.
"Serena?" I scan the area, first the skies, to see if she took flight, then the ground for any sign she walked away. "Where is she?"
Davi searches the distance, but there's nothing to see but large, sharpened rocks and the slosh we've landed in. "Serena!" he calls out.
Our voices echo off the open space while we trudge through the mud. The humidity here is stifling. Sweat coats my forehead after five minutes, and I'm wiping it from my eyes. Every inhale I take is covered with a thick earthly flavor, causing my throat and mouth to dry out quickly. Grabbing my water from my bag, I open it to drink

from only a drop that hits my tongue. Confused, I squeeze the leather pouch, but there's nothing left.

"Mine's empty, too," Davi says breathlessly. "They were nearly full when we left."

"It's got to be the environment here. Evaporated our water from our pouches just as quickly as it appears to be doing from our bodies."

He's right. I can feel the dehydration kicking in and look ahead for shelter from the sun. "We need to get out of this sun's path. Serena will find us."

"Where do you suggest we go?" Davi asks. I point to the mountain range just ahead. "Right."

The journey was arduous, navigating through the dense ground before it transitioned into solid rock. When shielded from the sun's rays, our bodies pressed against the exceptionally smooth stone, both of us running low on energy. "Without water, we won't survive this heat," Davi states. He's right; although he has magic, he's still human. I may come back from the brink of death, but not Puny. "The map shows a stream at the end of this valley. A sort of oasis by the looks of the trees. We make it there, hydrate, and then follow up to look for her."

The turmoil I feel for leaving where we landed without her has my insides twisting. That and the lack of water. Davi and I use the last of what we have to walk the shadows of the valley, keeping contact with the stone as it seems to be keeping us more relaxed. My ears twitch at the sound of water flowing, and I perk up the second I see it.

We drop our sacks together and race to the bank, dipping our hands into the surprisingly cold liquid. I cup my hands together and bring a small puddle to my lips, their dryness longing to taste its refreshing texture.

"Stop!" Serena's scream catches my attention, and she's next to me. She knocked the water from my hands, wiped them clean, and looked at me with fear. "Did you drink it?" I don't answer her immediately; I try to ensure she isn't an illusion. "Alwin, did you drink the water?"

I shake my head from side to side and gently caress her cheek. She pulls out her waterskin, pops the cork off, and holds it to my lips. The fresh, crisp liquid easily floods my throat, and I want more, but she pulls it away. "Not too much. We need to conserve what we have. Davi, you need some, too."

She reaches in his direction without looking, her focus mainly on me. I follow her arm and see the Rune Master violently shaking on the ground. Without my full strength, I can barely move. "Serena." My voice is scratchy.

"Don't speak. You'll need to be healed. Davi," she looks over and finally realizes why he hasn't answered her. Racing to him, she rolls him on his side. "You drank it, didn't you? Idiot." She scolds him while supporting his head until he finally stops moving. Using a cloth from her belt, she wipes his mouth before turning on his back and listening to his heart. "It's faint. We must return him to Master Mikao now, or he'll die."

"How?" My voice croaks, and I crawl over to them, hating my weakness.

"I don't know, Alwin, but without his runes and no Tarot Master, we're stuck here. Maybe you should call Braxor. Can't dragons fly across worlds?" Her tongue is sharp, and she's concerned about the Rune Master. Whether that be because Serena has a pure heart or our best chance at saving the Confessor, Rose is currently cradled in her arms.

"No. But I can try some Rieke."

"You know how?"

I've been watching Master Mikao for many years. I was learning his techniques and ways of using the essence to heal the sick and wounded. Looking down at Puny, I inhale sharply and let it go before taking more water from her just for the extra boost. I place one hand on his forehead and the other on his heart. "Serena, I'll need your help to heal him. If I use too much of my life force, I may not survive this."

"How does this work?" she asks. I place her hands in the same spots mine were, then touch her hands with my mind. Our skin buzzes to life with our essence.

"I want you to close your eyes and focus on your soul. Reiki works to create a state of equilibrium in our life-force energy. When you feel his soul reaching out to you, don't block it."

"How will I know?"

"Because I'll be there with you. Now, close your eyes and find your peace." I do the same, thinking of the ways Master Mikao would instruct others to clear their minds of everything and focus on the one thing or image that's always brought them peace. I searched my memories and found one of when I was a child, eating gooseberry pie fresh from the oven. It was my favorite. The bursting flavor brings a smile to my face.

I exhale on three counts and then repeat while inhaling. Davi's aura quickly finds me, and I reach out to him. Runes paint his pale skin, and his eyes are sunken in. He looks smaller than usual, and I see creatures of bones sticking prongs inside him. "Serena, where are you?"

She doesn't answer, and I'm no longer inside my body. Everything that is happening is going on inside of the Rune Master. I charge forward, trying to pull them from him, but they're stuck like a moth to the flame. "Dark One."

Davi's soul pleads for help as a shaky hand, nearly nothing but bone reaches for me. When I feel the last of him pulling away, a blast of fire knocks into a creature and appears, not in her regular form, but as a Phoenix, my mate. She blasts the other three from Davi's body and quickly lands. Her nails gently grasped my outstretched fingers.

I place Davi's hands over mine and Serena's chest while putting mine against his. "Let it flow, Serena. Give him some of your life force, or we'll lose him for good."

She makes a bird-like noise, which I assume means she understands, and in a few more seconds, I watch as my shadow and her flames dance along his skin like vines on a tree. The essence we've freed up, sinking into him, rejuvenating his soul again. I break the connection before he takes too much and is knocked backward.

I blinked the brain fog away and sat up, looking at Serena sit- ting beside him, appearing unaffected by what we just did. When I go back to them, I see the color come back to the Rune Master's face, his eyes no longer shrouded in darkness, and the pink tinge a human has surfacing back in his lips.

"Serena, are you okay?" She smiles at me.

"I am. I believe you just performed your first healing session, Rieke Apprentice." she said, pride glowing in her eyes.

"We don't know if it worked. Or how well it did. Plus, we used part of our essence to do it. I don't know what the consequences of magic like this could mean." I warned her.

"Guys?" Davi wakes, and Serena helps him sit up. "Don't drink the water."

"Yeah. I figured the name Sea of Souls would be enough warning." Serena deadpans. "Either way, the sun appears to be setting soon. We'll camp here tonight and plot our next move tomorrow."

"One problem with that," I say, and they look at me for further explanation. "Water. Your one water skin won't be enough for the three of us. We have dried meat left for food, but I imagine that is scarce here, too. It would be best to travel at night while the sun isn't beating down on us."

"Davi will need to rest, and so will you." Serena persisted. "No. I will carry him. I'm already feeling better, Serena. Trust me." She looks at me and then at the Rune Master before nodding in agreement.

"Then so be it. We only travel at night."

After getting Davi back on his feet, with both of us supporting his weight, we decided to head back in the direction we came. The island appears to be much larger than we anticipated. The Oasis of Trees is on the other side of the mountains and doesn't show us needing to cross a stream of soul creatures. That's what Serena is calling them, to reach it. We decided that climbing would take longer and more energy than we had to spare.

Ten minutes into our hike, Davi lets Serena walk ahead as he limps while baring his weight against me. It's awkward, and I bite my tongue with the many unkind things I could say to him because I know by the look in his eyes.

"Thank you, Dark One. For saving me." I roll my eyes.

"If Serena didn't ask me to, you'd be soul creature food, and I wouldn't shed a single tear for you. After all, what fate does an adulterous traitor have bestowed upon him?" It appears I can't hold my tongue when it comes to him.

"Whatever the gods decide, I'm sure it will be what I deserve." He answers in a humble tone that rubs me the wrong way.

"Who will take your place?" I inquire, genuinely curious, as there can only be one Rune Master at a time. He can name an apprentice, but the essence and relics don't pass on until he does.

"Trying to figure out how much longer I can be useful to you and your Phoenix?" he asks, but I don't entertain his question. A sigh escapes him as he answers, "There are a few ways to know when my apprentice is nearby or how to find them. One uses the runes themselves to locate their next master. But the other, well, it's much more. They have to be immune to all magic except for the Amazons. I didn't know that one until my first encounter with the Queen. But your shadow magic and Confessor powers."

"I see. So how did you get chosen?"

"The runes found me." he says. "When I was a boy, I ventured into a cave just beyond a waterfall while playing a game with my little sister. In the pool were shimmering white tiles that made me think of pearls. We weren't wealthy, so I figured they could benefit me. I was taken into another realm when I swam to the bottom and touched them. A world between worlds where only Rune Master's past, present, and future can venture. That was where I learned everything. When I was sent back, the life I once knew wasn't there anymore. The realm was overrun with pure blood, and I was a man. It felt like hours in the in-between, but on the outside, it was years

—something to do with time not existing.

"I went to find my family and discovered the village I grew up in was empty. Not a single livestock insight. That's when I used the runes for the first time. Portal me to where my family is." He stops for a moment, the pain of his past coming to life in his eyes, and I find sympathy for him for a moment.

"What happened?" My voice is softer than usual.

He turns to look at me. "They were dead. Their bodies were tossed into fire pits amongst thousands of others. I swore on them that day I'd get revenge on who did this to them. To our home."

"Did you ever find out?"

He nods. "Queen Lilac's father ordered the slaughter of my home so he could conquer that realm. They even built a palace and battalion there. I haven't been back since."

"What realm? I know you are not from Xora or Whitfrost."

Davi unhooks his arm from my shoulders and pulls his shirt off to reveal his inked torso. "Right between the shoulders. I got it tattooed days after I saw what happened." I read the word in my head over and over, knowing I'd never been there or heard of it until now. "Ulorea. The place where nothing but humans thrived until the former King of

Xora marched across our lands and destroyed it."

"Is that how you ended up in service to his daughter?" He covers himself back up and looks on ahead. Serena's bright flame kept her in our line of sight.

"Yes. Let's call it a failed assassination attempt. Lilac has magic. I'm unsure how it happened, but I hope to find out one day. Right before I gut her."

"Alwin and Davi, have you two passed out again?" Serena calls us, and we no longer speak about Davi's past. When we catch up to her, she's looking at the map, her small ball of fire illuminating it from the side. She moves her hand behind it, careful to keep it from catching. "Do you see that?"

"Unbelievable," Davi whispers.

"At least we're heading in the right direction." she says. Her little flame has revealed hidden ink showing the location of the one city on the godforsaken island. "Alistair's palace must be in the middle of the oasis. If we pick up the pace, we'll make it to the edge by morning."

"I'll carry, Puny." I don't wait for an object as I lift him across my shoulders and lead the way.

"A little warning would've been nice." He grunts, my shoulder digging into his gut.

"That's where you have me wrong, Puny. I'm not nice." "You're nice to Serena."

"She's my mate and the one who warms my bed at night. My future wife and mother of my children."

"Good point, Dark One."

# 20

# SERENA

Alwin and Davi continue to banter back and forth about senseless things. Meanwhile, I'm focusing on guiding us through a world none have ever been to while maintaining my fire.

The heat here didn't bother me. Something about my essence is protecting me, and I have no desire to drink as often as those two.

I don't mind knowing I can provide them with the necessary resources to survive in this place. As we approach the beginning of the tree line, I signal for us to stop. We don't know what potential dangers are lurking within those trees, and I don't have enough energy to go through another Rieke session.

Alwin and Davi catch up to me, silent aside from the shallow breaths they're taking. My mate shows strength even when carrying his bag and another person's body weight. I look towards the sky, trying to judge when the sun will rise, but nothing gives its position away. "We don't know what lurks in the shadows. I don't want to put us at risk."

Alwin gently sets Davi back on the ground, narrowing his eyes as I see him summon his shadow magic. His eyes go entirely black while the hum of essence vibrates from his body into mine. Our emblem comes to life on my chest as it recognizes its match. "There's nothing aside from a waterfall in the middle of the oasis. Any sign of life can't be for a mile as far as I can see."

"So we keep going?" Davi asks more than states.

I look at my mate, whose eyes fade to standard color, and he nods. "We keep going until we can't. Drink up. The fates might bless us with clean water once inside the shade of the trees."

Moving ahead, Davi walks alone, benefiting from the additional rest, and he enjoys full access to the water. Alwin made the same choice as me. At this moment, the Rune Master is more useful when alive than when dead. Since neither of us can port back home, Braxor has not come since Alwin called an hour ago. He believes the dragon will see if and when we truly need him.

I cautiously step over the wood line, keeping my flame ahead of us, and see an artificial path of stones leading further into the small forest. We kept as quiet as possible, moving at a pace Davi could tolerate. It doesn't take long for the water flow to catch my ears. I lead us to the sound; the desire to taste fresh water makes my mouth water. I've not gone this long without a drink since I was a girl. Days in Narborim weren't so kind to my mother and me. I am being fatherless, living in a rotting home with little to no food and scarce water rationed by the village elders.

The day the Gnaxtor came was a blessing and curse. Being taken in by Niya's family helped me stay alive, but it also meant never seeing my mother again. Those days have long since passed, and I have a new purpose. A new family that found me, and I intend to bring it back together before the end of this war.

Through the thick foliage, I see a shimmering blue glow coming from behind it. I push through, the sharpened thorns of vines pricking at my skin, but I don't care because I can smell the deca-dent taste of water. Pressing on, I bring my essence to help protect my skin, burning whatever touches it and race to the pool's edge. It's beautiful, clear, and soulless.

"Serena, are you sure it's safe?" Alwin asks from my right side. I cup my hands, dip them into the liquid, bring them to my lips, and sip. The fresh, crisp, cool water soothes my dry throat as I slowly swallow. I lock eyes with my mate as he watches me. I'm waiting to see if I'll react Davi did to the other stream. Nothing feels off, and I take another handful and bring it to Alwin's lips. After he tries it, we wait another moment before grabbing and filling the empty water skin.

I look to tell Davi, but he's dunked his head into it. A laugh bubbles in my chest at the sight of him. "Be careful, Rune Master, you might drown."

He surfaces, his hair sticking to his forehead, mouth dripping wet. "It tastes better than death."

"Doesn't everything?" I ask.

"Right." Davi fills the water skin he is holding and caps it.

After we all seemed filled to the brim with as much water as we could handle without dying, we were back on our feet again. "Should we rest here for the night?"

"Yes. Puny will need to rest and eat." Alwin replies.

"Davi set up for the night. I'll go get some firewood." I place my bag down next to Alwin's and get moving. Lighting the end of a fallen branch with my flame as I pile other dry ones. Next are fallen leaves for the kindling. I've been using my essence for hours, my power running dangerously low, and my stomach twists with hunger.

A nearby branch cracks, causing me to freeze. Scanning the area, I finally spot it—the creature with bramble-colored fur, almost melding into the night. However, nothing eludes my light. Crouching down, I empty my hands and approach slowly. With a flick of my fingers, I direct a fireball straight at its exposed side, relishing the satisfying sound upon impact. "Good shot." I cringe at the sound of Alwin's voice. "Didn't hear you coming."

He follows me to the game. "That's because darkness and I are like twin flames. I have control overshadows and everything to do with it. Using them to keep me hidden is one of the first skills I mastered as a boy."

"Tell me more." He takes a seat next to me in the soft grass. "About your life growing up. You know about mine."

He ran a hand through his long hair, whether from nerves or to get it out of his eyes; I couldn't tell. "There's not much to it. My father trained me since the second I could summon my first glimpse of shadow. Every day, it was the same: learning the history of our race, exercising for hours, and when I wasn't physically more assertive, he'd try to strengthen my mind by using different tactics to test my mental barriers. One of the worst visions, probably his favorite to use, was of my future wife dying and me not being there to protect her.

"A glimpse into my future if I failed my lessons. After weeks of feeling that loss tore me apart, I built a solid wall. When he got through torturing me with her, he moved on to my children. They would be more powerless, dragged off by humans to use as leverage against the next Shadow King. What I saw, it's something I wouldn't wish on any parent. Then, and I'm sure he regrets this one, it was my mother. He knew how close our bond was, and for a little while, I thought he envied our bond.

"He would have her beheaded for giving birth to me. That was her crime, and unfortunately, her death became a reality even though he couldn't stop." Tears swelled in his eyes, and I interlaced my fingers with him, providing him with comfort. "I guess that was the real test. When it came down to it, neither of us could protect the person we loved most."

"Alwin, you can't blame yourself."

"But I do." He snaps, then he sighs. "I'm sorry. It's hard for me to imagine her ever since the cave in the Fenix Mountains."

"She sacrificed her soul for me, and that's something I'll never be able to repay her, but I'm eternally grateful because it brought me back to you. To Niya, Rose, and even Davi." I smiled.

"Puny seems to be growing on you." he comments.

"Despite all the bad, there is good in him. I believe he can be redeemed."

"Second chance?" He quirked a brow.

"Everyone deserves one. He didn't kill Niya. Not saying that what he did was excusable because it wasn't." I sigh, cup Alwin's cheek, and look deep into his before saying this next part. I hope he understands it's more for him than the Rune Master. "No matter our mistakes, big or small, they all mean one thing… that we still have a soul. Davi is human; they tend to make many mistakes, but having lived with humans all my life, I've realized that's how they learn, how we all learn. The only difference is, we don't let it define or defeat us."

He leans forward, pressing his forehead to mine. "You have a way with words, Serena."

His lips meet mine. Our kiss is initially soft but grows more intense as our desire to mate surfaces. Alwin's hand landed on my hips, lifting me to straddle him. A growl of hunger interrupts the beginnings of what I can only assume would be a heated session of sex against a tree. "We need to eat."

"I'm hungry for you, Phoenix."

"Ah, but the rabbit will give me the fuel to keep you up the rest of the night." I wink and move to get off him, but his fingers dig into my sides, and he pushes me down on his ready cock.

"How long will you tease me?"

"We're on a mission, and as much as I'd love to strip you down and make love to you in that pool of water, we're pressed for time. Besides, we must wash and have enough energy to face whatever fate will test us when the sun comes up."

He whimpers, pleading in his eyes, but lets me go.

Back at the camp, I get the fire going while Alwin tends to the rabbit. I was skinning it and getting it cleaned for us to roast it. There isn't much to the meat, but enough for us to enjoy along with the leftover portions we brought.

"I'll take the first watch," I state, and Alwin nods. The one thing I've always admired about him is that he doesn't try to control me. And most certainly doesn't treat me like a damsel in distress. He respects my need to contribute to the team.

The noise from the water. I have to stand so I do not fall asleep.

It drowns out the snores coming from Davi, which is a bonus. There is no gap in the canopy of trees, which prevents me from gazing at the stars. With nothing else to occupy my time, I pull out the tarot deck that's been burning a hole in my pocket since I placed it back there a few days ago.

I try to remember watching Niya's technique as she shuffled them. I know she usually pulled three cards for herself and then interpreted them. Growing up with her, she taught me the meaning of the cards or potential interpretations of them. Their feel is smooth, but there's a heaviness to them. One wouldn't think parchment could weigh this much, but when the fates play apart–

"Show me something," I whisper and pull the first card. Staring back at me is the *Temperance*. An image of a woman in robes with angel wings pouring equal parts liquid into two vases is painted on it. I rack my brain trying to remember what Niya said this could mean. Next, I draw *The Emperor* and then *The High Priestess*. Both honorable and regal cards by the looks of the figures painted to sit on thrones. All three cards sit placed on my lap as I study them.

This reminds me of when Niya gave me my first reading just one month after I got to the church.

We were sitting on the rug in her room; she was dressed in white robes, shuffling her deck. I was wearing pants and a shirt gifted to me by the family.

"Are you ready?" she asks. "Go for it," I replied.

She lays out three cards, all painted with funny little images. One at a time, she explained them to me.

"Temperance could mean inspiration or protector. You could be destined for a greater purpose." Greater purpose, how could she mean that for a poor half-elf orphan girl? "This next one," she pointed at the one with the painted lady on it, "the High Priestess means you have a sense of mystery about you. Or in need of enlightenment. But don't be afraid because The Emperor has many meanings, too. One could be leadership.

Maybe you'll become some Illuminate."

I sighed. I'm unsure why this raven-haired girl wanted to play nice with me or give me false hope for *a brighter future*.

"That's it. These cards again." My voice is louder than I meant for it to be, and Davi stirs while Alwin pops a brow at me. "Go back to sleep."

He sits up, placing his elbows on his knees before speaking, "I can't sleep knowing we'll be heading into unknown territory and tomorrow to tell a man that we were originally sent here to assassinate him." I gesture for him to come to me, and he does. "Playing with cards like the Confessor?"

"Not playing, learning. I was meant to have them, but I don't fully understand why they chose me."

"Because, like anything I have seen you do since meeting you six months ago, you exceed everyone's expectations." I smile at him.

Alwin pulls me in for a kiss, and then the bright light of day begins to rise. I am highlighting the steady flow of the waterfall. After putting my deck back in my pocket, I pulled the map out and looked at the next spot, but nothing appeared except that the city was marked where the falls were.

"Good morning." Davi's rested voice fills my ears.

"I think we need to head into the falls. Looks like the entrance to the city is through there." I point directly ahead of us.

"Then into the unknown we go," Alwin remarks.

Once we packed and ensured the fire was completely out, we headed to the pool's edge. "We'll need to swim there. I'm unsure how deep the water is, but don't stray from the bank."

My gaze drifted to Davi. "I can swim. A little. Okay, good enough to keep my head above water. Stop worrying about me."

He leaps, and my stomach lurches, watching his entire body submerge. My eyes frantically searched for him to breach, but nothing happened. "I'm going in."

Without another second, Alwin dives headfirst, and I follow.

The water is clear once the wake of our entrance dissipates. I try to find them, but something is pulling me deeper. I kick and scratch towards the surface, but it doesn't work. My lungs burn for air, and I can hear my heart pounding in my ears. Darkness clouds my vision, and I feel it when I'm about to give in.

The burning flame of my phoenix comes to life inside of me. My arm crunches as feathers of flame form on each appendage. Each finger twists until turning into long talons. I can feel my legs shrinking until the firebird takes over my body.

Taking flight, I shoot out of the water, taking to the sky. When I return to the pool, I see the reflection of the most beautiful animal ever. But then my eye catches the dark ribbons of ink spreading through the clear liquid.

*Alwin.*

I tried to call his name, but my voice didn't sound normal.

A hand breaches the surface, and I glide down, my talons gripping the thick wrist. I flap as hard as I can, their weight increasing the higher out of the water they come. Davi is wrapped in Alwin's arms, taking in deep gulps of air while coughing up water.

"Serena!" Alwin calls to me, and I caw at him. His black eyes meet mine, and we both feel relief. I drag them half-body to the bank and wait until they're safe again before shooting to the sky. I'm looking across as far as I can see. Something flickers in the distance, and I fly towards it. Reaching out, the edge of my claw feels a vibration coming from that part of the sky. I press forward and watch with amazement as it disappears.

*False barrier.*

With this knowledge, I land and will my figure to transform. Nothing happens. I try to concentrate, but the phoenix has her claws in too deep.

"Serena, what's wrong?" Alwin asks. I come up to his chest and frantically make a noise. "Calm down."

I signal for him to follow me and look over my shoulder as they do. Once we are standing in front of the barrier, I meet his eye, a silent plea to trust me before I fly into it.

# 21

# ALWIN

As I try to recover from the traumatic experience of almost drowning in the powerful waterfalls, I keep my eyes fixed on
the majestic phoenix. Its vibrant colors and graceful movements leave me in awe as it glides effortlessly toward a wall of illusion, gradually fading from my view.

"Move it, Puny." I grip the back of his collar and race forward.

Beams of light swirl around as our bodies are lifted from the ground, transporting through what I can only describe as a tunnel. I keep my hold tight onto Davi, the pull growing stronger the further we fall.

The sun's light hits my eyes just before we're dropped onto a soft patch of grass. My grip on Davi falters upon impact as we roll a few feet. I roll onto my back, blinking away the bright rays before standing. "Serena! Where are you?"

"She's over there," Davi answers, and I look in the direction he's pointing. Perched on the silver gate is my firebird. "It's apparent that her phoenix is still in charge. It must think she's in danger."

The Rune Master has a point, and I think about that as my gaze travels to the city behind the wall. It's bustling with life past a stone bridge that runs over a stream of water that matches that of the pool we nearly drowned in. I approach the gate, reaching out to touch it, when Serena caws at me. Our eyes meet, and she flaps her wings before gliding over the entrance.

"What's she doing?" Davi asks.

"A flyover." Because that's exactly what that meant: she could cover more ground faster than we would walk. I push the gate, but nothing happens.

"Perhaps try a password."

"If I wanted your input, Puny, I'd ask." He raises his hands in a signal of defeat. I'm hard on him, but it's because I don't trust him. Serena has a particular affection for him. Her ability to forgive is one thing I'll never be able to do.

While watching from a distance as Serena's form grows smaller the further she flies, an elf dressed in violet armor approaches us with a jagged spear. "What is your business in Silver City?"

My hackles rise. I bare my teeth, but he doesn't appear to be phased by my warning.

"We're just humble travelers looking for a place to stay for the night. If you would be so kind as to show us a fine tavern or inn." Davi's irritating skill at manipulating others into doing something could be in our favor.

"We have a certain disdain for those we deem as threats." His gaze assesses me from head to toe. "Sanctuary is something we grant but only to those in need." he states.

Davi limps forward, gripping his stomach, and it could be partially faked, but I won't say a word to contradict him if it will get us inside. "Let me clarify. We do seek sanctuary within your walls because, you see when we were stranded here three days ago by an evil witch, she left us with no water, and with us not being from here, we nearly died from drinking from the sea."

"You did? Only a child is foolish enough not to know better. Those waters are infested with soul creatures. Their main job is to trap more unfortunate victims in their dark abyss. How did you survive?" The guard seems trapped by the Rune Master's dramatized accounts of what happened. "This big oaf is a Rieke Master?"

I raise a brow and go to speak, but apparently, I have lost my tongue to the annoying man at my side.

"Apprentice. But he picks up on things quicker than most. That's why Master Mikao chose him."

The guard's eyes widened in surprise and admiration. "You work with the legend?"

I laugh on the inside. Master Mikao will find this humorous. Or won't react at all to the humble bastard.

"Why yes, we're close friends with him. If word got back to you, what's your name again?"

"Joana Greyson."

"Right, Guard Greyson was the one who granted us sanctuary in Silver City; the Rieke Master would show his gratitude in some way. With a spiritual healing session or other means."

Greyson looks between us, then at the gate, the city, and with a sigh, removes a key from the ring attached to his belt. It swings open smoother than expected, and he lets us through before securing it again. "Promise me you won't cause problems? King Alistair will have my head if he finds out I helped two enemies into his realm."

Davi laughs, and I scoff, but the severe nature of the guard tells me he's serious. "Oh, definitely not an enemy."

"Right. If you cross the bridge, follow the main path ten buildings down; the Firebird Inn and Tavern is the brick building on the left. You can't miss it, as there's a large phoenix painted across the rooftop."

"Your King has an affection towards the legendary bird?" I ask. "He considers them to be rare signs of fate. If one were ever to cross your path, it would be like looking at a god or goddess." The guard didn't know how close he was to one.

Walking away from the front, I remain quiet, not wanting to praise Davi for his cleverness. I listen for *her*. *Please pay attention to the people we pass, how they dress, and the way they whisper to one another about the newcomers.* When we make it to the door, I take one last glance at the skies, hoping to see her. *Where are you, Phoenix?*

"Come, she'll find us." Davi taps me on the shoulder as an old friend and walks inside. I follow, ready for drunks and loud music, but what greets us is surprising. A front area with one person and adjacent to that is a small seating area with four tables all filled with people eating.

"One room? Or two?" the human woman asks.

"One room, two beds." I get out before Davi can even attempt to escape my sight. "We'll take our food in the room."

She nods and hands over a brass key shaped like a firebird. "Up the stairs, last door on the right. Dinner will be brought up in an hour." She sniffs us and wrinkles her nose. "And I'll have them bring you both fresh clothes."

Davi sniffs himself and then coughs. "We smell like shit."

"Worse than that. It smells like you two took a swim in the bog." She states. I tire of the back and forth and trek to the room without another word.

It's one of the most lavish establishments I've ever stayed in. The smell is something like cleaned linen; there's not a speck of dirt to be seen, and aside from the two beds, there are two wardrobes, each with a four-tier candle stick on it. I set my bag down and moved to the bathroom, not caring for Davi's protest to bathe first.

I need to connect with Serena, and the only way I can do that is to find some peace. With the door locked, I strip down and look for the basin to fill, but there's something different about this bathroom. Everything is shiny and looks new. The soaps smell funny but better than my current state.

With the hot water pouring down me, I sit on the floor, cross my legs, and focus on my mate.

"Serena, where are you? Are you safe?" I wait for her to answer, but the longer the silence, the more worried I get.

"Alwin!" Her voice is panicked, and I try to connect with her visually. To make out what she is seeing. Flashes of bars, humans, and elves surround her, a reflection in their armor showing me she's still in her phoenix form. *"He has me. You need to run!"*

"Where are you?" It flashes again, but I can barely make it out.

My ears twitch to listen to what is happening. I can only make out one voice, one name spoken as a face comes into view.

*"Now the universe will know that fates favor me, firebird."*

*"Lord Alistair, what would you have us do?" He* smirked, reaching a finger into the cage. *Serena pecks at his finger, drawing blood, but he laughs.*

*"Don't let her out of your sight until I return."*

My eyes snap open. The rage I feel is boiling inside me; before I know what's happening, my fist connects with the wall, shattering the tile and leaving a hole.

"Alwin? Are you okay? Did you fall?" I push to my feet, leave the shower, not caring it's still on, and grab the towel before entering the main chamber. I dry off quickly, ignoring Davi's presence entirely. "What happened there?"

I find the clean clothes folded neatly on the right wardrobe and quickly put them on, tossing my hair into a high tail at the back of my head.

"Um, hello, you're bleeding." It takes his touch on my wrist to remember where we are. My hand around his throat as a growl vibrates in my throat. "Dark One, snap out of it!"

I blink a few times, the red color of rage clearing my vision, and release him. The Rune Master is heaving and gasping for air.

"They have her. He has her." I say, swiping a hand down my face.

"Who?" He croaks, standing.

"Alistair. He's got her..." I pause, my fists curling at my sides. "In a cage."

"Fuck. Alright, I'll get ready, and we can go." Davi heads to the bathroom, but I don't have time to waste on him.

Looking at my bleeding knuckles, I grab a spare towel and quickly wrap it before pulling my sack on my back and heading out the door.

I need to secure a weapon first, which may prove more difficult than I anticipated, being that I'm a stranger here and the greeting at the gate doesn't give me any hope that they'd be willing to sell one to me.

"I see my son's clothes fit you well." The woman who gave me the key catches my attention as I pass her.

Looking down, I see I'm wearing all black, the shirt and pants fitting me well. "Yes. Thank you."

"Are you in a hurry?" I furrow my brows. "You look like you're making a quick exit. Something wrong with the room?"

"No." I approached her. "I just need to find an armorer or a blacksmith."

She clears her throat. "Why?"

"Are you always invested in your customers' business?" "When they want to seek a weapon, yes." I hum, and she elaborated, "Vwriynn, the main island, was destroyed because of strangers with access to weapons. King Alistair has made Silver City a safe place for anyone to live, and there are rules we must follow. To include no weapons. There is no need for any. The guards have them, but that's to protect us. I'll have to report you."

"I wouldn't." I snarl.

She smiles. "Or you could tell me why you're here."

This woman is old, but something about her tells me she isn't messing around. "I don't take it kindly to be blackmailed."

"And I'm just trying to ensure you're not here to cause trouble." She backfires.

"I'm looking for someone." You might as well start with a half-truth. "She's critical to me and the person who took her. Well, he isn't unarmed, and I fear the only way I can get her back is with force."

"I see." She rubs her chin. "If she is in the city's gates, you must report it to the Watch. They'll be able to help you locate her."

I shake my head from side to side. "No. I know where she is. It's getting her back that's the issue."

"And you think this will be resolved with violence?" "If need be," I reply under my breath.

She sighs. "Give me a reason to trust you, and I might be able to help you out."

How can I convince a stranger to trust me? As if the fates are on my side, I hear Davi walk beside me, freshly showered and dressed in new clothes.

"And I see my daughter's clothes fit you well." the woman comments, and I laugh. Davi scowls but then thanks her. "I suppose you'll be seeking a weapon as well?"

"Me? No. But I see my friend has told you why he needs one?" Davi responds.

"He was just getting to the part about convincing me not to report you both." she states with a judgmental eye on me.

Davi reaches out and touches her arm; simultaneously, I see him dig into his rune bag. "You can trust us." I feel magic in the air as a ringing sound briefly hits my ears. The woman's eyes widened, and then Davi let her go. She pulls out a parchment and ink pen, scribbles something down, and then digs her pocket for something.

"Take this and go here. Ask for Cordelia." I look down and see the name of a building. A golden coin decorated with a firebird sits on top of it.

"Thank you." Davi nods and then grabs the stuff before guiding me outside.

When we're far enough away, I go to ask what he did, but he speaks before I can.

"A small Rune Master trick."

"Though they were just for portal-ling?" "And that's why they never chose you." "Care to explain further?"

"No, Dark One. Some secrets of the Runes are more important than any threat you could ever give me."

I can respect him for that.

We approach the building, and they all look the same, except this one has a golden phoenix carved into the door. I knock three times, and the eyehole slides open. "We request a visit with Cordelia."

The piece slams back into place, the locks turn, and the door opens. We walk inside, and then a chill runs up my spine. My vision changes to see through the pitch black, but at the last second, I see someone coming at me with a large log; I catch their wrist, but don't see the one behind me as pain erupts in the back of my head before I fall forward. Davi's limp body lies opposite mine, and my vision fades as unconsciousness envelops me.

# 22

# SERENA

As a little girl, I watched the Bird keeper across the path feed and sell different kinds of food. The prettiest ones were the blue jays and cardinals. Their feathers would shine brightly when the sun would hit them to ride. I always wanted to run my hand across them. One day, I ventured out alone when no one was watching. There was a cage at my eye level, and I reached inside. The feathers felt better than I imagined in my head. Smooth, silky, and clean.

They made the bleakness of Narborim fade away for a few minutes. At that moment, I wasn't a half-elf girl trapped in the isolation of her rotting house. I was just a girl petting a bird in those few stolen minutes.

And then that moment ended.

The Bird keeper reached my wrist and clamped down as hard as she could before tossing me into the mud. I was scared, humiliated, and trapped. That's how I feel right now. Caught in the clutches of an elf who believes I'm a gift from the fates. Aside from his president ogling from the other side of these iron bars, his intentions are unknown.

*I don't understand why I haven't changed back.* The mind-numbing thought has been running on repeat since it happened. I'm not sure how this happened, or why I can't seem to control the essence inside of me, but I'm starting to fear that I may never transfigure again.

*Alwin! I call through our bond. Please give me a sign that you are still connected with me.* I reached out to him. Our tether strained from the distances and iron separating us. Even with all my fire- power, I feel cold without him, like a wall of ice blocking me from getting to him.

The door to the room creaks open on its hinges, and in comes to my captor. Alistair McCain, King of Silver City. That's how he introduced himself to me when the net shot into the sky took me down. His hair is trimmed short above his pointed ears, and his eyes are blue grey, almost like Alwin's. He has a beard and mustache, the color of snow. Come to think of it, he looks nearly identical to Alwin aside from his age.

"Hello, firebird," he greets me with a smile, a tiny piece of meat pinched between his finger and thumb. I eye it, but nothing about it seems to be appetizing. "You must be hungry after flying here from the outer realms. Where do the fates reside?"

I don't acknowledge him. Turning my beak up at the raw food he's trying to feed me. Closing my eyes, I focus on returning to my regular form. Nothing happens, and I don't know why. What happened between jumping in that pool and breaking the surface?

"When you're hungry, truly starving, you'll eat whatever I give you." He sighs, tosses the meat onto a plate, and picks up a vine of grapes. Their vibrant purple color and fruity scent make my mouth water. An involuntary noise escapes me, echoing through the room, and he smiles. Juices from his half-eaten food dripped down his chin. "A fruit lover? Very well." He presents it to me, and I greedily peck one off the vine. "Good. Eat. You'll need to refuel your energy before I suggest you to the people. They've worshiped you for decades.

"Did you know you're a legend around here? An inspiration to my citizens. That's why you see the phoenix painted everywhere." I swallow the pieces of grape, look around for something to drink, and notice a small bowl of water. We continue to share the delicious fruit while he rambles about why I'm here and what it means to this city. "I've been around for a few centuries, Firebird. When I learned about you, your power, and the endless possibilities that your existence could mean, I vowed to myself that if I ever saw you, I'd make you mine. That's why I invented the perfect cage.

These bars," he said, gripping one while putting the empty vine down, "are not just made with pure iron.

"It's infused with the essence of two tarot cards." Alistair digs into his pocket and pulls out a deck. He was shouting at them while keeping his eyes squarely on me. "The thing that non-tarot masters don't know is how powerful these painted parchments are. Each one has power of their own. You can't control exactly what they gift you with, but they learn from you after many years of bonding. Your mind, body, and soul." He stops shuffling and pulls the top two cards, revealing them to me without looking at them.

"*The Chariot* and *The Hermit*. Both have multiple meanings, but know I needed to level up this cage and the net used to bring you down." That's how these items are so powerful. I can't feel my essence at all. "And that's why you aren't in your true form." I caw at him, asking him to elaborate and question how he knows I'm not a bird. He gives me a pearly white smile. "Yes, Firebird, I know what you are. Inside that fire-feathered bodice is a two-legged being ready to break free. That won't happen until I let you out of this cage." My wings flap, trying to get him to understand that is precisely what I want.

Alistair laughs, pushes to his feet, and puts his cards back into his pocket. "Don't fret; I will free you once I know why you're here. Then, when you agree to stand by my side as my Queen, you'll be presented to the people in whatever being you are. Elf, human, dwarf, it makes no difference to me." The doors to the chamber swing open, revealing a man who seems to be a guard.

"My Lord, I apologize for the interruption, but there have been reports of two strangers wandering around the Front Market." the Guard states.

"This place is a sanctuary, and you know my policy. They're meant to be here if they make it through the barrier." Alistair responds.

"Of course. It's just they're here inquiring about purchasing weapons." Alistair rubs his beard at this. "And..."

The Shadow King approaches the guard, giving him his full attention. "Spit it out."

"One appears to have the same essence as you, My Lord." "Who says this?" he asks.

The Guard's eyes darted to me and then back to his king. My chest tightens as I try to diffuse the rampant thoughts racing through my head. Alwin wouldn't use his powers openly if he thought it wasn't safe. I don't believe Davi is foolish enough to reveal who he is. But as the saying goes, whatever fate decides is already set in stone. "She did. The innkeeper."

Alistair seems to ponder this momentarily before nodding. "And these two have been subdued?"

"She sent them to *her*."

"Very well. Have them brought to the cells." Alistair turns on his heel and approaches me. His eyes narrow as a smile breaks free before he says, "Something tells me you didn't come alone, Firebird. Don't worry; you'll see your companions again." By the sinister look reflecting in his eyes, I try to call upon my power, but a bucket of numbing balm has been poured all over me. My wings flap frantically as my chest tightens, and the screeching tearing through my throat causes tears in my eyes.

The rest of the day went on slowly, leaving me thinking of endless terrible possibilities. I attempted to transform through the bleak loneliness multiple times, but nothing happened.

My powers are failing me.

I only lifted my head when Alistair came waltzing inside with a trail of people following him. Servants, guards, other members of his court, and then finally, two men, bagged and bounded, were ushered inside. I knew the instant I saw the tall one that it was him. He was here. Alive and appearing unharmed.

Alwin and Davi were forced to the marble floor; Alistair took his throne, the impact of their knees resounding in my ears. Two women, wearing a silver mask covering their faces aside from their eyes and nose, stood at either side. They were dressed in pure skintight clothing matching the color of their mask.

I looked around the room, memorizing each face I could so that if any harm came to my mate, I'd know who to turn into ash. "The trial for the two trespassers has begun." one of the guardsmen spoke.

"Tall one," Alistair started pointing at Alwin, although he couldn't see through the bag over his eyes. "Remove the bag."

The woman on Alwin's right does as ordered. I watch him blink at the brightest, his hair falling across his shoulders. Something that resembled the color of blood coating his forehead. I squinted to see better, and my fire came alive when I did.

Each head turned to me. My rage and flames burning through the bars echoed around the room. I could see the bars beginning to bend against my essence. So I didn't stop.

No matter the terror I was causing. No matter what Alistair would do.

The only thought coursing through my head was that they hurt my mate, and now they have to pay.

"The Phoenix, it's melting the bars." someone said. "Not possible. They're pure iron." another responded. The fright in their voices only fueled me further.

*Good. Be afraid of me. Fear my power.*

I push and push as the metal begins to melt. Each drop brings me closer to freedom. A shadow comes over me; two dark hands grip the bars and pull them together.

"No!" It comes out in my normal voice. "It's a she-elf." one of the guards exclaims.

I look down, seeing that I'm standing on two feet, my body draped in a dress of gold and crimson flames. Wings of fire burn brightly at my back while fire sprays from my palms. My eyes lock with Alistairs as the fight for control continues. I snarled, and he sneered, sweat beading across his brow.

"Kill them!" he commands.

"Stop!" I scream, my gaze cutting to the two men kneeling on the floor. Alwin's eyes meet mine, and a blade comes across his neck. His body falls to the floor, blood pooling around him. Those eyes that ensnared mine every time we made love, blinking, his soul fading.

"Murderer."

My essence tears through me in an explosion of flames and light, knocking everyone into the walls and causing debris to fall from the ceiling. All I see is red.

I lock eyes with the woman in silver closest to Alwin and approach her. She stands with a blade in hand, her bright eyes revealing no fear, and I catch the subtlest movement beneath her mask. She's mocking me with a smile.

I don't give her mercy. Pointing one finger at her, I let my fire go, but she dodged and struck my neck. My shield of heat burns her hand, and she screams, stumbling backward. This time, I see it. The fear and it's intoxicating.

"You should've never touched my mate." I snarl before igniting the spot where she stood, my fire consuming her body, screams, mind, and soul. A single sound resounded throughout the hall when the hilt hit the floor. Beside it, a pile of ash.

"Serena." I hear Davi call my name and turn to him. His bindings are free, his bag removed, and his eyes widened, a mix of admiration and trepidation shining back at me.

"Did they hurt you?" I ask him. He shakes his head from side to side. Then I look over to the Shadow King, the pads of my feet leaving a trail of cinders in the floor. He stands before me, his deck of cards out in preparation to fight me. But he doesn't know I have my essence of tarot ready to defend me.

"Pheonix, I meant no harm. If you let me, I can heal him, but I must move quickly." Alistair pleads. The taunting and belittling tone from earlier was replaced with terror.

"If you're lying to me, you will join my mate in the afterlife," I warn, and he nods his understanding.

Alistair moves swiftly, rushing over to Alwin's limp body. He does exactly what I saw my mate do with Davi—touching his heart and forehead. Incoherent words pass his lips, and I watch, pleading with the fates to not take him from him. We've been separated for far too long.

Golden light shines under his palms, and the hum of magic dances in the air between us. I watched and waited for hours, which were only minutes. My attention was solely on his chest. When it finally rose, relief and tears flooded me. I raced to his side, lifting his cold hand to mine and kissing it. Brushing the hair from his face, I saw him blink a few times before he fell into a deep sleep.

"He'll sleep for a day or two. I had to pull him from the edge." Alistair explained. "I will set you up in guest chambers."

Alistair attempted to move, but I swiftly grabbed him by the neck. My sharpened nails sank into his skin as I lifted him off the ground while pushing myself to my feet. His feet dangled in front of me, hands desperately scratching at my arm, urging me to release him. "You ordered him to die. We came here for help, but your first instinct was imprisoning us. No one touches him without paying the price."

Something deep inside of me that I didn't know was there rose its head up. I latched onto it. A branch contacted me from my ancestor's past, showing me this was the right thing to do. This was the power of the true Phoenix, and to use it only when necessary because it can't be undone once I do this.

"Phoenix, please!" I saw my reflection shining in him. My flames consumed my body aside from the hand around his throat.

"You've abused the gifts you were given, and now, I shall take them away." Inhaling deeply, I pushed the essence into him, whispering the spell of undoing, "Has ego potestates a te."

Alistair's screams of pain are far off in the distance as I feel the shadows leaving him. I was detached from his soul, dissipating against the light of my flames. It's alarming and empowering. His body slumps over, and I let him fall to the floor.

"What did you do to him?" Davi asks, his voice low with caution.

"I did the only thing worse than death." Davi looked at me as I stared into the Rune Masters's face and continued, "I burned the essence from his soul. The Shadow King is no more."

"You mean he's non-magic?" Davi asks, and I nod. "Oh, my fates."

"Alistair is still a tarot master in skill, but he has no power of the cards in his pocket. He can no longer command the power of healing through Rieke. So, yes, Davi, he has no more magic." I explained.

A groan came from Alistair as he struggled to his feet. I was immediately looking smaller than when I first laid eyes upon him. "You... you bitch. How could you? After I saved him."

"You killed him. And so many others." I responded, uncaring what insult he would come up with next.

"For someone who loves the ancient firebird so much, you know so little about her true power. And messing with her mate was the dumbest thing anyone could ever do." Davi said to the King. "Now, what should we do with the rest of them?"

I turned to face the crowd, all paralyzed with fear at my feet. "You may all return home. There is nothing left for you here."

"All except you two." Davi pointed to the other woman in silver and another dressed in black and brown leather. The two fell on their knees at my feet.

"Go home," I commanded; they looked at me confused at first, but then scrambled to their feet and took off out the door.

"Why?"

"Davi, shut it. Or you will need to find the next Rune Master before your time is up."

## 23

## ALWIN

"I still don't know how she did that." I hear Davi's hushed tones as I blink away the brain fog.

My neck is sore, and I swore I could remember dying. I sit up slowly and examine the room I'm in. Davi is in the corner speaking with no one? Or himself? I'm not sure, but that doesn't matter because I'm no longer chained, nor is he. No bars surround us, but one thing doesn't make sense.

"Where is she?" I hoarsely ask. I rub my neck and try to clear my throat. Davi turns to me, stuffing something like his Runes back inside his pocket before walking over to me and picking up a cup of water. "What happened?"

"You died. Serena saved us. Killed the lady in silver that slit your throat and then burned Alistair's essence from his soul." I blink three times to ensure I'm no longer sleeping. "Your mate is powerful. More so than anyone has ever known since the first Phoenix walked the universe."

Did she burn his essence? Not possible. "Where is she? What do you mean I died? How am I sitting here talking to you if that were the case?" I sip on more water, slowly trying to calm the aching in my throat. Each word feels like I'm dragging nails across my windpipe.

He sighs. "Serena is waiting in the throne hall for you."

Immediately, I stand. Initially, I am a little dizzy, but I brush that off and move towards the door. "Alwin," Davi's concern makes me pause as I turn the handle and look at him over my shoulder. "There is something different about her since we came here."

"It's been a day; how much could she have changed since the last sunrise?" I don't wait for him to answer, and I take my leave of him. At first, I noticed how lost I was until a guard pointed me in the right direction. If that isn't daunting, I'm not sure what is.

"Dark One," another guard bows, and I'm unsure what else to do.

"The Phoenix Queen is waiting for you." another states, escorting me down a narrow corridor and through an arched open doorway that leads directly into the throne room. The last place I remember seeing her alive, behind bars in her firebird form.

As I walk in, my breath is caught at the sight before me. There is no longer a trapped bird in a cage but my beautiful mate, sitting on a throne of flames with a dress made of fire covering her. Her hair is braided in two, the tails just brushing her navel. I swallow down the lump in my throat and make my way to her. She catches sight of me and is instantly on her feet, soon in my arms.

Her fiery scent engulfs, but her flames do not. "Alwin." "Serena, what happened? Puny said some crazy stuff, but I'd

rather hear from you." She pulls back from me, her hands cupping my face as she pulls me in for a deep kiss. Our tongues collide in heat and passion. Her hands move to the hem of my shirt, ripping it from me as my back hits a wall. "Fuck now, talk later."

My hands skim her body, the flames disappearing to reveal her naked form to me. "It's been too long, my mate."

Serena pulls my pants to my ankles, my cock springs free, and she wraps her long fingers around my shaft, pumping me up and down as I devour her mouth. My shadows come to life as my mate bond recognizes her. I run my fingers through her soaking pussy and insert two fingers, pumping before moving my hands to her hips and lifting her so she can wrap her legs around me. My tip nudged at her entrance, and in one move, I thrust inside of her, making us both moan.

Our foreheads press together for a brief moment before I spin us, pushing her into the wall and pumping in and out of her at a fast pace. I feel her nails raking down my back as my tongue trails the length of her neck. "Alwin." she moans my name, which awakens my need for her.

"Serena." I capture her lips as I palm her breast with one hand and use the other to tease her bundle of nerves that I know makes her go crazy. My mouth waters to taste her. I lean forward after moving my hands back to support her hips and claim each nipple. Nibbling until I swirl my tongue around them and sucking until I leave my mark. She begins to clench around me, and I know she's close to her first climax.

I capture her mouth with mine again and move one hand to her clit, pinching and rubbing until finally, she squeezes my cock, moaning my name. She opens her eyes, looking at me with all the love I feel for her, reflecting on me. Her feet are lower to the ground, but I'm not done with her yet. I pull out, then lift her into my arms, carrying her to her new seat of power.

"They call you the Phoenix Queen." I sit down; she positions herself in front of me with her back to me, then sinks. I pull her back to me, my arm across her chest, and the other snakes around her waist. Her wings of flames are gone; just like any additional time, I touch her from behind. "I always knew you were a Queen, Serena. Mine, and right now, I'm going to fuck you on this throne while you scream my name so this entire city knows exactly who you belong to."

I don't wait for her response as I move in and out of her, our bodies building sweat and my pace speeding with each thrust. I sink my teeth into the side of her neck, causing her head to fall back against my shoulder and her nails to dig into my thighs. Every pleasure I give her matches the small pinches of pain she brings me. Serena is my mate, and I can only consider pleasing her. Feeling her pussy clench down and milking me until her womb is filled with my seed.

"Alwin," she moans, and I move the hand from her chest to her mouth; she sucks on my fingers, and I groan, pumping faster. I'm getting close as I feel my balls seizing up, but I know she needs to climax with me. I gag her, then use my hand around her waist to move to her clit and rub until I feel her orgasm building.

"Now, Serena," I command, and with her teeth biting into my fingers, she brings us both over the edge; I spill my seed into her as she clenches down around me through her climax. We sit there for a few heartbeats, our bodies relaxing as we come down from our high.

I trace my fingers up and down her back, causing gooseflesh to rise, and she sighs. I'm unsure if she's ready to talk, but I know she will once she's ready. Serena interlaces her fingers with my free hand and brings the back of my hand up to her lips for a soft kiss. "Alwin, there are some things I need to tell you."

"I know, Firebird. When you're ready." I assure her.

"Let's get cleaned up, and then we will talk." After untangling ourselves from one another, I redress, and she covers her body in those flames again. I watch as she moves over to a table and pours liquid from a decanter into two cups, handing one to me. She seems nervous, and I hate that she feels this way when it's just the two of us.

"Tell me, Serena. Nothing you can say will keep me from you." She flashes a half-smile and begins.

I listened to every detail from beginning to end, starting from when she went through the wall to when I was taken to the infirmary. "And it just clicked when I saw your soul leaving your eyes. A well of power overflowing as a damn that was blocking it burst open. It was unlike anything I'd ever seen or felt before. I heard ancient ones speaking inside my head, filling it with different spells and visions of past phoenixes. When I killed that woman, I could see nothing but red. Every thought that passed through my head was turning her to ask for what she did to you. Then, when I faced Alistair, the man who is the reason we're here, the reason that child was dead, and who captured me, I knew what I had to do."

Her eyes met mine in a flash of worry. She was afraid to confirm what Davi had told me. I reached for her, and she didn't shy away, allowing me to pull her close to comfort her emotions, guilt, shame, or power.

"Tell me what you did, Firebird." She lowered her chin, but I lifted it, keeping my gaze locked. "I know saying it out loud will make it real to you, but I need to hear it, and so do you."

Tears swelled in her eyes, and I could see it. The turmoil she was feeling for what she had done. What she had taken from another like us. "I burned... I burned his essence from him, making him a nonmagic."

I wiped each tear from her cheer before reassuring her, "You did what you thought was right, Serena. There is no shame in that."

"I'm a monster, Alwin." She backs away from me, looking at her hands like poisonous vipers ready to strike. "This power inside of me, it's dark."

"But it's also light." I step towards her, but she halts me with her hand up. I keep forcing her until her back is against the wall, the tips of her toes are brushing my boots, and our chests are rubbing against one another. "You're my mate, Serena, and I'm called the Dark One. The darkness inside you is part of the balance of our bond." I pull my shirt aside to reveal our imprint. My shadow swirls, dancing around her phoenix form. "You were born from the light, and I from the dark.

Our bond gives us the equilibrium we both need to survive. Neither one of us is tipping the scale in either direction." I'm so close to her now; our breath mingles, and her scent is washing over me. The smell of our mixed cum was still strong inside of her. "You saw me die, that made the scale lean to the shadows, and you discovered a new gift. And to me, it is one because now we have a secret weapon that can be used to defeat not only Queen Lilac but also the Amazon Queen. Those two thrive on their ability to use essence."

"Because death is too good for the likes of them." she whispers. "That's right, Firebird." I wink, and that coaxes a smile out of her. "Keep that smile, Serena. Don't let anything or anyone take that from you." I lean down and kiss her. I am pouring all my strength and love for her into it because that's what she needs from me. And I realized long ago that I would do anything for her. Be anyone to her because she is my fate; she will be the next Queen of this universe, and I'll be right by her side. If not only for her to mate with but as a weapon for her to use at her will.

Someone clears their throat, causing us to break apart, and I roll my eyes as Puny's scent fills my nose. We both turn to look at him. "Sorry to interrupt, but he's asking for you."

"Alistair. You have him locked away?" I ask her.

"Seemed only right to do to him what he did to me. Powerless and behind bars." She shrugs, and I smirk, can't help but feel pride swell in my chest. "Bring him here or have the guards do it. I think it's time for Alistair, the former Shadow King, to meet the new one."

She links her hand with mine, walking me over to the throne before taking a seat. I stand over her right shoulder, keeping a protective arm across her chest. Not that she needs it.

\*\*\*

## ALWIN

Alistair looks strikingly familiar to me. Only he has white hair on his head and face. He's kneeling before us, and Serena looks him over a few times before signaling Puny to let him speak.

"I see the throne suites you." He croaks out.

"What do you want, Alistair?" Serena asks, sounding annoyed. "A pardon or a chance to work on an alliance with you and your mate." He points to me but doesn't look at me. He appears to be afraid to meet my eye. This could be due to his weakened state now that he is no more than a nonmagic elf.

"There's nothing you could offer me except for your head. Which I'm still inclined to take. I need it to free someone very dear to me." That catches my attention. She doesn't feel threatened if she reveals that to him.

"So, your purpose for coming here was an assassination?" He accuses.

"My purpose for coming here would've been friendly if you hadn't captured first and asked questions later." Serena snaps. "Give me one reason why I should keep you alive. Your people have welcomed me as their new Queen within less than the sunrise I've sat on this throne. Your armies and guards pledge their loyalty to me and every council member. What could you possibly offer me?"

Alistair's eyes cut around the room as he looks for the answer on one of the walls. "I used Reiki to heal him. There are so few masters left in the universe. I can teach you." He spits out.

"Without your essence, the ritual is useless. I have no desire to become a healer." she retorts. Alistair fumbles for another answer.

"What about shadow magic? There are things your mate doesn't know I could teach him."

I answer this time, "There's nothing that I don't know, old man." "Be that as it may, I'm still older than you, boy." This time, our eyes lock, and I get a clear view of his face. I study it while he continues to ramble on about training me in ways my father taught me—an image of when I was six years old flashes in my head. A man is standing next to my father; they're identical twins, but this one has a scar across his right cheek. I return to the present, and my feet move on their own accord as I close the distance between him and me. When I reach him, I lift him, brushing my fingers through his beard until I feel the uneven skin.

"How did you get that?" I ask.

"What? None of your business, and put me down." He snaps. "Where are you from? Did you have a twin?" The questions pour

out of me as I realize who this man is to me. "Was your brother Alfred?"

His eyes widen at the mention of my father's name. "How do you know that name?"

"Answer my questions first." I challenged him before dropping him to the floor.

"Alwin, do you know him?" Serena asks.

Alistair's eyes meet mine as he rubs the spot on his cheek before standing. "My older brother gave me this scar when we were children. It was during a dagger training session, and he went too far. Of course, my father never stepped in to stop him until he saw the blood."

Fuck.

"We can't kill him," I whisper to my mate. "He's my uncle."

# 24

# SERENA

After the revelation in the throne hall, we retired to the dining hall and had food brought in so Alistair could reconnect with

his nephew, who hadn't seen him in over two centuries. I keep forgetting how old Alwin is compared to me, but he was never half-human.

"Alfred, damn him, kept me from you when I tried to stop him from following down your grandfather's path," Alistair said between sips of water. "He wanted to make you unbeatable mind and body like we were. Then, when the time came for me to stop him, I was banished here to Vwriynn. There was nothing here but what you've seen. I came to this small, secluded island and made it mine. Slowly returning to the mainland to find any locals I could that were willing to help me build Silver City, and in return, I grant them sanctuary."

*Fuck, he sounds like a saint now.*

"Who taught you to be a Tarot Master? And where did you learn Reiki? As far as I know, Master Mikao is the only Master alive." Alwin stated.

Alistair smiled at the mention of the Reiki Master. "Well, I've had a few run-ins with Master Mikao. He's taught me a few tricks here and there because I needed something to teach the people within these walls if we were going to thrive. The tarot, that's something different." He pauses, reflecting, and I can see sadness and fondness mixing in his eyes. "I had a teacher, and his name was Master Runk. He was human, honest, and very in tune with his cards. Every time he spoke about one, it was as if he was reading it from one of the ancient scrolls. He passed down everything he knew, including his deck, to me before he passed."

*Now, I feel humiliated. What was I thinking?*

Alwin must've sensed my distress and placed a calming hand on my thigh.

"Do not fret, Phoenix Queen, you taking my essence from me is not the end of the world. I have many talents, as I told you, that can be useful to all of us. Including the Puny one." I chuckled at using Alwin's nickname for Davi as we watched him scarf down a chicken thigh. "What role does he play in this little trio?"

"Puny is a Rune Master." I answered.

"A Master of Runes, how rare a find. There is great honor in your practice." Alistair says to Davi, who has just finished swallowing a mouthful.

"Thank you." he responds.

"Now that we're all being honest with one another, why don't you start telling me why you are here?" Alistair asked before biting into a piece of bread.

I look at Alwin, who nods for me to take charge. "To make an incredibly long story short, the Amazon Queen has captured our friends, and the only way to get them back is by bringing your head to her."

"I see." He hums, his lips pressing against the rim of his cup. "We weren't going to. We plan to ask you for your allegiance in the fight against her and Queen Lilac of Xora." Alwin added. "Uncle, is there anything you can tell us about her? How do you fight her and win? My powers are useless against her."

The three of us wait while Alistair ponders his response. "I have a way, but without my essence, it's pointless."

"Tell us, and we can figure out something." I plead.

"You," he points to me, "must pardon me and grant me permission to stay here, seeing this is my home."

"Done," I state.

"You." He points to Davi, "need to power up every Rune you have. I can get you whatever ingredients you need aside from dragon bone. That is very hard to come by." Davi acknowledges him, and then he moves on to Alwin. "You, my dear nephew, must return to Master Mikao and become his apprentice. The only way for us to be ready is if one of us has the power to heal the other."

"Leave here? Without my mate? No." Alwin states, crossing his arms.

"Fine. Bring him here; I'm sure Serena knows how to summon a portal using the Moon Card." At the mention of using my cards, I look away. He doesn't know I'm not a master, not even a novice. "I see. She doesn't know how the cards work. I can train her, but it will take time. For now, I will work on helping you learn one card that will help free your friends. The Devil card will be the one we focus on. Since your Rune Master can summon portals, we should be all set in about two weeks."

"Two weeks? But Niya and Rose may not have that." I protest. "Is there another Tarot Master or apprentice we could call upon within this realm?" Alwin asks.

Alistair shakes his head from side to side. "I'm not saying it will take that long for Serena to learn how to work with the card, but it may take that long for your Rune Master to restore his blank tiles. Especially since getting access to dragon bones means a portal link to Xora, the only known dragon colony."

"I may have a way of getting it faster," Alwin states, and I grip his wrist.

"Are you sure?"

"Braxor and I have a pact." he responds.

"Then it's settled. Alwin will work with getting the dragon's bone here while Davi begins getting the ingredients ready for the restoration spell, and Serena and I will begin our training. Oh, and Alwin will need to have Master Mikao come here." Alistair sounds more pleased with himself than we are feeling now.

\* \* \*

Back in our chambers, shown to us by Alistair, I fluff a pillow before walking over to the wardrobe and looking at the emptiness inside. A sigh escapes me, but the smell of bathing oils has me perking up as I feel Alwin's heat pressing against my back. His teeth nipped at my ear, and our naked bodies pressed together.

"We'll have new clothes brought to you tomorrow." he whispers. "Although, I do approve of flames or nothing at all."

I turn in his arms, my smile faltering. "I didn't have to take his powers."

"Don't do that to yourself."

"But it's true. If he had his essence, we wouldn't need to worry about me training to become a novice Tarot reader." I sigh and lean into his bare chest, soaking in his presence.

He grips my hand and walks me to the bathing chamber. There's a tub big enough for both of us to fit comfortably. I nuzzle in between his legs, his half-erected cock digging into my back. Alwin lathers his hands in oils and presses his fingers into my back muscles. I begin to relax, closing my eyes and letting him take control of my body.

"Are you ready for your coronation tomorrow?" he asks, and my eyes pop open.

"What? When was that discussed?"

"When you left the table, Alistair informed me that for you to become Queen of this realm truly, there needs to be a ceremony, which must happen quickly. He knows you were bluffing about the loyalty of his armies and guards. He thinks having the ceremony tomorrow will ensure they pledge themselves to you."

"I don't deserve nor want to be anyone's Queen." I sigh. "You're mine already, Firebird. And I think it's wise to take

control when offered. We need more power to fight a war against Queen Lilac's armies." He's right, of course.

"If I am Queen, what does that make you?" His fingers stopped, and I feared I may have insulted him, but then he shuffled behind me, making water splash, and I went to turn, and what I saw had my breath catching momentarily. "Alwin, is that?"

"I know the timing may not be right, but we've already accepted each other as mates, and I figured this could be the next step." In his hand is a gilded ring with phoenix wings and an obsidian stone at the center. "Serena Ozark, will you do me the honor of becoming my wife?"

My eyes drifted between the ring and my mate, and as I said, "With all my heart, Alwin, I will marry you."

He slides the ring on my left finger, and I wrap my arms around him, our lips meeting as I straddle him. "Is this truly what you want? For us to become Queen and King of a realm we're not from nor familiar with?"

Alwin's hands rest on my hips under the water, and he looks at me. "As long as we do it together, there isn't anything I wouldn't do with you, Firebird."

"So, we have a plan?" I ask.

"Indeed, we do. You become a Tarot Master, I a Reike Apprentice, and Puny will restore his pieces of rock to portal us back to Whitfrost to save Niya and Rose. Until then," he pauses, then I feel his cock twitching beneath me. "I intend to spend every moment I can worshiping you as my Queen." He lines his tip to my entrance and pushes me down onto him in one move. "My wife." He thrusts, and my head falls back in pleasure. "My mate."

I let him remain in control, his mouth, tongue, teeth, and cock bringing me to my first orgasm. Alwin thrust inside of me, his grip on my hips hard enough to bruise as I kept my grip on his shoulders, our tongues dancing while I rode him. One of his hands finds my clit, and he rubs it just like until I'm clenching down on him. "Alwin."

"Serena." He moans, capturing my left nipple and teasing it between his teeth. "Fuck, I can't wait to taste all of you."

Then he stands, bringing me with him. He walks us over to a bench where our towels are hanging over, sets me, then kneels between my legs, lifting each one so my knees are aligned with his shoulders, giving him the perfect access to my pussy. Alwin runs his tongue over the center, causing me to shiver, and I grip his hair. His fingers tease my inner thighs while he sucks and licks, his tongue diving into my soaking entrance, and I begin to move against it, riding him shamelessly.

Two of his fingers move inside of my pussy while the other explores my ass. A territory we have yet to talk about but one I'm willing to go to with him. "Alwin."

"Only if you wish to." I nod, and he begins to prep it with my previous orgasm. With his mouth on my clit, he has two fingers pumping me in and out while the third still nudges slowly. He inches forward, and there's a burn, but I can take it. Alwin goes to his knuckle and picks up pace before beginning to add a second finger to my ass. My body is stretched, and I'm on the verge of climax again. "Ride my fingers, Firebird. Make yourself cum."

His words lit a fire inside me, and I did as he said. Taking control, riding his fingers while he sucks on my clit, and I feel my orgasm building until I release it. Clenching down hard on him and moaning his name. I don't get time to relax before the hunger in- side of me has me pouncing on him. He falls to the floor, and I straddle him, sinking, and I fuck him. My nails dig into his chest as I move up and down, bringing us both to oblivion. When he's done spilling his seed inside of me, I get off and lick him clean before crawling up to him and kissing him.

We lay on the cold floor for a few minutes before returning to the bath to clean ourselves. I use my fire heat to dry us entirely before we get into our bed, neither of us caring about being naked. Alwin wraps his arms around me, his hand resting on my belly while the other is under the pillow where I have my head. An image of our future comes to mind and has my thoughts buzzing with possibilities. I'm afraid to voice one, but not because of the reasons any bride would have.

"Tell me what's on your mind, Firebird." "Trying to read my thoughts?" I tease.

"You can let me in if it would make it easier." He suggests, and I let my mental walls down, sending him the images and words I won't voice. "One day, when our world is safe, I will gladly fill your womb with our children. A Prince or Princes of shadow fire would be a force this world won't be ready for."

I turn to face him, my heart growing more prominent at the thought of being a mother to his children someday. I cup his cheek, press a chaste kiss to his lips, and look deep into his eyes as I say with all the truth and courage I can muster, "I don't want to wait, Alwin. Tomorrow night, I want to start trying to be a mother. It would never prevent me from doing my duty to this world or the next. I am to be your wife, a Queen, and even if I become with child, I know they will be safe inside of me when the day comes for us to go to war."

Alwin looks at me and smiles, then rolls on top of me nudging my thighs apart. "Why wait another night?"

I laugh. "Have you not had enough of me?"

"Never, Firebird. I'll remove the spell of contraception, right," he closes his eyes, and I can feel the magic coming from him. "Now." He reaches down and lines his tip up to me. I thought I'd be sore, but I'm not there, and he pushes inside of me. "Once I spill my seed in you, that's it. There is no turning back. You will become with child. Are you sure you want this?"

I don't hesitate to answer him, "Yes, Alwin."

Our lips meet only instead of the lust-filled hunger from earlier; it's slow and full of love. As is the rest of the night. As we begin a new chapter, we make love under ribbons of fire and shadow. In nine months, a child of Shadowfire will be born.

\* \* \*

The following day, I was busy preparing for the ceremonies tonight: a wedding and a coronation taking place all at once. Alistair had brought clothes that fit my new status, but he also added some shirts and pants, knowing I would only wear dresses during ceremonies. Or I assume that's what Alwin told him.

There would be no training for me today. Davi was already working hard with the Royal Apothecary, letting the restoration spell start. Alwin went off privately to contact Braxor and hopefully get a message to Master Mikao. I took my alone time to explore some of the castle, but there wasn't much to it. A bunch of extra rooms meant for guests.

When I stumbled upon the training yard, I found Alistair training with a wooden dummy. "Now that I don't have my shadows, I can't let my other skills get rusty."

"I hope someday you can forgive me," I said as I approached him.

"There is nothing to forgive. If I met the person responsible for killing my mate, I'd have done the same thing." He smiles, puts his blade down, and then waves me to a table. "I think we can do some training with The Devil card, right?"

I nod and sit across from him as he pulls it out and places it in the center.

"A few things to know about this one. It means false truths, but there are several other subsidiary meanings to that as well. The one I intend for us to use it for would be to create a truth that the Amazon Queen will believe." I raise a brow, not understanding.

Alistair stands and walks over to the training armor, picking up a helmet to bring it back to the table. He sits again. "The Queen will look upon this helmet and believe it to be my head."

"I've seen someone use this card before. She used to disguise herself as another person. I initially believed it, but something about her gave it away." Odith was a vile person.

"That makes being a Tarot Master a gift and a curse. There is a temptation in this power, Serena. If you treat them right, they will protect you and provide for you, but if you abuse them, they will—"

"Turn against you." I interrupt, remembering what happened with Odith.

"So you do have some experience with them."

"You have no idea," I mumble, but he still hears me.

"Someday, if you want you can tell me, but for now, I want you to focus on your deck. You can't use mine, but imagine this card. The first step is communicating with them. Once you accomplish that, then we can move on to step two." he states.

"And how many steps are in this process?"

"Just focus on this one." I do as I'm told, pulling my deck from my pocket and imagining The Devil card. When there's a magic zap between my fingers and the painted parchments, I pull the card but sigh when it's wrong. "You won't get it in one day. You have a couple of hours before you need to get ready. Use this time and keep trying. Once you accomplish this, tell me, and we will continue."

After Alistair leaves, I keep trying, and with each card I pull, it becomes apparent I'm not the only one with the cards. Hours pass, and my fingers become numb to their feel as my eyes grow weary. Just as I contemplate giving up, I draw one last card, only to be interrupted by Davi calling my name before I can examine it.

"It's time to get ready for your wedding." I stand and walk over to him. "Also, Braxor has arrived with Master Mikao and the dragon bones I need."

"Alwin's connection to him is strong," I admit.

"Practicing your pulls? What card did you get?" Davi looks at my hand, and I eye the card.

"The Devil."

"And that means?"

"Step one is done." I push past him and race to my chambers.

Excitement fills me, as well as nerves.

*I'm getting married and becoming a Queen all in one night. Mother would've never believed this.*

# 25

# ALWIN

I never thought I'd see the day of my wedding. Before Serena, the idea of finding my mate and wife hadn't crossed my mind. The priority was always ensuring the freedom of those born like me—half-bloods or, as the humans called us: half-breeds. The world I pictured had a half-blood sitting on the throne, banning any laws against us. In a perfect world, no unnecessary bloodshed or prejudices would exist.

With Serena by my side, that vision has become more apparent and vital than last night. Deciding to bring a child into this world was quickly the fastest 'yes' I could've given to my mate. Everything and anything she's ever desired is going to be delivered to her on a silver platter. I wouldn't be standing here dressed in a finely tailored black suit if that weren't the case.

My hair is combed and pulled back in a half-up fashion. There is no color on me, and that is alright with me. The boots I'm wearing have been shined bright enough. You can see my reflection staring back at me, and I was given a scented oil to wear. I chose not to because it smelled too much like spiced rum, and I didn't want my bride to think

I needed to drink to survive this march down the aisle.

A knock sounded at my door, and Davi peeked his head inside. As our designated ring carrier, he was given a position of honor to stand at the altar with us. Alistair would be in with the crowd as it wasn't deemed appropriate for the former ruler to be seen with the new ones. The announcement of his stepping down so that his nephew and nephew's new bride would take over the reign of Silver City came as a shock to most of the citizens. As I stood by his side when we made the message from the balcony of the second level, I was anxious.

Would they revolt against us? Can I truly trust my uncle? So many thoughts were coursing through my brain that I didn't hear most of what he said until there was an uproar of cheers from the people below us.

"When my nephew found me, I was overjoyed by the news of his survival of the purge of our kind. I want you all to show your love and support for him as he takes my place as the new Shadow King of Silver City. His bride and fated is the Phoenix Queen we've all been waiting for." Alistair finished.

I scanned the crowd and saw a mix of admiration, intrigue, anger, and disappointment. It was unsettling.

"Say something." My uncle encouraged me.

I moved forward and, looking at no one in particular, began, "Thank you, Uncle. I first would like to commend you all on how fine a community you've helped build and maintain. I've never seen anything like this back where I'm from. Serena and I come to you willing to aid in whatever ailments you need resolving."

"We don't have any!" One person shouted.

"This city is a peaceful, thriving place. We don't want another King." Another protested, and others agreed, making the gathered crowd restless.

"Our intentions are not to rob you of your ruler. Alistair will remain at our side to advise and guide us in the ways of this wondrous city. There are threats outside of your barrier some of you don't know about. But I assure you, they are genuine." I swallowed as that made them go silent. Every eye on me, every ear hanging on each word passing my lips. "Those of you that are not of pure-blood, meaning coming from a sole lineage of a single species, there is a mighty Queen in the realm of Xora that would have you killed or go through convergence. Death is the likely result at her hand. It has been my mission for a century to rid this universe of genocide against our kind. I've lost many friends in this quest, but they've each taught me something before departing this world." I think of everyone that we lost during Odith's attack as it's the most recent.

"You have sanctuary here, which I don't intend to jeopardize. But I only ask for your help in return. Serena and I intend to fight this Queen's armies and overthrow her reign of terror, but for us to do so, we need an army. One that is willing and capable to fight against those that have essence. Whether it is the simplest form of controlling a single element or being a Tarot Master, all wielders are welcome to join us in this fight to free our brothers and sisters from certain death." Head turns, and whispers echo throughout. "Please do not feel obligated. But I ask that if you are volunteering, you come to the palace the day after my wedding and submit your name.

"There is great honor in serving a cause as noble as this. Freedom comes at a price, and some of you will pay it. The God of Death doesn't give life without intending to take it. Thank you for your continued support and loyalty during this haste transition."

"Alwin? Hello, oh fates, are you getting cold feet?" Davi's hand waving in my face has me blinking away the memory of this morning.

"No. Has Braxor arrived with Master Mikao?" That was another eventful hour. Calling on my friend used a lot of my strength, but when I finally reached him down our bond, the reception was clear. It turns out he's been in this realm before, and although he didn't like the sound of using dragon bones for a spell, he understood the need for it.

"Yes. They know to speak with you after tonight's proceedings." he answered.

"Okay. Let's get this thing started." I follow Davi to the throne hall, where both ceremonies will occur. One right after the other, and see it's packed with no one we know besides Master Mikao. Braxor, I imagine, is somewhere on the outside because he's much too large to fit inside this hall. The Master of Ceremonies is at the center, dressed in a white suit with golden floral imprints sewn into his sleeves. He looks about my uncle's age, only in human years.

"Welcome, Sire." He bows respectfully, and I grimace at the word.

"Thank you, but I'm not King yet," I whisper.

"True, but in an hour, you will be," I smirk at the older man, unsure how to respond. Alistair said this man had performed several weddings over the years and even knighthoods, guard hoods, and cruising of newborns.

Trumpets sounded, and the crowd rose as the announcement of my bride entering caught all of our attention. When the double doors opened, I couldn't believe my eyes. Serena was dressed in an off-the-shoulder gown of black and crimson feathers. All are sewn to perfection, representing the colors of our imprint, our essence. When she reached for my hand, I gladly took it, unable to concentrate on anything or anyone else but her.

"Beautiful." Is what I whispered, and I saw a pink color rise in her cheeks. Her hair was pinned to the top of her head to expose her face.

The words exchanged between us comprised traditional vows of devotion, duty, loyalty, and love—sentiments already deeply rooted between us. However, it was the sealing kiss that truly made it all feel real. Our lips meet in desire and passion. My wife and I didn't hold back, dipping her, skimming her body with my hands until I could lift her into my arms. Serena retained some semblance of control as she broke from my embrace.

"Alwin, we have an audience and still need to move on to the coronation."

"It's your fault, Firebird. If you wouldn't look so damn editable right now, I'd have control over my need to taste you. To fuck you on that throne again." She gasped, and I smiled but nodded my understanding. "To be continued."

The Master of Ceremonies gave us both a look of curiosity before gesturing to his helper to bring forth the two crowns and scepter. They laid on a velvet pillow of blue and looked heavier than I expected.

"With the power gifted to me by the fates and our former sovereign, Alistair, Shadow King of Silver City, I crown thee, Serena Ozark, Phoenix Queen, and her mate, Alwin, King of Shadows." Serena let out a heavy breath when her crown was placed upon her head, and as we took each other hand and hand, scepter in her other free, the crowd welcomed us with an uproar of cheers. When the ceremony ended, I carried my new wife to our chambers and discarded our clothing on the floor.

When I was on top of her, my lips meeting hers as she wrapped her legs around me, I could think of no better way to end this day than buried inside of her. I peppered her body with kisses until landing on her navel. A new life would soon blossom inside her womb, and I wanted our child to know me by voice.

"This is your father speaking." Serena giggled. "One day, you will be born, and things will be expected of you, but don't be afraid because you will have a wonderful mother to help you navigate this chaotic universe."

"Alwin, we don't know if I will immediately become a child. It could take months."

I smiled at her and moved back up her body, looking deep into her eyes as I said, "Then I guess we better keep practicing."

Our night was long, but I wouldn't change it for anything. After spilling my seed in her on the bed, we moved to the bath, then against the wall, and finally finished with her bent over the balcony looking out at our new home. We fell asleep that night in pure bliss, thoughts of war and destruction completely abolished from our minds as we looked forward to our family's future.

\* \* \*

"Alwin and Serena must stay here while they continue to train.

It's the only way to ensure the victory of this upcoming war." Alistair starts our meeting of council members.

Braxor is on the edge of the courtyard, which we decided was the best place to have this meeting. Davi is close to finishing the restoration spell, which means that Serena needs to fine-tune her power over The Devil card for our deception to work.

"I agree. Alwin has much to learn if he intends to become a healer. Although powerful, Serena still needs to trust in herself when mastering the cards." Master Mikao adds.

"Why are you two talking as if we're not sitting across from you?" she asks. "I pulled The Devil card yesterday and have many times over today. I'm ready for the next step."

"We'll see about that. Turning one object into another requires a lot of essence and concentration." Alistair argues. "If we send that boy into the lion's den with a faulty illusion, he'll be killed, and your friends will never be freed."

"First off, I'm a grown man; secondly, Serena, as much as I admire you, and believe me, I do, I am powerless against the Amazon Queen, and I don't want to walk in there thinking I have his head in my bag when it's just a rusty old soldier's helmet." Davi inputs.

"Fine. Give me another day to learn this new skill. I don't want to waste any more time debating on when to act when Niya and Rose have been with those druids for almost two months. Please, Alistair, I must try at least to summon the illusion. I want it to be ready by the time Davi's Runes are finished being restored." Serena pleads.

I look towards Braxor, who is unusually quiet.

"Will your dragon armies be ready for when we need them?" I ask him.

"Don't worry about my colonies, Dark One. If we're needed, we'll be there." Braxor garbles.

"Then it's settled. The Queen and King will stay here to master their skills while the Rune Master sets forth to free the Confessor and Pixie. The war strategy will begin once we're all safe within Silver City's confides." Alistair finishes.

With the meeting finished, Davi races off to the Apothocary chambers, and Serena follows Alistair to begin training again. Braxor bids me farewell until my need for him to return is called upon, leaving me and Master Mikao in the courtyard. He's silent, and I know it's because he is finding words of wisdom to reassure me that everything that has happened up to this point was always meant to happen.

"Your mate is with child, Dark One. Sending her into battle may not be wise."

"How do you know?" I ask.

"My connection to the spiritual world is strong. That's an advantage and blessing when one becomes a Reiki Master. There's a soul already blooming inside of her."

"It's been a day, maybe two, since we, you know." I don't wish to talk about fucking my wife with one of the most respected men of my time.

He chuckles. "Being a celebrity does not deprive me of the knowledge one becomes with a child. But although the seedling is just that, you will feel the child's soul in time just as easily as I do."

"I see. Is that the first lesson in my apprenticeship?"

"As much as I would like to take you on as my apprentice, Alwin, there are things that you need to do to earn that honor. I can't simply give it to you because we're old friends. As much as I value our relationship, it would be a disservice to you and those around us to take you under my figurative wing without testing your intentions."

"My intentions are honorable."

"That is what you say, but to know one's heart and soul is different than knowing one's mind, as the three can be at war with one another." Master Mikao approaches me, placing a gentle hand over the beating organ. "You have great darkness inside of you, Shadow King, but being that your mate is full of light, that can balance it out. I know you know this, but Reike has powers beyond healing. Like all magic, it can be manipulated and used for darker deeds."

"What does that mean? I've never heard of Reiki being used for nefarious means."

He sighs. "That's because each master has done their best to prevent such occurrences from happening. But it didn't erase the past."

"You mean someone has used it for evil?" Master Mikao separates himself from me, stepping back before pulling out a chair to sit.

"There was an incident many centuries ago where a young pupil discovered necromancy. Which is the opposite of what Reike is.

Your uncle has pulled you back, but it was a matter of minutes. That's the fine line between the two powers. Necromancy is used after days of death, but Reike can be used within minutes. If you combine the teachings of the two, the result is catastrophic." I take my seat from him, showing him I'm ready to listen and learn. No matter what he says, I will do whatever it takes if I need to prove myself to him. "I'm hesitant to teach you, Alwin, because of the shadows inside of you. Your power is one of the closest things to death there can be, aside from the darker arts. Reiki is about light and healing. I would be more inclined to teach Serena."

"But she's already getting her feet wet with the cards; adding this one might be too much," I state. "What must I do to prove I am the right pick? That I can use my essence for good."

Master Mikao lowers his momentarily and meets my eye before saying, "You must purge the shadows from your soul. Then and only then will I be willing to teach you."

# 26

# EPILOGUE

*A Rose will rise, a Raven will cry, and the skies will bleed when the Rune Master dies.*

In this next chapter, the Rune Master Davi must take the hard-headed pixie Rose to the Realm of Masters so she can take on her destiny as the next Rune Master. Meanwhile, in the clutches of the Amazon Queen, Niya's situation grows more dangerous as she tries to free herself and her Griffon. With the growing power inside of her, leaving the ship proves more difficult than she was prepared for.

What will happen when these three unlikely friends meet fate end? What do the cards store for our young Confessor and her mate? Will Davi do the right thing and hand over his title and power to the one the Runes have chosen?

# About the Author

**About The Author**

C.M. Hano is a talented writer and a dedicated mother of three wonderful children. Her love for Disney, magic, and princesses is reflected in her writing, full of romance and adventure. She is an expert at weaving magical tales that transport readers to enchanting realms of wonder and excitement. In many of her stories, dragons play a central role, which is no surprise, given that they are her favorite magical creatures. C. M. Hano's writing is a delightful blend of imagination, creativity, and heart, and her stories will surely captivate anyone who loves a good fairy tale.

**Stay In Touch**
  Facebook: C. M. Hano
  TikTok: @cmhanoauthor
  Twitter(X): HanoCera
  Instagram: @cerahano
  Facebook Reading Group: C. M. Hano's Reading Warriors

**You can connect with me on:**

- https://linktr.ee/cmhanoauthor
- https://x.com/hanocera
- https://www.facebook.com/cmhano
- https://www.tiktok.com/@cmhanoauthor
- https://www.instagram.com/cerahano

Milton Keynes UK
Ingram Content Group UK Ltd.
UKHW011102010424
440421UK00005B/456